PRAISE FOR EARL JAVORSKY'S FIRST NOVEL DOWN SOLO:

"Earl Javorsky's bold and unusual *Down Solo* blends the mysterious and the supernatural boldly and successfully. The novel is strong and haunting, a wonderful debut."
– T. Jefferson Parker, *New York Times* bestselling author of *Full Measure* and *The Famous and the Dead*

"Awesome."
– James Frey, *New York Times* bestselling author

"Don't miss Earl Javorsky's *Down Solo*. It's kick-ass, man. Excellent writing. This guy is the real deal."
– Dan Fante, author of the memoir *Fante* and the novel *Point Doom*

"Javorsky's dark and gritty prose is leavened with just enough humor to make *Down Solo* a compelling story that will take readers to the outer limits of noir."
– San Diego City Beat

"Javorksy's writing reminded me of the Carl Hiaasen novels I'd read sprawled out on the deck on one sunny Florida vacation. Perfect entertainment, with the right amount of action to keep me alert (and to keep me from snoozing myself into a sunburned state). But there's also a deeper layer in *Down Solo*, which left me thinking past the final page."
– Bibliosmiles

TRUST ME

TRUST ME

⬇

EARL JAVORSKY

THE
ST●RY
PLANT

Studio Digital CT, LLC
P.O. Box 4331
Stamford, CT 06907

Copyright © 2015 by Earl Javorsky
Jacket design by Barbara Aronica Buck

Story Plant Print ISBN-13: 978-1-61188-214-8
Fiction Studio Books E-book ISBN: 978-1-936558-66-7

Visit our website at www.TheStoryPlant.com

First Story Plant paperback printing: July 2015
Printed in the United States of America
0 9 8 7 6 5 4 3 2 1

This one's dedicated to the ones who didn't survive the ordeal

When he talks like this you don't know what he's after . . .
—Leonard Cohen, "The Stranger Song"

PROLOGUE

⏁

How could it have come this far? She had sworn it would never happen again, and yet here she was, climbing the stairs into the open air at the top of the building. It was nighttime, cool, still, and starlit. She followed, hand trapped in his—if she could only find some strength, pull him down and watch him tumble to the landing, she could step over him and go home and forget.

She was here, she told herself, of her own free will. This would be the last time, and it would be easy to say so.

They stepped out onto the roof. He put his arm around her, nuzzled his face in her hair, and then led her toward the wall at the perimeter. He leaned her against it and moved up behind her, close, his face in her neck as she looked out over the blazing lights of Westwood. They were directly up two flights from her apartment, fourteen stories from street level. His arms crossed in front of her and his hands cupped her breasts under her robe.

How did this happen? I despise this person! Yet she shifted her shoulders to accommodate his embrace from behind. She had liked him once. With reservations, yes, but he had been so charming. He had helped her when, without even knowing it, she most needed help.

She felt his left hand slide down past her belly, grazing the soft hair with his fingertips. He placed his right foot between her feet, prompting her to set them farther apart. A finger curved and found its mark—she gasped and realized she was moist, betrayed by her own body as it reacted, as if in pleasure, in spite of her feelings.

Her hair was still wet from a bath. He liked her freshly bathed for these sessions. Our little times together, he called them. As if they were lovers, but without the love.

She concentrated on the rough texture of the stucco wall. He withdrew his hands and turned her around, then lifted her so that she sat on the wall. *This is the last time, you son of a bitch.*

Absentmindedly, she placed her hands on his shoulders as he parted her robe and bent to brush his lips high against the inside of her thigh.

The wall was narrow and uncomfortable to sit on. Behind her, LA's affluent Westside stretched all the way to the ocean. It had all seemed so thrilling when he first brought her up here—the danger, the craziness of it—she had convulsed in orgasm before falling into the safety of his arms and weeping in relief.

Now she felt nothing, not even fear. Just an odd detachment, like staring out a window into the rain, or waiting in a long line at the market. Soon she would simulate an orgasm so that it could all be over.

There was a pressure at her stomach and she felt herself tilting backward. It happened so suddenly she lost hold of his shoulders, and now she felt the sharp points of the stucco scrape the backs of her calves.

Falling, she thought of her brother, Jeff, and the time he saved her life. They were teenagers, bodysurfing at Santa Monica Beach, and he plucked her out of the ocean after a wave tumbled her for so long she thought her feet would never find the sandy bottom.

Her last thought before she hit the ground was of the man on the roof. How clear, how perfectly clear, that everything they had done together had always pointed relentlessly toward this.

CHAPTER 1

⍗

Jeffrey Fenner found out about his sister's death while
waiting for a plane to take him home.

By the time he arrived at San Francisco Airport it was almost
midnight, and now he had to decide between a nearby hotel and
the redeye special. He needed a drink but the airport lounge was
closed. He opted for the flight back to LA. He bought his ticket
and headed for the men's room. Locked in a stall, he sat on the
toilet seat and put his briefcase on his knees. There was over an
hour to wait, plus forty minutes on the plane, then the taxi ride
home meant another forty minutes—it all added up to at least a
half-gram of coke required for the duration. He opened the briefcase and pulled out a bank deposit bag, inserted the key into the
lock, and pulled the zipper. Inside were a variety of neatly labeled
vials and plastic bags. He located the bag marked "personal"
and the orange vial that said "Valium." From the bag he pulled a
flake of soapy white crystal the size of his thumbnail. Resealing
the bag, he took out two Valiums, placing one in his mouth and
the other in his pocket. He fished in his left shoe in the hollow
of his arch and located a small amber glass vial. Using the vial,
he mashed the piece of cocaine into powder and scooped it onto
his driver's license, which he then bent into a curve as he tapped
the powder into the mouth of the vial. When the vial was full, he
capped it and replaced it in his shoe. He transferred the rest of the
coke on his license to the back of his left hand and lifted it to his
nostril, inhaling sharply.

Refreshed, he closed up his briefcase, checked his nostrils in the mirror, and went back out to the lobby.

The lighting was grim and everything looked dingy. The people had an equally grim look, as though lost or sentenced to an endless purgatory for travelers. It occurred to him that he hadn't eaten in a long time.

In the middle of the lounge was a fast food stand. He joined a line of ten or twelve people who stood, zombie-like and silent, waiting for a Middle Eastern-looking guy with a red-and-white striped cap and matching apron to microwave a new batch of chilidogs. The food looked plastic, like the permanent display meals at a cheap chain restaurant.

He stared ahead and listened until the sounds around him merged into an abstract buzz. He looked forward to getting back home, although in fact he wouldn't be going home; he had to stop by Rich's place first and make a delivery. At least he could relax, have a drink, while they weighed product and did the math. Then he could finally go home and go to sleep. Sleep—he hadn't slept in three days. Muscles in his leg twitched with exhaustion and toxins; he felt creaky and brittle, cranky, jumpy, and increasingly sour.

From the background of babble, one particular noise seemed to be demanding attention. It had a red flag on it, like a loud knock in the middle of the night.

"You are wanting something, sir? We have veddy good chilidog. You are wanting how many chilidog?" He found that he was at the counter, oblivious to how he had arrived there. In a moment of panic he realized his hands were empty; he looked down and saw his briefcase on the floor, locked between his ankles.

"Two." He held up two fingers to verify. The guy handed him a pair of paper boats containing long lumps covered with something that looked like steaming dog food. Jeff paid, scooped up his briefcase, and turned away.

The food was ugly, but he was surprised at how good it smelled. He devoured both dogs, wolf-like, sitting in the row of hard plastic seats farthest from the other waiting passengers. Afterward, he headed back to the men's room to wash his hands. It was large and very bright, but vacant, so he took a quick blast from the cap of the amber vial.

There was still some time to kill, so he pulled out his cell phone and thumbed Rich's number.

"Hello?" Rich's girlfriend answered on the first ring.

"Hey Lilah, it's Jeff." His voice echoed weirdly in the bathroom stall.

"Where are you? Rich waited, but he had to go out."

"I'm at the airport in San Francisco. Things got a little hung up but I'll be there by two thirty. Think Rich'll be back?"

"I haven't been able to reach him. Are you still coming by?" He pictured her, with her high cheekbones and pouty little mouth. Her crazy mess of hair. They had been friends for years, but someone else was always in the way.

He went to a concession stand and bought mints and a paper, then went to sit by the terminal at Gate 5, where Southwest Airline Flight #3714 would be leaving for Los Angeles at 12:10 a.m.

It was in the Metro section of the *LA Times*:

SUICIDE IN WESTWOOD

Twenty-eight-year-old Marilyn Fenner, a research assistant at UCLA, was found dead Monday morning, apparently after jumping from her twelfth-floor balcony.

Shit, he thought, no way.

CHAPTER 2

Holly Barnes sat on the edge of her bed and watched Tony as he dressed.

She had come home from an audition—a small production of *Speed the Plow*, but a great part—and found her apartment meticulously clean. The screen door to the balcony slid properly in its tracks, the spots of mold were gone from the shower ceiling, and fresh gladiolas in a vase accented a beautifully prepared meal on the kitchen table.

They had made love afterward. It had been quick but spectacular, and now, looking at him, she found herself thinking that there was still hope here, that he really was a decent person, that mistakes had been made but perhaps they could both learn from them and move forward together.

"So, you got a meeting tonight?" Tony brushed his hair, long and jet black, his back slightly arched because he was too tall for the mirror. He wore tight, faded jeans with an old silk aloha shirt and scuffed eel skin boots, but his dark and chiseled features made her think of the leading-man type of an earlier era.

"Yeah, over on Franklin. Where are you playing?" Tony played bass in a band. They played the best showcase spots in town, had a good following, and had just finished recording a demo.

"Some weird pub called The Club Foote off Highland somewhere. Used to be a punk-rock dive, Hal's Bar or something like that. We'll be done early. Want to see me?"

She didn't want to see him again that night. Seeing Tony after a gig meant staying up until nearly dawn while he paced and talked off the manic energy that always came with an hour in the spotlight. They would finally make love, but she would be angry, knowing that she would be underslept and off balance the next day.

"Call me. If you get the machine it means I'm sleeping." She smiled and kissed him, realizing that she was stepping on thin ice.

"Oh well, yeah, who knows what'll come up," he said. "You better get your beauty sleep." What he meant was that if she didn't invite him over he was free game for any bimbo at the club that met his criteria—a sliding scale of standards that dropped a notch each hour after midnight and two notches per shot of Wild Turkey. The thought sickened her, but she would deal with that at the meeting tonight.

"Maybe tomorrow night. Anyway, knock 'em dead," she told him, and kissed him lightly on the lips, while with her right palm at his chest she held him at a distance. *Just like that*, she thought, *in the space of two minutes, and I hate him again.*

She watched him go out the door and waited until he was halfway to the drive before closing it, as though she wasn't quite safe until he had gone some minimum distance. Now she felt like she owned her own space again, not having to walk on eggshells for fear of offending Tony.

She turned on some music and, whistling along to the first song, shed the oversize tee shirt she had been wearing and headed for the shower, thinking about how they didn't even share a taste in music.

CHAPTER 3

Once the plane took off, Jeff tilted his seat back and closed his eyes. The cabin was dark, lit only by the scattered reading lights of a few of the passengers. He was grateful to have a row to himself. At liftoff he had pulled out the amber vial, felt the powder hit high in his sinuses, helping him breath and think clearly again.

Okay—so, it didn't make any sense, his straight-arrow sister taking a dive from her balcony. He knew he was a fuck-up; his life was certainly swirling in the bowl at the moment, but Marilyn had it all going for her. He glanced back at the paper. They had her name right, her age, her job, and yes, she lived on the goddamned twelfth floor, but something was wrong somewhere; he just couldn't find it yet. He was too burnt out to even think about it.

There was a time when he was the protective big brother, three years Marilyn's senior and always there to comfort her when their parents flipped out, a job fell through, or a boyfriend left. Then Marilyn stabilized, made it through college, and found work she loved, while he floundered as a photographer at the edge of the entertainment industry and drifted more and more into the drug world.

Years before, he had made a bundle in the LSD trade. He took Marilyn to Hawaii once and his parents to San Francisco for a weekend, making up a convenient story about his affluence. He had lost it all since then; the ride had gotten dark and rocky as he floundered in the cocaine business. Now he had a chance to start over. He had located his long lost San Francisco connection, contacted his old distributors, and borrowed money from Rich to invest in a batch of the best LSD available. There was a resurgence of psychedelic drug use throughout the country. On a wing and a prayer, this could launch him back to the way things used to be, erasing a thousand mistakes as he rebuilt his little world. He put the newspaper on the empty seat next to him and willed his sister out of his mind.

He thought about Lilah as he endured the cab ride to Rich's Brentwood apartment. She was the kind of girl every man wanted to have but no one wanted to have around. She flirted openly with Jeff, but it seemed to him she was like that with every male.

Before going up to the apartment he went to the underground parking and located his car. He opened it and groped under the passenger seat, grabbed a paper sack, and locked up again. He carried, besides his briefcase, another half-pound of coke, twenty-six-and-a-half thousand dollars, and a Walther 9mm. It was spooky in the garage; he didn't see anyone but it felt like there were people there. Things were on the verge, he thought, of flying apart. He needed a drink and some sleep badly.

▽

The door opened just as he was about to knock. Lilah stood in the doorway dressed in a silk robe that hung loosely open, exposing most of her breasts. He stared, standing in the hallway at two forty-five in the morning with his briefcase and his gun, at this beautiful girl and had the insane wish that Rich was far away.

Lilah presented her cheek for him to kiss. She turned at the last moment so that their lips brushed and then stepped back to let him in the apartment.

He took the briefcase and the bag into the first of the two bedrooms down the hallway. This room had just been vacated by Rich's roommate Doug, a drunk who couldn't make the rent. It was now empty except for a single bed and a Dial-O-Gram scientific scale on a shelf in the closet. The air was thick with the humidity of an August heat wave. He set the briefcase and the bag next to the scale. He would deal with it all later.

▽

Lilah poured him a big glass of Chivas on some ice, and now they were settled on the living room couch. She lounged across from him, smoking a cigarette.

"Rich called. He says he's on a boat somewhere out of Marina Del Rey, doing business. He'll be back tomorrow or something."

He poured a little pile from the amber vial onto the glass table and divided it into neat lines with a credit card. They used a short piece of a straw and Lilah put the residue on her finger and stuck it in her mouth. She pooched her lips and sucked in her cheeks. He pictured her on the cover of Cosmopolitan magazine.

Lilah started rubbing his thigh. He had dreamed of this but never entertained its possibility. It was probably a very bad idea, but the booze was working and he was feeling great. He held the drink in one hand, her left breast in his other, and started to tell her about the San Francisco trip. He needed, however, to go to the bathroom. He walked down the hall and suddenly felt dizzy, disoriented; his stomach was queasy and the room blurry. He returned from the bathroom and sat down heavily. Lilah asked him what was wrong and he told her to get a bowl, quick. He threw up into the bowl and lay back, his heart pounding. His hair felt damp and hot; everything was swirling. *Goddamn chili dogs* was the last thought he had before he passed out.

CHAPTER 4

⍗

Holly didn't even bother with make-up. With her hair towel-dried and pulled straight back, tied with a rubber band, she put on some jeans and a Gold's Gym sweatshirt. Tonight's meeting was not an affair to get all done up for. Still, she thought, with a last glance at the mirror, she was lucky—she still looked good: tan, slim, and healthy. Her gray-green eyes looked out over high, carved cheekbones; her nose was straight, and her full lips, when she smiled, showed perfect teeth. Her modeling days were over, but acting was so much more real, more substantial and satisfying.

She went out to the carport and thumbed the button on the remote device on her keychain. The woop-woop sound from her little BMW convertible told her the alarm was disengaged. Holly loved her car; she loved driving in the warm LA nights, with music blasting and her hair blowing crazily in the wind.

She drove up to Olympic Boulevard and turned east, then north when she got to La Brea. By the time she got up to Sunset and over to Franklin it was nearly dark; she would be just on time if she could get a parking spot.

The meeting was in a church annex. Some people filed into a door in the side of the building. When Holly got there a greeter she had never seen told her "Welcome" and shook her hand.

Inside, about thirty people sat in folding chairs arranged in a circle. At one end of the room was a table covered with books, carefully displayed, and a tray with coffee, cups, and sweetener.

She nodded to the several people she knew and took one of the few vacant seats, opposite the side where the table was set up.

A woman with a notebook on her lap cleared her throat and said, "Greetings, and welcome to the regular Wednesday night meeting of SAVING OUR LIVES." She was reading from a format, Holly saw; the same format that all the meetings used, with small variations according to each group.

"My name is Cynthia and I'm here to save my life."

"Hi, Cynthia," the group intoned in unison.

"Our purpose," Cynthia continued to read, "is to learn to live free from the injuries of our past and find our potentials as fully expressed human beings. We are here to take charge of our lives, having spent too many years giving our power to other people, or to concepts like money and prestige." There was more, but Holly stopped listening as she began looking at the other people in the room.

It seemed to be an affluent group, no down-and-outers, and she was glad of it. Of the thirty in the circle, about twenty were women, ranging from their early twenties to mid-fifties, with a couple of attentive teenagers just to her left. Then there were the men. It seemed odd to her that men would come to hear information like this; to talk about honesty and emotional issues, about trust and fear of abandonment. It struck her as courageous and wimpy at the same time.

"I will now share for ten minutes and the meeting will open up for discussion." Cynthia wrapped up the reading from the notebook and cleared her throat again. She looked about forty, very thin and rather smart looking in a gabardine suit.

"Okay," she began, "I'm a little nervous. I've never spoken in front of a group before. I guess I'll begin with how I got here.

"About two years ago my life just seemed to be coming apart. I had been divorced for five years and every man I had dated since turned out to be a bigger jerk than my ex-husband." She paused. "Or else he was totally boring." This got a laugh from at least half the room. "My daughter had just gone off to college and my home seemed intolerably empty. I had a decent career in advertising and couldn't stand going in to work, and nothing seemed to have any meaning for me—I was dying inside. I had been in therapy and . . ."

She lost track of what the woman was saying. She had noticed a man gazing at her from across the circle; he was sitting several seats to the right of the speaker. He didn't look away when she noticed him. Instead, he smiled and nodded slightly, as if encouraging her or drawing her into complicity.

He was interesting looking, she thought. Not the type to come to this group—he looked far too self-assured. She guessed he was in his mid-fifties, tanned and athletic looking and could pass for much younger. His hair was combed straight back in a European style and he wore a cream-colored suit. She looked away. He had a distinguished look, not someone she would ever go for, but interesting. His nod had been somehow reassuring.

". . . and my friend told me about Bobbi Bradley's work and how Bobbi's book had changed her life." Cynthia paused and looked up at the ceiling, as if recalling her favorite childhood memory. "So I read that book and when I was halfway through I came to my first meeting. That's when I discovered that other people felt the same way I did and that they had found a way out. Then I read about how there was a little child in me . . ." Here Cynthia's voice cracked and the room went silent. Inaudibly at first, she began to cry, and then she covered her face and a great sob blurted out from between her hands. The girl next to Cynthia patted her on the back and offered her a Kleenex.

"That child"—Cynthia's voice came out in a high-pitched croaking—"had been smothered by the expectations of my parents. I realized that I had been shut off from joy since I was eight years old and had paid for it in every aspect of my life."

She wasn't sure she liked this speaker. It embarrassed her when they cried, but then she had to admit that she had been clearly instructed at an early age that crying was foolish and wouldn't get her what she wanted. She started to wonder if she was going to hear anything useful tonight.

"So I learned that this program was based on Bobbi's technique of accessing the inner child and that by reassuring the child that she was okay I could have a new experience of life. And I could have a spiritual life, for the Bible says 'and ye shall be like children.' So, by following this program I have reclaimed power over my life. I have learned to set boundaries with other people. Once in a while I still get episodes of anxiety, but overall I seem to be much more in control."

Holly glanced over at the man in the cream-colored suit. He seemed to have looked her way at the same moment, and he gave a smile and a little shrug as if to say, "Oh well, who knows?" She frowned. She disliked Biblical references.

"Thank you for letting me share. The meeting is now open for participation." Cynthia looked relieved that her ordeal was over. Several hands shot up; Cynthia pointed to a large, soft man to her left.

"My name is Ted. Thank you so much for sharing. I got so much from what you had to say. I always seem to hear just what I need to hear. The part about giving your power away to other people is exactly my issue . . ."

That was in the part she read, she thought. Who are these people? What am I doing here? But then she considered the man in the nice suit—and several of the women—very composed and smart looking. They had an air of knowingness about them that intrigued her.

Others participated. One of the teenagers had a stepfather who got drunk and fondled her. A man said that since he had come to SOL he had managed to stop drinking hard liquor and was now able to ration his beer. One very distraught woman had just been left by her boyfriend and was talking about her abandonment issues. The man in the cream-colored suit raised his hand.

"My name is Art, and I'm here to save my own life." He had a deep and resonant voice with a cultured flavor to it. Holly sat forward, listening now with full attention.

"I'm sure you're all familiar with Bobbi Bradley. Hopefully you have each read her book, *Saving Our Lives*, from which this program came into being." He paused and looked around. Members in the group were nodding their heads in acknowledgment. "If so, then you know that this work has drawn from twelve-step programs, time-honored spiritual disciplines, and the latest work in psychology and neurolinguistics."

She hadn't read the book but she felt hopeful that there was something substantial here, possibly something that could solve her problem.

"We bring our problems here," Art went on, "our insecurities and fears, our addictions and self-destructive behaviors, and expose them to the light of day. But that's only the beginning. There is something available here, a map to navigate by, to get us to a safe haven of sanity and rational living. It's charted out in Bobbi's book, but to really experience the power of her ideas there's nothing like seeing her in person. So I just wanted to share, for those of you who didn't know, that Bobbi will be giving a seminar on the course tomorrow night at the Beverly Hills Playhouse. I have flyers if you would like to know more about it. Thank you."

Cynthia checked her watch and then announced, "That's all the time we've got." She buried herself in the format for a moment and then added, "It is a custom after this meeting to get together at Hamburger Harry's for fellowship. We welcome the new people to join us."

Everyone stood up and joined hands. "I already have the power to change," the group chanted in unison. Holly, embarrassed, joined in: "Together, we can save our lives." The room burst into a cacophony of scattered chattering and the folding and gathering of metal chairs.

She thought of saying hello to the few people she had met before, but they all seemed to be engaged in conversation. People throughout the room were hugging each other. She headed for the door, which was blocked by a knot of people gathered around Art, who cheerfully handed out bright orange flyers for the seminar.

"Hello," he said, and then he held out his hand. When she took it he gently drew her around in such a way as to separate the two of them from the rest; it even seemed quieter, she thought, as though they were in a cocoon. "I sense that you're new here." His gaze was very direct, but he drew her in in a comforting way, his smile friendly and reassuring.

"Yes. I've been to two other meetings before tonight." He was still holding her hand. "I'm Holly. It's very nice to meet you," and she shook his hand, expecting him to then let go. Instead, he brought up his other hand and now held her palm between both of his.

"Holly. How very nice that you're here." He still smiled, but his voice became grave. "Something quite painful is usually required to bring us here. The path to freedom begins with sharing your pain."

His hands were warm and dry, comforting, even though she felt a bit foolish. "Yes. Things are a little confusing. It seems like the parts of my life definitely don't fit together like they should."

Art let go of her hand, only to take her shoulder and propel her toward the other people by the door. "Everybody, this is Holly! She's new and she's joining us at Harry's."

After reluctantly allowing herself to be hugged by five or six people whose names she immediately forgot, Holly felt Art take her by the elbow. "Why don't you leave your car here and drive with me? It's really much easier than trying to find the place by yourself. I'll bring you back."

"Well, I think I'll just follow—" she stammered, but Art interrupted her.

"Holly," he seemed suddenly stern. "It's okay. It's different here. It's safe, and it's crucial that you believe that, starting right now. You need a place where you can begin to trust."

She hadn't intended to go, but found herself intrigued. He was clearly a leader in the group, and she felt flattered to be included. She allowed him to guide her out to the parking lot to where his car was parked.

He drove a gleaming new Jaguar, low slung and forest green. It smelled of leather, mingled with a pleasant, spicy note that she took to be Art's cologne. He pushed a button and Miles Davis's *Sketches of Spain* started to play. She knew it because it had been one of her father's favorite records.

"So," Art began, as he wheeled out of the lot, "let me guess. You have a boyfriend, but things aren't quite perfect." He was turned toward her as though they were still parked, but drove with perfect assurance. "Maybe he drinks a bit more than he should. He's exciting, but he hasn't found success just yet; in fact, he's not in great shape financially. How am I doing?"

She was very uncomfortable—she felt exposed, as though her life had been shown to be transparent and trite. She had experienced a distinct sensation of falling as he spoke, but anger provided the solid branch that she needed to steady herself, to come back into her own.

"Actually," she replied, "I do have a boyfriend, and the fact is he's about to become very successful. He is also a very decent person." She wondered why she rallied to Tony's defense in the face of such an accurate assessment.

"I'm sure he can be," Art said, seeming amused.

"You certainly go out on a limb with your presumptions." She needed to nip this in the bud before the man started plucking more data about her life out of thin air.

"Oh, let me venture a bit further. This limb bends, but it never breaks, and below it are other limbs. The question is, what tree am I up in?"

"Maybe you're up a tree of bullshit," she shot back.

"Oh, feisty, that's a very appropriate tactic. Tell me, which of your parents was the alcoholic and which was obese?"

She felt like she had been punched in the gut. Her father had died of cirrhosis of the liver, but was certainly not an alcoholic. Her mother, however, was definitely overweight. Holly was baffled at her reaction. An overweight parent would have been easy enough to guess, but there was something relentless in Art's approach; she was under siege.

At that moment the Jag turned into the parking lot of Hamburger Harry's. It looked like the whole group had shown up, and some of the members that she had just met grinned and waved as Art parked the car.

"This is not about me attacking you," Art said, turning toward her as he switched off the ignition. "This is about finding the chink in the armor that you're so unwilling to reveal. Even if I am mistaken in my guesswork so far, something impelled you to come to our meeting. It has a face. It has a description, it has a background, and you have a part in it. That's why it's so hard to be honest about it. Relax. Let's go in and eat, enjoy. I promise I'll lighten up." He made a face of mock seriousness and it seemed to her that she was looking at a very little boy trying to look grown up. She smiled. He smiled back, and it occurred to her for the first time that he was attractive in an odd way. His nose was too large, his lips too full, his features were rough, but it all added up to a strange appeal.

She allowed Art to take her hand as he helped her out of the Jaguar. They joined the others in the lot and entered the restaurant. Other members of the group were already seated in a section where all the tables had been pushed together to make one long row. Art led her to the far end of the row and seated her in the last chair. He then sat at the end of the table, to her right, as though he were the host of a dinner party.

"The salad bar here is excellent," he said. "Follow me and do everything I do." She did, even though she wasn't hungry.

They returned to their seats with identical plates, each covered by little piles of chili, pasta, artichoke hearts, salad greens, and sourdough bread. "To faith, fellowship, and food!" Art proclaimed, and the others, now all seated, laughed and raised their water glasses, their ice teas, and their diet cokes.

▽

It was past midnight when Art brought her back to her BMW in the church parking lot. He had held court for hours; Holly, like the others, had refilled her plate several times, and the serious mood of the meeting had evaporated. The whole line of approach Art had pursued earlier, during the ride to the restaurant, seemed to be finished as well.

"Holly," he began as he again held both of her hands, standing at the open door of her car, "it has been delightful having you along tonight."

She felt flattered. Throughout the evening he had treated her like a special guest. The meeting had been kind of a downer, she thought, but the get-together afterward was quite pleasant.

"I had a great time. Thank you." She meant it.

"Holly." He was stern again, intense, saying her name as if he didn't already have her attention. "I think that you are about to embark on a major voyage of discovery. About yourself and about the world. Tonight was a beginning, but you need a real introduction to this work, and tomorrow night's seminar is perfect, crucial even, for you at this moment in your life." He let go with one hand and, reaching in his jacket pocket, pulled out an envelope. Handing it to Holly, he told her, "Please be my guest tomorrow night. Seven sharp, at the Beverly Hills Playhouse. There's a ticket in the envelope, along with my card. Call me if you would like a ride."

She was flustered. Something in his manner almost commanded her to go—it seemed too forceful; he certainly wasn't attractive in this moment. And yet she couldn't say no. She thanked him again, took the envelope and, disengaging her other hand from his, got into her own car and closed the door. She put the envelope in her purse and started the BMW.

▽

She listened to music at full volume as she drove—in order not to have to think—but her mind just shouted louder. "Who the hell does he think he is?" His personal interrogation came back to her, with all its attendant discomfort. What an asshole, she thought, shaking her head as she turned into her building's driveway.

Tony's car was parked in her spot. It was a decrepit Volvo station wagon, parked askew with its tail end sticking out into the traffic lane. All of his gear was visible in the back—amplifiers and instrument cases—and the driver's side window was open.

She parked in visitor parking and hurried up to her flat. Music was blaring from her stereo—it had that noisy, messy quality she had come to know as belonging to a live recording of one of Tony's club gigs. She started to let herself in when the doorknob flew out of her grasp.

"Hey, Miss nighty-night-early-tonight made it home. I know. You tried to sleep and couldn't so you made the bed and got dressed and went for a FUCKING DRIVE. AM I RIGHT?" *He's shouting at me,* she thought, *inside my own home.* He stood holding her door open but blocking the doorway. In one hand he gripped a bottle of Wild Turkey. The words "Get it while it's hot . . ." came in a distorted roar from the stereo behind him—it was the chorus to a rock song he had co-written.

She brushed past Tony, surprised at her own audacity. He let her through and followed her into the living room. She hit the off button on the stereo and turned back to him. "I want you to leave here right now."

"Whoah, baby. Aren't you glad to see me?" he taunted as he stepped toward her. "I called and I called and then I thought to myself, well why don't I just go over and sneak in real quiet-like and snuggle up with her in bed. Wouldn't that be nice? But nooo. Check it out. The bitch flew the coop!"

"Get out of here, Tony. You're drunk. I hate it when you're drunk. Go home."

"Where were you?"

"I went to a meeting."

"Bullshit. Fucking meetings are over at nine. BULLSHIT." Now he was yelling again

"Look, I went out with the people from the meeting afterward. We went to a restaurant."

"Bullshit." Tony lunged forward and grabbed her purse. He reached in and pulled out her compact. "Nice," he said, and threw it over his shoulder. He followed with her wallet, hairbrush, and address book, throwing them aside, until he got to the envelope.

"Hey now. What have we got here?" He opened the envelope and pulled out a business card. "Dr. Art Bradley, Psychologist, Licensed Family Counselor, Co-dependency and Substance Abuse Specialist, hey, in Bevahlee Hills, dahling. Oh, and look here!" He pulled out the ticket. "The Bevahlee Hills fuckin' Playhouse. Well, isn't that nice. Tomorrow night." He stepped up to her and lowered his face to her, then moved around to whisper, "I thought we had"—his tongue flickered warmly in her ear—"a date tomorrow night."

"Tony, goddamnit, cut it out." She turned her head and tried to pull away, but Tony's hand shot out and caught her hair. She felt a shock of pain as he wrenched her around and flung her, by the hair, back into the stereo console.

"Tony, please, you've got it all mixed up. Stop." She was pleading with him, but somewhere in the back of her mind she was furious, ready to push a brick in his face if only she could get her hands on one.

"All mixed up. You've got it all mixed up," he mimicked. "All mixed up? Mix this up, you little cunt," and his hand shot out and caught her right above the eye in a backhanded slap that she heard before she felt.

At that moment a voice came from the door. "Holly! Holly, is everything okay?" The voice had a lisp; it was Arnie, her next door neighbor, very sweet, very gay, and not her first choice for the moment, but Tony simply said, "Oh Christ," and turned around and left. As he passed Arnie at the door he said, "What a fuckin' joke," and then he was gone.

CHAPTER 5

Jeff was startled out of oblivion by a bump against his mouth. It had started out lips on lips, but caress turned into collision; teeth had gnashed against his teeth. He looked up and groaned. Lilah was standing over him, swaying, a goofy look on her face, teeth bared in a crazed grin. He knew that look. It meant that she had taken one, probably several, of his Xanax bars. He also realized that she had gotten into his bank bag.

"So, man, you're busted," she managed, with effort, to enunciate. "You're doing heroin."

"What the fuck are you talking about?" he yelled, wide awake now. He jumped up and marched off into the spare room, Lilah following. His briefcase was open on the bed, its contents scattered everywhere. On the floor were a magazine and a long clear glass vial. The vial's contents were arranged into little piles and lines—more than half was in the carpet. It was the LSD. The humidity was beading on it; the part in the rug was gone forever. The substance, in its pure form, had represented over ten thousand doses. Lilah put her finger into one of the little piles and leered at him, triumphant.

"You're a fuckin' junkie, man. That's why you got sick."

He couldn't believe what he was seeing. "What the FUCK is the matter with you?" he yelled. Lilah stared at him as if he had a poisonous spider on his nose. "What the fuck are you doing?" She put her finger in her mouth. That amount alone could have sent thirty people to Mars for twenty-four hours; God knew what she had already ingested.

He grabbed her by the wrist and yanked her up and out of the room. He slammed the door while she yelled something about how the color of the powder had clued her in that there was heroin in the vial.

He locked the door and started trying to salvage what was left. The LSD was almost half gone. Rich's investment was in the toilet. He took stock of the rest of the room. The large bag was still in its spot on the shelf. That was good. He counted the Xanax; there were three missing. With the coke it was hard to tell; he didn't keep close tabs on his personal stash. He snapped one of the bars in half and ate it, along with a Valium, put everything back in the briefcase, and cleared off the bed.

He lay down, his heart thumping like a basketball on a gym floor.

▽

The next thing he heard was shouting from outside. He looked at his watch; he must have slept for an hour. There was a brief silence, then a crash and the sound of breaking glass, and then he heard Lilah shout, "CAST THE DEVIL FROM YOUR HEART. THE DEVIL IS IN YOUR HEART." This was followed by a voice from the neighboring apartment building—"Give it a rest, Lilah!"—and laughter. A different voice yelled, "Party time at Lilah's again!" followed by, "Shut the fuck up, all of you."

Another crash. BOOM. Something heavy this time. He could picture her throwing things out of the living room window.

"CAST THE DEVIL FROM YOUR HEART." There was a muffled thump, as though a large piece of furniture had just been pushed over. Jeff dozed.

He woke to a scream. "AAAH! GET AWAY FROM ME! FUCK YOU, DEVIL." This was way past out of hand. He reached over to his briefcase and fished out another Valium. He needed, and intended to get, at least ten more hours of sleep.

▽

This time he was awakened by a new sound. It came from the direction of the front door and had a crisp authority, a staccato rhythm of great purpose. After a silence, it resumed. He sat up on the edge of the bed. There was another silence, followed by, "POLICE! OPEN THE DOOR!"

"Shit." He froze. He heard the unmistakable sound of the front door frame giving way, followed by heavy footsteps and the squawking of a police radio.

"YOU," he heard Lilah shriek, "CAST THE DEVIL FROM YOUR HEART." She was really out of her tree. More footsteps. A female voice said something he couldn't hear. A male voice laughed, the walkie-talkie blared, and the footsteps fanned out throughout the apartment.

He got up and shut the closet door. Then he put his ear to the wall, trying to hear what was going on in the living room. He considered the window, but throwing out the bag and briefcase would surely attract attention. Climbing out was out of the question.

He couldn't hear much, but things seemed to be settling down. The female voice asked questions, Lilah's voice responding in a singsong fashion. He reached in the pocket of his trunks. The amber vial was there. He whisked it out, unscrewed the cap, and inhaled what was left inside, savoring the medicinal smell as he put the vial under the mattress. He licked his thumb and index finger, then used them to clean his nostrils in a pinching motion. A hard object rapped against the door to his room.

He opened the door and saw a cop holding a big nightstick. The cop was huge. Jeff was six feet tall and he had to look up at the guy.

"What's your name?"

"Jeffrey Fenner, sir."

"What's been going on around here?"

"Well sir, I don't know."

"You don't know? What the hell have you been doing?" The cop was incredulous.

"Sleeping. Well, trying to, anyway."

"You slept through this?" The cop gestured for him to step out and look down the hall into the living room.

He looked out and saw four other cops standing by the door—one was the woman he had heard—and Lilah bound onto a stretcher on wheels. The living room was a mess, with stuff all over the floor and the couch and chairs tumbled over. He stepped back into his room. "It's probably better if she doesn't notice me," he said.

"Why is that? What's going on here, anyway?"

"Well, sir, ah . . ." His nose was about to drip. He started to reach for it, then let his hand drop. "I'm in grad school over at UCLA. Uh, biology, sir." He saw an opening. "Anyway, I saw an ad for a roommate in the campus newspaper. I've only been here for ten days and I'm already looking for a new place. This girl," he jerked his thumb in the direction of the living room, "just parties too much." He was on a roll now. The cop looked bored but was clearly waiting for more. "So this weekend I was in San Francisco, visiting my folks. I had to take the midnight shuttle home and I think I ate some bad food at the airport 'cause I was sick as a dog by the time we landed in LA." All this time he was standing in the doorway, eyes locked with the cop in the hall.

"So I get home and she had just gotten back herself. She was fighting with her date and seemed pretty loaded at the time. I needed to sleep so I just stayed in here and locked the door." He had no idea where the story came from—it just flowed. He remembered the disappointment of not qualifying for college.

The cop looked at him in silence, softly tapping the nightstick into his palm. He thought of the scale—it was right next to the gun in the closet, along with the coke and the money. A voice from the front door said, "You ready?" and the cop replied, "Yeah, let's clear out." He looked at Jeff and said, "Get some sleep," then turned around and left.

He heard the front door pull shut, then creak open on its broken hinge. In the outside hallway, footsteps receded until finally it was quiet. He waited for ten minutes, then got dressed, gathered his bag and briefcase, and walked to his car. As he rolled out of the driveway, he shook his head, thinking about what he had just pulled off. He had skated on some thin ice before, but this morning was a capper.

Driving through Brentwood toward the beach, he grimaced at the brightness of the day. It was hot, but he didn't care. His apartment was four miles away. If he made it there, he could sleep until dinnertime, or maybe all the way through to the next morning, and things would be different. He would be rested, he would eat, and then he would figure out what to do.

CHAPTER 6

⊽

He found it buried in the third page of the Metro section of the *LA Times*:

SUICIDE IN WESTWOOD

Twenty-eight-year-old Marilyn Fenner, a research assistant at UCLA, was found dead Monday morning, apparently after jumping from her twelfth-floor balcony.

Joe Greiner put the paper on his desk and wondered who made the decisions about whose death made which page and how much of a story it would get. Didn't this girl have a life, a family, a history? He sipped at his coffee. It was sweet, loaded with sugar and powdered creamer. Like a liquid candy bar, he thought.

The phone rang. "Homicide, Greiner." He didn't really feel like talking.

"Joe? Ron Pool. I catch you in the middle of something?"

Pool, from the *Times*. Decent guy. Wrote the piece on the girl. "Always, Ron. In the middle of a sea of shit. What's up?"

"I got curious about the girl, is all. You call it a suicide, we print it's a suicide. But it bugged me so I did a little checking."

"Yeah?" Pool was a thorough guy, a professional. "What kind of checking?"

"Well, I haven't come up with much. Except that the suicide rate for women in her age group on the Westside took a big jump in the last couple of years."

"Yeah, so it's a fuckin' epidemic. What of it?" Pool usually came up with better.

"I don't know," Ron said, "but it's got me like an itch. I pulled files on a few others but don't really have much. Fax me what you've got and I'll keep you up to date if anything shows up."

"Hey, maybe it's a suicide conspiracy." Joe wasn't big on hunches. You show up, look around, ask questions, weed out the bullshit; what starts out as a puzzle always gets dumb and simple. Except here there wasn't any puzzle. "Hey, what the hell, I'll pull suicide files, last two years, Westside, female, twenty to thirty."

"Thanks. I'll get back to you." Pool hung up.

Joe started to put the phone down, then changed his mind and punched a number instead. He was relieved to hear his ex-wife's answering machine pick up.

"Janey, I'm at the office. Be here 'til four. I'll come by to pick up Robbie at six. See ya." It was so much simpler leaving a message.

He had two hours worth of paperwork to do. A few calls, then gathering the files for Pool, would take him right up to four. Then, he thought with relish, he would get some time at the gym. His hand went automatically to his gut; he grabbed it and hated the way it filled his hand, pushed over his belt. He had powerful arms and legs but couldn't get rid of the flab in his middle.

A few hours later, Joe finished the paperwork and accessed the database. He entered the password "RAIDERS" and then the keyword "suicide." A few more parameters narrowed the range to what Pool had asked for. The cursor blinked and then a message came up: "Search indicates 8 records." He punched in the print command and walked over to the printer. Eight very lonely young women, eight desperate acts. He took the list down the hall to where the files were and started pulling the folders, getting more depressed as the stack grew.

CHAPTER 7

⩡

Holly blasted up Roxbury drive. It was only a short hop to the Beverly Hills Playhouse; the evening was warm, she had the top down, the music turned up, and everything seemed just right: mysterious and full of promise.

She had gone to bed the night before with a bag of ice clutched to her eye, angry with herself, hating Tony, and even angrier at Art, as if he had been responsible for what had happened. And that awful meeting—what in the world did they have to offer?

In the morning, she had awakened thinking about the meeting again, only this time it seemed as though something had happened there that she couldn't quite put her finger on. It was vague, tenuous, and she couldn't find it in any particular thing that she had seen or heard. It was just a sense she had of a promise of relief.

The ticket to the lecture was in her purse on the passenger seat. She had found it on the floor in the living room—Tony had dropped it when he grabbed her hair. After he left, Arnie had come in and comforted her, telling her that Tony was a wanna-be, a has-been that never was, and that even though he was sexy he was too much of a loser for someone like her. Arnie had smoothed out her hair, talked to her in the bathroom as she undressed, and patted her blanket when she was in bed, turning out the light and whispering good night.

She turned up Canon Drive and found herself in a long line of cars all waiting to get into the same parking lot. She drove around them, noticed the line at the Playhouse, and circled the block. A parking spot materialized for her on the next street over; she locked the BMW and walked back to Canon Drive, glancing at the expensive displays in the storefronts as she passed.

The line on the sidewalk was long and she didn't see a soul that she knew. Taking a place at the end, she picked fragments of conversation out of the general buzz:

". . . absolutely haven't had a shouting match since we read her book";

". . . It became clear as daylight I was in the wrong marriage"; and ". . . wonder what her own personal life is like."

Yes, she wondered, what can life be like when your ship comes in, your book is selling, people line up to see you at $45 each, and you have all this knowledge that helps others? Is it quiet at the center?

"Holly!" She turned and saw Art, dressed in a dark blue suit this time, looking even tanner than before as he smiled at her. He took her by the hand and led her toward the theater door, saying, "I'm delighted you came. Let's get you to a decent seat before I have to go running off to play stage manager again." He whisked her past the line of waiting people, professional people, she noticed, well dressed and attractive, interesting looking. Many were hugging each other. Over and over, people nodded and smiled as they passed. Some seemed to clamor for Art's attention. He walked her past the ticket taker, through the crowded lobby, and, once in the theater itself, down the aisle to the front row. The front section was generally full, except for two seats by the center aisle. Next to these were several people Holly recognized—they were from the meeting the other night and the restaurant after.

"Holly, how great you made it!" It was Ted, the man from the meeting. "Have a seat. This is definitely going to change your life."

She sat, still holding Art's hand, as though he were a parent who had just safely guided her across a busy street. "I'm off," he said, "to orchestrate madness into order. A special talent." He kissed her hand before letting it go.

"A very great man," said Ted from behind her as she turned to see where Art was headed. The theater was filling rapidly. "He was my group's facilitator at a weekend workshop." Ted seemed to be proud of this fact.

"What happens at a workshop?"

"We go through Bobbi's program step by step. It's a truly amazing experience. Everything I thought I knew and all the opinions I had ever formed had to be reevaluated and for the most part thrown out. When my turn came, I got so in touch with my feelings that I was in tears within five minutes. I had so much energy invested in protecting myself from those feelings that it was a tremendous relief to just surrender and let myself be entirely vulnerable."

"Where did this all happen?" she inquired, not at all sure that what Ted was describing sounded attractive to her.

"Oh, up at Serra Retreat in Malibu. A perfect setting. I'm going again in October, if I can afford it."

"Why, is it expensive?" She couldn't imagine spending money to break down and cry in front of a group of total strangers.

"Oh, well, of course there's some expense involved. But considering what happens to you in here—" he gestured to his heart "—and in here—" he tapped his head "—there's really no way to put a dollar value on it. I mean, it doesn't even equate."

She sensed that there was something defensive about Ted's response. "Well, if I wanted to go, how much will I need to spend?"

"The food is excellent and the view is amazing. It's like a great vacation, except you're getting all this critical work done. The whole thing runs fifteen hundred dollars." He stared at her as if this were a challenge: Dare to say it's too much.

The lights dimmed and the room became quiet. She felt annoyed at the possibility of being pitched on a fifteen-hundred-dollar workshop that she would absolutely never join.

A woman walked up to the podium and adjusted the microphone. She was of medium height, slightly stocky, and dressed in a rather drab business suit. With her short-cropped hair and black-rimmed glasses, she looked like a no-nonsense executive secretary in an investment banking firm. Holly had expected something quite different, a more commanding, glamorous presence.

"My name is Bobbi Bradley and I'm here to save my life."

"Hi, Bobbi," came back in unison. Holly was surprised to realize she had said it too.

"There's a reason we do the things we do," Bobbi began. "It traces back to when we were very small, when every time we were frustrated in our legitimate expectations for safety, love, and physical affection, for the attention and reliability of the adults around us, we made an adjustment. We protected ourselves. We built a suit of armor. Eventually we confused the growing of armor with growing up. We never realized that the growing of armor is the development and solidification of deformities in our psychic make-up. So we think that we have grown up, we look like adults, we may or may not have the responsibilities associated with adulthood, but we have this pain, and we don't know where it comes from and we don't know what to do with it. So we overeat, we drink, we feed the flames with drugs, we immerse ourselves in obsessive relationships; anything to dull the pain, to live with our condition. You see, the fact is, our armor is our prison."

Something about the woman's voice had picked up and carried Holly's attention from the moment the lecture began. It must be the same for the others, she thought, as the room was imbued with a quality of rapt attention. For the next hour she found herself laughing with the audience at Bobbi's perfectly wrought ironies, nodding her head at connections she had never made before, and tearful as Bobbi related the childhood experiences of a convicted serial rapist.

"The point," Bobbi was saying, "is that we need to consciously become as children again, because underneath the armor that's what we have been. And it's only from that place that we can then build in order to become adults in the best sense of the word, able to live responsibly and have real relationships. So, we need a method for becoming children again, and a setting. And, crucial to the process, the setting must be safe, and the method true.

"The SOL movement, born out of my first book, *Saving Our Lives*, offers the method and setting required. We use a synthesis of psychoanalytic principles, metaphysical concepts, twelve-step work, and groundbreaking new technology to effect powerful long-term change in anyone who is committed to the process. The intensive workshops provide the framework for the initial catalyzing effect and later ongoing development. Many of you have already been to an intensive. We now have meetings all over the city and in many other states, in which we continue our work and commence to show, by example, how much for the better our lives can change. Thank you."

There was a silence for several seconds, followed by an explosion of applause. People around Holly stood, still clapping, until she was the only one in her row sitting. It made her feel conspicuous so she, too, stood.

Bobbi Bradley remained at the podium with her hands slightly outstretched, palms up, as though encouraging the audience. With a simple twist of her wrists, her palms faced outward and the room fell silent. Holly, like the rest, settled back in her seat.

"All right, now it's your turn. Who's got something to say?"

At this point Art appeared in the aisle with a microphone. Several hands shot up, and Art handed the mic to a woman a few rows behind Holly.

"My name is Denise and I'm here to save my life," the woman said.

"Hi, Denise," the audience echoed. Denise was in her late thirties, well dressed and self-assured, Holly thought.

"I just wanted to share with you that I first came to hear you two years ago because my friend thought it would be good for me. I was in complete denial at the time and perfectly convinced my life was okay."

"And was it really okay?" Bobbi asked.

"Somewhere in your pitch, when you spoke of having to undo the armor, I found that I was feeling scared and angry. I actually left the room. The next day I realized that what I was afraid of was being unprotected, and that you had told me a truth about myself."

"So what did you do?" Bobbi encouraged from the podium.

"I called the SOL hotline and they signed me up for the intensive. My life has totally been rocketed into a new dimension since that experience. It's not something you can describe; it's something you've just got to do." The woman sat down and more hands went up.

Holly listened to more glowing testimonials of the SOL intensive workshop experience. She had the feeling she was being set up for a pitch and was not surprised when two women began passing out flyers. Sure enough, there it was—fifteen hundred dollars for three days at the Malibu retreat.

Bobbi chose a man in the back. He was attractive, maybe fifty but trim looking, and when he took the mic he said only, "My name is Ron." There was a moment where Holly expected to hear the rest of the SOL statement, but it never came and the group remained silent.

"Bobbi," Ron continued, "I paid forty-five dollars to be here tonight. Your workshops cost fifteen hundred dollars. A set of your tapes runs ninety-five bucks. Don't you think there is something fundamentally inconsistent in offering work of this depth at such great profit to yourself?" Holly wondered the same thing but hadn't wanted to draw attention to herself.

Bobbi seemed unruffled. "The most useful thing for you to bear in mind is that the results of the work stand independent of the cost. In fact, putting up the money will intensify your commitment to the work. And that in turn will result in a greater sense of being a part of our fellowship, an increased sense of well-being, of wholeness that will launch you into so much higher a state of creativity and productiveness that the few dollars you pay here will be the best investment, the wisest placement of that energy we call money, that you ever made. Furthermore, I invite you, once you've got it, to give it away."

It was a smooth response, Holly thought, to Ron's challenge. A higher state of creativity, wholeness, well-being, rocketing into a new dimension—it all sounded so very attractive.

Bobbi thanked the audience to new cheers and applause and then left the stage. Art walked up to the podium and took the mic.

"Okay, does anyone not have an application for the next intensive?" He held up a copy. "Look around and you will see someone in your section standing and holding up one of these. Take your application to them and they will walk you through the enrollment procedure. Don't go home and think about it. The time to save your life is now."

The house lights went on and the theater burst into commotion. Holly turned to see Ted: he had a look of triumph on his face. "Really something, wasn't she?"

Holly wasn't yet sure what she thought—she was baffled by the juxtaposition of serious issues, tantalizing promises, and blatant hucksterism she had just seen. She was saved from having to answer by the appearance of Art.

"Holly, deck the halls. Why look so dour?" He really was very charming, she thought. "You're worried about the price of a miracle. Put it out of your head—we'll have a talk about it later."

CHAPTER 8

⏀

Ron Pool left the theater and walked to the parking lot. He unlocked the door to his old Land Rover and stepped up into the seat. In the quiet interior of his car, he closed his eyes and tried to still his thoughts. Instead, they took him back to a particular night in what almost seemed like another person's past, the end of a twenty-year nightmare, the night of his last drink nearly fourteen years ago. He remembered his first few weeks off booze, the horror of the first sleepless nights, the shaking hands. The thoughts, the guilt, and the pictures that wouldn't stop.

Driving home, he decided to give Joe Greiner a call.

"Joe. Ron Pool."

"Hey, Ron, 'sappening?" Joe was at home, probably drinking, never drunk. "Did you get my fax? Eight girls in less than two years, including Marilyn Fenner."

"I got it. Hell of a coincidence, don't you think?"

"Yeah, like they're in some damn club or something," Joe said.

"Joe, I'd really like to look at each file, photos and everything. This is worth looking into, and those case summaries aren't enough to go on."

"Ron," the detective replied, "I don't see it. Matter of fact, I think you're chasing a dead tale," and he made a garbled laughing sound that turned immediately into a fit of coughing.

"Jesus, Joe, you get worse all the time."

"What, this cough? It's nothin'."

Ron turned up Beachwood Canyon. "No, I mean your god-damn sense of humor."

"Come over to the station tomorrow and spend some time with the files. It's depressing, is all, so I have to make funny to get by, you know?"

He pulled into the driveway of his small canyon home and turned off the engine and the lights. Sitting in the still darkness, he realized how much he liked the cop at the other end of the line.

After a pause, he said, "You okay tonight, Joe? Something getting you down?"

"Naw, fuck no, same old same old." The Land Rover was still making its cooling off pops and clicks. "Where are you, anyway?"

"I just got home from a lecture. It was good except for the goddamned sales pitch at the end."

"You like all that New Age shit, don't you? Me, I think it's a waste of time." Ron could hear the clinking of ice cubes through the phone. He pictured Joe at his computer with a bottle of Tanqueray.

"Joe," Ron said, "you know what they say about contempt prior to investigation. I like to go out there like the world is a big banquet and I can pick a little of this and a little of that and come back with some useful information. It's kind of like digging for gold."

"More like scrounging in the fuckin' dump, if you ask me," Joe replied. "Hey, I'll bet these New Age shindigs have great looking chicks, am I right?"

"Well, now that you mention it . . ."

"Yeah, contempt prior to investigation my ass. Hey, Ron, catch me tomorrow—my inner child has to take a piss." Ron heard a chuckle and a click, and then there was nothing but the sound of a solo cricket chirping in the darkness.

CHAPTER 9

⏀

Jeff woke for the fourth time and decided this time he would get up. He had made the same decision earlier, but then revoked it because it was dark outside—too early, he had thought, and had gone back to sleep.

For some reason, the sun wasn't up yet. Puzzled, he looked at his clock and saw that it was 9:30—he had slept all day. His cell phone said that he had twelve messages. Usually that was good news; it meant people were ready to do business. Right now, though, it filled him with dread. He ignored it and left the ring volume off.

He realized that he was still dressed. Gradually, the pieces of the previous three days began to assemble themselves, culminating in his arrival home from Rich's at nine in the morning. God, what a nightmare. He must have fallen asleep right away.

He stripped and made his way through the dark room to the bathroom, where he finally turned on the light. Squinting in the bright illumination, he turned on the shower, waited for the hot water, and stepped in. The water felt good as he let it beat on his face—he had a moment of pure luxury before the reality of his situation began to filter into his thoughts.

Aiming straight down between his feet, he urinated into the drain for what seemed like forever. He was lightheaded from hunger and knew he needed to eat so he could think more clearly. Several things were very clear to him: that Lilah could cause him a lot of trouble if she talked, that he was short on the San Francisco investment now that most of it was in Rich's carpet, and that the messages on his phone were probably mainly angry calls from Rich. And that none of it mattered: only Marilyn mattered now.

He cleaned up, then dried off and dressed in jeans and, because it was still hot, a tee shirt. The shirt was white with a logo on it that said Channel Island Surfboards. He chose a contact from his phone's list and thumbed the dial icon.

"Hello?" He heard voices, laughter, and music blaring in the background.

"Gary, hey, it's me. Gotta see you. Meet me at Pop's in half an hour; can you make it?" Jeff felt a little shaky—it seemed like a long time since he had talked to anyone.

"Bad timing, man," Gary said through the noise. "We're like, ah, already committed, you know?"

What Gary meant was that he had company, probably a friend and a couple of women, and that they had already ingested enough drugs to make leaving the house impractical.

"I'll make it worth your while, big time. Listen, do something that'll straighten you out, leave some for the chicks, and tell them you'll be right back. Really, you'll be right back." He knew that Gary was only five minutes from Pop's, and that Gary's visitors weren't going anywhere.

"Worth my while, eh? Well, okay, I'll see you there," Gary said, and he hung up.

During the whole conversation, Jeff had been staring at the bag on his desk. Now he pulled out the large zip-lock baggie full of white chunks. He reached in the drawer and got a spatula and then opened the bag. He poked around until a long ridge of flaky powder sat on the flat end of the spatula. He looked at it and thought of the night before at Rich's, then placed it back in the bag. No, he wasn't even going to start. In fact, he should probably avoid it for a while, get rid of the whole bag of goodies, maybe even go to Kauai and chill for a while after he had taken care of business. Tonight, he would eat, work with Gary, relax with a couple of drinks, and maybe get back to sleep so he could wake up on a decent schedule.

He pulled an Ohaus triple beam scale from under the desk and carefully weighed the bag. He then inventoried the contents of his briefcase and added the coke to it. He put the inventory list, the cash, and the gun in a false-bottomed waste basket that was filled to the top with nasty trash: beer bottles with cigarette butts in them, Burger King wrappers covered with crusted cheese, and a dried-up apple core.

CHAPTER 10

꜔

Holly walked into the most beautiful living room she had ever seen. An entire wall was filled with recessed niches, each about twenty inches square and subtly lit from within to display an exotic carving or statuette. She recognized a bronze Kali and a four-armed Shiva, next to which was an African carving with a wooden phallus so massive it looked as if it were about to tip forward. A tapestry depicting a medieval court scene hung above a gleaming grand piano. Four people were present, seated around a marble coffee table. Art led her across the room to them.

"Holly, I'd like you to meet our hosts Joanie and Diane." Two women stood up and welcomed her. Joanie was a petite blond in her forties, beautiful, thought Holly, and yet unpretentious. Diane was at least six feet tall, with thick black eyebrows and very pale skin. Joanie took Holly's hand warmly and told her she had come to the right place.

"This," said Joanie, gesturing toward a thin balding man with very bright eyes sitting on the sofa, "is George . . . and Amy." George and Amy greeted Holly without getting up—Amy had Tarot cards spread on the table in front of her in five groups of three, Holly noticed, and the rest of the deck in her hand.

"We've been waiting for you," Joanie said, "and Amy has been entertaining us with the occult." She smiled slightly at this, as if amused, and then said, "Perhaps we should do your cards, Art. The hanged man and the tower have figured so prominently for the rest of us—perhaps you are the key."

"Joanie my dear, you're still looking for the Mark of the Beast on my forehead, after all these years. The only card that consistently shows up for me is the Fool. Now, Holly, have a seat." Art gestured for Holly to sit at the end of the sofa next to Amy and then brought a leather wing chair over and sat next to them.

"Those are the strangest-looking cards I have ever seen," said Holly, peering at a picture of haughty woman on a sled pulled by a leopard, all angles like shards of glass.

"The set was designed and commissioned by Aleister Crowley," Joanie said.

"Who is that?" asked Holly.

"The most brilliant psychopath of the twentieth century. A nasty man," said Art. "I have no taste for anything he produced except these brilliant images."

"Art, you have every book he ever wrote in your library," Joanie said.

"Of course. It's necessary to explore the darkest corners of the human heart. The path to wellness must always begin with recognition of sickness."

George put out his hand, palm forward, and intoned solemnly, "A riddle." The party looked toward George expectantly. He wore a black silk shirt buttoned to the throat. "What did Madame Blavatsky get when she ate some bad pork?" He suppressed a smirk as he looked around for an answer.

"Uh-oh," Art said. "Watch out."

"Tricky Gnosis," George burst out gleefully.

Everybody groaned and then burst out in laughter. Holly had no idea what they were laughing at or what they were talking about as they chatted on about Theosophists and Yeats and the Golden Dawn, about the Platonic Ideals and Aldous Huxley.

The conversation was interrupted by a small Hispanic woman carrying a tray. She silently placed it upon the table, looked to Joanie for further instructions, and left the room.

"Okay," said Joanie, "who would like some tea?"

Tea was poured, the cards put away, and the room was silent for a few moments, except for the murmurs of "sugar only," "yes,

that's perfect," and "thank you." Holly took tea and several cookies. She felt comfortable and yet apprehensive, as if something
were in the air that everyone was aware of except her.

☡

Only an hour earlier, after the lecture in Beverly Hills, Art had
suggested to Holly that she mingle, and then he led her to a group
that was conversing in the lobby. Art merely presented her and
said, "Holly. New." The others introduced themselves. Art told
her he would be back soon and disappeared.

A tall man with a gray beard held out his hand and said,
"Welcome to SOL." A student-type in a corduroy jacket told her
she was in for the ride of her life if she stuck around.

"I'm not so sure I will stick around," Holly replied. "I'm
certainly not going to spend fifteen hundred dollars to find out
what's next."

"Holly, what are your aspirations?" asked Frank, the man
with the beard.

"I'm an actress."

"Since you've not yet graced the cover of People magazine, I
imagine you have some measure of success yet to achieve ahead
of you, yes?" He looked at her patiently, she thought, and did not
seem to expect an answer.

"Holly." It was the guy in the corduroy, Nick. "How would
you feel if you had a suspicion that everything you think you
know was wrong? Everything you know about how the world
works, about how other people work, what they think, what they
are. Like a flat earther just beginning to figure out that something
wasn't right." He grinned.

"The point," continued Frank, "is that people come here
because they feel stuck in the problem that is their life, but are
unwilling to admit that, at the most fundamental level, their
thinking is the problem."

"Yeah," said Nick, "who wants to give up their thinking? It's
all we know."

"Yet what you know may be entirely false," added Frank, "and what you think you know generates what you call reality. Talk about staying stuck. There's no way out of the box."

Holly looked around for Art. She wished he would come back, yet she was angry with him for abandoning her to this onslaught.

"I just came here out of curiosity. Who said I was stuck?"

"Oh yes, the retreat into 'I'm okay, my life is fine, I'm just auditing this deal like I'm auditing the rest of life.'" Nick was derisive. "Okay, a riddle. What do you call a sound that you've heard ever since you were born?"

"I have no idea," Holly retorted.

"Silence. You would call it silence because it would be the threshold below which you can never hear anything new. The sound of the chatter of your own thinking is what you think is silence. Think of the possibilities of what you're missing."

"It all seems very arrogant," Holly told him. "You're all talking to me like I'm an infant."

"That's the point, Holly." Frank was lighting a pipe as he spoke. "I was, figuratively speaking, an infant before I did this work. Tenured professor of philosophy at a university, three published books, lecture tours, educated at Harvard and Cambridge, and yet I was an infant. So we're not here to insult you. We're here to invite you to step through the door, make a commitment, trust someone, and let life become a constant surprise."

At that point Art had returned and, taking her by the elbow, guided her to the exit. She turned to see the group smiling beatifically at her. Frank gestured a goodbye with his pipe.

"Do you know who that is?" Art asked her.

"Not a clue," she replied, biting her tongue at the choice of words.

"That is Frank Dixon. His book is number one on the *New York Times* bestseller list."

"Yeah, so he can afford to blow fifteen hundred bucks."

"Actually, Holly, he finished the book after completing the work in SOL. He came here three years ago in a suicidal depression, incapable of facing his computer screen."

They were outside. Art's green Jaguar was parked right in front of the theater—she hadn't noticed it earlier.

"Holly," Art turned toward her and placed his hands on her shoulders, holding her at arm's length, "I'd like you to come with me to visit some very special people. Will you join me now?"

$$\forall$$

Holly sipped her tea and reflected on the drive through the narrow, twisting roads of Stone Canyon, past the huge walled and gated estates, and up into the hills. They had finally come to a wrought-iron gate set in ivy-covered brick walls. Art had pushed a button and announced himself; the gate swung open and they continued up a driveway that was at least a city block long. There was a fountain in the middle of a circular drive in front of the house.

"Holly," Art broke into her thoughts like a wake-up call. "Still with us?"

"I'm sorry. I was thinking how lovely the house is."

"Holly, we're all going to stand up now, and I'd like you to join us." Art reached for her hand. She put down the cup of tea and stood.

The others joined in a circle and Joanie took her other hand.

"We are here to save our lives," Joanie intoned.

"We are here to save our lives," the others repeated.

"We must trust," said Joanie.

"We must trust," they echoed.

"Surrender," Joanie's hand gave Holly's a little squeeze.

"Surrender," she joined in the reply.

Art broke from the group and brought the ottoman that matched the wing chair into the middle of their circle.

"Holly, I'd like you to stand up on this for us," he told her as he offered his hand in support.

"Why?" she asked, suddenly uncomfortable.

"Because this is the beginning. Your entry into the work. I absolutely guarantee your safety." He took her hand and helped her step up on the ottoman.

She stood awkwardly, feeling naked and exposed. The others moved so that Art and Diane were in front of her and to her left, George and Amy to her right, and Joanie, who stood back a few paces, was facing her.

"Now, Holly, if you would close your eyes," Art suggested softly.

"Holly," Joanie began, "I am going to take you on a guided meditation. When I tell you to fall, I want you to fall straight forward. Keep your eyes closed—we will catch you. There is absolutely nothing to be afraid of."

"I don't want to do this," Holly replied, but she kept her eyes shut and made no move to step down.

"I hear you," said Joanie. "You don't want to do this. I've got that. Now, you are walking up a road through a beautiful mountain forest. The trees are tall and full and green against the clear blue sky. It is very peaceful. Ahead, to your right, is an old stone wall. It is about ten feet tall. There is a castle beyond it. Something is very wrong. The castle is being demolished."

Holly stood still, actually seeing the trees and the wall, and felt a sudden anxiety that danger approached.

"You begin to walk more quickly. Over the wall you glimpse a monster. It is half beast and half machine. It has destroyed the castle and is tearing down the wall. You begin to run. Without looking back, you know it is chasing you. The road ends at a meadow; you run through tall grass and flowers. When you look back, you see that where the beast has run there is only scorched desert. You run to the end of the meadow—the edge of a cliff is before you. You look down and can see only a shimmering golden fog. Behind you is destruction. It is time, Holly, to jump."

Holly, standing with her arms outstretched like a highdiver, eyes still closed, shook her head in a small tremor and said, "I can't."

"Why not?" asked Art.

"I just can't."

"Holly, tell me what you're feeling right now," he persisted.

"I'm feeling . . . panic. Anger. I feel like this is some of the silliest bullshit I've ever heard."

"I hear you, but that is not a feeling. Stay with your feelings, Holly. Where are you feeling this panic?"

She concentrated for a moment. "In my neck."

"Where else?" Art prodded.

"In my jaw and my shoulders. And I have a headache."

"A headache. Where is your headache?"

"In my head, goddammit, where else do you get a headache?" Holly snapped.

"In the front of your head?"

"Yes."

"Where?"

"About an inch in from my forehead."

"How wide is it. How thick?" Art persisted.

"It goes from temple to temple. Maybe an inch thick."

"Does it have a shape?"

"Yes, it's oval." Holly was entirely inwardly focused.

"Does it have a color?" Art's voice was gentle but persuasive.

"Yes. It's orange. No, it's changing. It's bluish."

"How big is it?"

"I don't know," she said. "It's getting smaller."

"How about your jaw, your neck and shoulders?"

Holly moved her shoulders and turned her head left and right. "They feel okay. I'm okay."

"And your head? Do you still have a headache?"

"No. No, I feel fine." She flexed her fingers as though they had just begun working.

"Okay," Joanie resumed, "you are standing at the edge of the cliff. There is nothing but destruction behind you. Ahead is a golden mist. All you need to do is fall into it. There is nothing to lose. It is quite beautiful."

With no intention of cooperating, Holly felt herself pitch forward and then, after the briefest second of flight, she was picked out of the air by five pairs of hands and gently lowered to the floor. A sob welled up from deep in her gut; it came out like a bellow but she didn't care. She had a vision, first of gemstones glinting from the bottom of a mountain stream, then of a child, herself at six years old. She was looking at a man squatting, pointing a camera at her. She saw herself through the camera, and then the picture tilted to a crazy angle. A brilliant light flashed.

Holly lay on the floor and wept, effortlessly and unrestrained.

The others knelt around her, hands still on her body. After a moment she turned over and sat up.

"Holly," Art began, "what did you see?"

"Jewels. Jewels in water."

"Ah. Very nice. What else?"

"Me," she said. "I saw myself. Someone was taking a picture of me. But then I was looking through the camera at myself when I was little."

"Yes?" Art encouraged. He handed her a handkerchief.

"Then the picture tilted." She cocked her head at an angle. "I think I fell over."

"Who fell?"

"I must have."

"Who fell?" Art commanded.

"Daddy fell."

"Why did he fall?" Art asked, almost in a whisper.

"He fell because he was drunk." She cried and dabbed at her eyes with the handkerchief.

"Yes," said Art, as he lightly brushed the bruise under her eye, "Daddy fell because he was drunk."

CHAPTER 11

⩜

Jeff drove up Santa Monica Canyon to San Vicente, heading east toward Pop's. His aging 280Z was nearly out of gas and the registration had expired, but he figured he could fill the tank later.

It was half past ten and the lot at Pop's was full—Thursday night was ladies' night. He parked in the market lot next door and walked back to the entrance of the club. There was a line at the door, people waiting to get their IDs checked and pay to get in. Jeff walked past them to the door.

"Hey, Jeff, come on in." The bouncer at the door was a big guy, looked like a football player, clean cut and all-American. He also moved—through Gary—a lot of coke for Jeff.

"Hey, Freddie, thanks a lot." They ran through a series of arcane handshakes that Jeff always hated. "Is Gary here?"

"Yeah, he's in back at one of the tables. Better hurry in if you still want to eat." Freddie had seen Jeff race in for dinner at the last moment dozens of times. "Hey, man, is anything happening?" They were still clasped in the last stage of the handshaking routine, and Freddie pulled in to ask this discreetly.

"Maybe, man, check with Gary later on, okay?" Jeff moved toward the inside of the club.

Pop's was a fixture in Brentwood, a sports bar with a large regular crowd and a magnet for out-of-towners. Most of the regulars were college types or young professionals—a straight crowd, at least in appearance. It was packed tonight, the dart board games already jammed, people three deep around the main bar, and the sawdust floor crowded with people standing, holding their drinks and yelling to be heard.

He pushed his way through the crowd toward the back room, which was darker and slightly less crowded. He saw Gary sitting alone at a booth.

"Hey, man, what's happening?" Gary gestured a greeting with his Heineken bottle. He had long red hair and a handlebar moustache and looked out of place in the club; he belonged in a rougher place, with pool tables and "Sweet Home Alabama" blaring from a jukebox.

Jeff slid into the booth. "The joint is jumpin'," he grinned. Already, the night seemed full of possibilities. "So what's up at your place?"

Gary shook his head, rolled his eyes, and grinned back. "Skippy showed up with the twinbos. I figured I'd let them stay. You know, bird in the hand, right?"

The twinbos were Jeri and Sherry, the twin bimbos. "Shit, Gary, they make Lilah look like Marie Osmond." Jeff told Gary about the night before at Lilah's. A waitress came and he ordered a cheeseburger, fries, and a bottle of Kirin.

"Listen, Gary, I got something for you, but I don't want things to get fucked up."

"Hey, no problema," Gary said. "I got it under control."

"Listen,"—Jeff moved in closer to Gary so he wouldn't have to speak loudly—"I'm going to lay everything I got on you. Can you move it by Saturday?"

"How much is there," Gary asked.

"An even half-pound, some weighed ounces and a bag full of Xanax," Jeff told him. "Just move it by Saturday, don't front any of it, and don't cut it in case I have to take it back. Okay?"

Gary said "no problema" again just as the waitress came. Jeff started on the burger.

"Best fuckin' burger in town," he said with his mouth full.

"No shit," Gary said as he ordered another beer.

When he had finished the burger and the last of the fries, Jeff drained his bottle of beer and motioned toward the door. "Let's head out."

They went to Gary's Mustang, which was parked around the corner, and drove to the market parking lot. Gary pulled up next to the Z. Jeff got out, took a quick look around the lot, and got in his car. He handed the bag through the window as Gary leaned across to grab it.

Out of the corner of his eye, Jeff saw a dark-green Ford sedan pull into the parking lot from the side street exit. It had a big antenna, blacked-in wheel-wells instead of hubcaps, and two men in the front seat. The vehicle turned so that he looked straight into its headlights.

"Shit. GND," Jeff said, and he released the bag.

He heard it land with a rustling sound. Gary was still stretched across the passenger seat of his car, hand reaching out the window. "Fuck," said Jeff, "what's the matter with you?"

The Ford pulled into the spot right next to Jeff and the doors opened. Of all the possibilities to tangle with on the street, Gang and Narcotics Division was the worst. If they smelled fear they knew they didn't have to treat you like an ordinary citizen.

"So, you going to the beach tomorrow?" Gary asked, loud enough for his voice to carry over to the cops.

Jeff yelled back, "Yeah, I'll be at the pier playing volleyball at eight," and he started his car. He heard the Ford's doors slam shut. He froze, wondering if they would knock on the passenger window or come around to his side where the bag was in plain view on the ground. He heard Gary's car start.

The cops, two big guys in sports jackets, headed toward the market, ignoring Jeff and Gary. Gary opened the door to his Mustang and, lying across the seat now, picked the bag off the ground and pulled it into his car.

"Fuck you, man, how could you just drop it like that?"

"I thought you had it," Jeff replied. "Call me tomorrow and let me know what's happening."

Gary pulled out of the parking lot. Jeff got out of his Audi and walked back to Pop's.

He needed a drink. His heart was pounding—he hated those guys. They never went for the "Oh, hello Officer, how can I help you?" routine.

Freddie nodded him in again at Pop's. He went to the table in the back room and ordered a Jack Daniel's. It took two more before he felt normal enough to venture out to the main room and see what was happening. Maybe he could still salvage the evening.

▽

He noticed a woman he used to date sitting at the bar and managed to edge in next to her.

"Hello, Janet."

"Jeff. Hi. What a surprise." She smiled.

Jeff said, "Christ, this place is a zoo tonight." He needed to plant the seed of possibility here, just in case nothing else was happening by last call. Janet brought him up to date on her life since he had stopped calling her. "Well, Jeff, I don't want to bore you with my hum-drum story. How about you? Your life is always so much more interesting."

He looked at her and drew a total blank. Nothing was very interesting. His sister was dead and he was drinking in a bar. He was out of money and living in a dump. He was driving a heap and he owed money to the wrong people. "Oh, the usual, you know . . ." He looked at her and shrugged. She looked so pretty, with her dark hair pulled straight back, her smartly tailored jacket, and her breasts pressing against her silk blouse. She had always had such high expectations of him. "Let's see if we can find a table where it's a little quieter."

"Yeah, let's move. Don't look now, but there's a guy across the bar that's been staring at me ever since I got here. It's giving me the creeps."

"You know, it's funny seeing you here—I was just thinking about you earlier in the evening."

Several drinks later, he led Janet out of the club. Freddie looked at Janet and gave Jeff a surreptitious thumbs-up gesture. Jeff said, "Why don't you give Gary a call," and walked Janet to her car. She drew him to her and they kissed, her breasts pressing against him as she opened her mouth. Jeff closed his eyes and felt himself sway. "Whoa, there," Janet said, "are you going to be able to drive?" The plan was that he would follow Janet to her place in the Palisades.

"Hey, I'm fine," he told her, but he wished he hadn't turned all of the coke over to Gary.

Janet drove him around the corner to his car. They pulled out of the parking lot together, heading back down San Vicente toward the beach. Janet's place was only a few miles past his apartment.

On the long stretch through Brentwood Janet suddenly raced ahead of him. He put on some speed but the taillights of her car were still receding. He realized that she was probably as drunk as he was. He slapped his face and it felt numb. He had that bad feeling in his stomach again.

The Audi stuttered as it hurtled through the darkened upscale neighborhood. He was doing about seventy but could no longer see Janet's taillights. The stutter happened again and he began to lose speed. He pumped the gas and picked up some power for a moment, but then the engine quit and he was coasting, out of gas.

"Shit. Unbelievable. Shit." He hit the steering wheel with both hands. He had pulled over into the bike lane, miles from a gas station. He opened the door to step out but his leg didn't support him and he rolled onto the street instead. He thought of Janet. *Fuck her*, he thought. *If she hadn't gone so damned fast she could have given him a ride.*

He stood up and brushed off his jeans. He was only about a mile from the Canyon.

He had only been walking a short time when he heard a car coming up behind him. He turned around and saw a new Lincoln Continental slow down, then stop, in the middle of the street.

The window slid down. "Would you like a ride?" It was a man. He looked small, older. Jeff was grateful and let himself in.

"Where are you headed?" the man asked.

"Canyon, almost to the beach," Jeff replied.

"Oh, well, that's lucky. So am I." Jeff noticed a softness to the man's S's. There was a cluster of gay bars in the Canyon. He put his head back on the plush leather headrest and hoped that the spinning would subside. He was glad that the driver didn't try to make conversation.

When they got to the bottom of the Canyon, he asked the man to drop him off several buildings away from his apartment. He said, "Thanks a lot," and closed the door. The window slid down again.

"Can I do anything for you?" the man asked.

"No, thanks, I'm all set," Jeff replied.

"Well, I mean, is there anything you would like?" The man smiled this time.

"Yes," said Jeff, "I would like to never feel like this again." He turned away from the car.

"I know what you mean," the man called out. "I'll probably be saying the same thing in the morning."

Jeff watched the man's taillights fade as he walked the short distance to his apartment and then quickly let himself in. He crossed the dark room to sit at his desk and put his head down on its hard surface. He sat like that, wondering how anyone could wake up at nine at night, almost get busted, run out of gas, and drink until he was sick, all before one o'clock.

He glanced at his phone, which now told him he had sixteen messages. He couldn't put it off anymore, so he dialed voicemail.

"Jeff, are you there? Jeff, pick up the phone. It's your dad." There was a click, then the voicemail recording telling him his options. He chose delete and played the next message.

"Jeff, call us at home, it's . . ."

The next message was his mother. "Jeff, call us right away. I don't know where you are but this is very important." Christ, he thought, I can't handle it. I need to straighten up just to call them.

The next call was the one he was worried about.

"Jeff, Richard." *Okay,* he thought, *how pissed off is Richard about his money?* "Listen, man, sorry about your sister. I read about it. But you know what? I need some money tomorrow or you're in deep shit."

CHAPTER 12

⏃

Ron Pool woke early Friday morning and considered the day ahead. He would begin with a bowl of oatmeal and then head over to Griffith Park to run. He had a six-mile circuit that he ran four times a week. Then he would return home and shower, get dressed, drink some coffee, and drive downtown for an interview with a possible witness at the county jail. At lunchtime he would cross town to meet Joe Greiner at the station. The evening was open ended.

At half past noon, Ron headed toward the Westside. It was another hot and humid day in the seemingly endless sweltering summer. He got on the Santa Monica Freeway and turned on the air conditioning.

Work had been uneventful. National elections were coming up in November and there was the usual feeding frenzy as the candidates turned up the heat on each other by plumbing the depths of negative campaigning. He had been given a piece to write on a city councilman who had been caught in a police sting. A policewoman had posed as a hooker, and, within three hours, twelve men had been arrested for offering her money. The councilman, one of the twelve arrested, claimed that he had known it was a sting and was doing his own investigative work on police procedure. Writing it up would be a snap, he thought. Nobody believed the guy, but his audacity was so great and his political entrenchment so solid that no one questioned his re-election.

He took the 405 north to Wilshire and headed west again. He pulled over and parked just past Bundy drive, locked his truck, and put some money in the meter.

The Bicycle Café was one of his favorite places to eat. It was typically Californian, all wood and hanging plants, but he liked the bicycle motif. An antique bike with a huge front wheel hung suspended by wires above the table he chose.

He looked around the restaurant: there were a few power lunchers—men in suits, briefcases at their feet. At a table nearby four businessmen were receiving drinks from the waitress. Ron wondered how they could start drinking in the middle of the day and then walk away from it, go back to work without needing another, and another.

The waitress came over to his table. She was attractive, healthy looking with freckles and chestnut hair.

"Hey, Ron, how are you?" She smiled.

"Really good, Leanne. How about you?" He always liked seeing Leanne. She radiated a quality he liked, a contagious optimism that he was convinced was real and fundamental to her nature.

They talked about running. She was training for a marathon but had a problem with her ankle. Taking some classes at night, history and philosophy; really liked it. She took his lunch order and walked toward the kitchen. He watched as she left; she had runner's legs, long and slender with powerful calves.

He took pleasure in his meal and decided not to review his notes on the suicide files while he was eating. He had long ago learned that his intuitive faculties worked best when he was feeling balanced—his mind seemed to work more efficiently if he kept things simple.

After he had finished and paid, Leanne came back as he was standing to leave. "I miss our runs together," she said.

"Yeah, me too," he replied.

She pressed her lips together and looked down for a moment. "Sometimes I wonder if you ever think of calling." She looked up at him, her eyes clear and gray, and held his gaze.

"I'm thinking it would be crazy not to," he told her, and she put her fingertips briefly to his chest to say goodbye.

He drove south on Bundy Drive. Everything north of Wilshire Boulevard was pretty upscale. By the time he got to Santa Monica Boulevard and turned he could feel the change in ambience. A wild-haired man in a pea coat clutched a sleeping bag as he sat at a bus bench and stared at his fingers. Ron wondered if the guy even felt the heat or if he was too removed from sensation to even register discomfort.

Traffic was thick and people were impatient. He stopped at a light; there was one at every block and he seemed to be stuck in an endless line of cars. He heard a loud horn blast directly behind him. A woman in a seedy older Cadillac pulled up on his bumper and the back half of her car blocked the cross traffic. The driver of the first northbound car that couldn't get past the Cadillac leaned on his horn. Two more horns added to the noise. The woman in the Cadillac inched up behind Ron until her bumper made contact with his. He looked in his rearview mirror and watched her as she honked in short repetitive bursts and motioned to him to move forward. Which of course he couldn't do—nobody was moving.

There had been a time, he reflected, when this would have made him homicidal. He had chased people on freeways, leaning across his passenger seat to shout obscenities at them through his passenger window, for lesser infractions than the woman behind him committed. He could no longer afford that kind of indulgence. An old-timer in AA had asked him to write a list of all the people that had ever made him angry. The list was so long he realized he had been totally dominated by people and events. "Scary, isn't it?" the old-timer had chuckled, then adding, "Trouble is, you stay pissed off, you'll drink again."

Six blocks and ten minutes later, Ron turned into the parking lot of the West LA police station. In the past fourteen years he had been here many occasions on assignment and it always brought back memories of the times he had spent in drunk tanks. Four in this station alone, twice for drunk driving.

He entered the police station, passing two cops in street clothes as he went in. They recognized him and nodded. A young black woman in uniform talked from behind the counter to an older black man.

"I'm sorry, there's nothing I can do. He's already on the bus to downtown," the woman said.

The man shook his head and said, "They told me I could come down here and post bond for him until five. I took time off work, I got the money, I drove all the way over here, it's two o'clock and now I want my boy."

The woman simply handed the man a sheet of paper and said, "You call this number right here first thing in the morning. It'll take that long to get him processed." She turned her attention to Ron.

"I'm here to see Joe Greiner," he told her. She asked him to please wait, and then picked up the phone on the desk behind her. As she spoke, the black man said to Ron, "There's people out there killin' folks, and these clowns got to hassle my boy." He walked out the door, still shaking his head.

Joe Greiner appeared in the hallway to the right of the counter and motioned for Ron to follow him. They wound their way through a maze of desks until they reached Joe's office. It wasn't really an office but a cubicle, much like his own at the *Times*, only the desk and wall panels were even older. They sat down in the only two seats the tiny cluttered space could hold.

"Hey, buddy, you're lookin' fit as ever. Still eatin' that rabbit food?" Joe liked to give him a hard time about eating salads.

"Joe, you spend two weeks with me and stay out of those Fatburger joints, you'll never have to grab the flab again."

"Oh, you seen me do that?" Joe looked down at his belly and patted it.

"Used to do it myself. I got tired of it, though. My back was always going out on me."

"Oh, right, you got tired of it. So what'd you do? Let me guess—you're not the Weight Watchers type. Speed? Nah. Binge/purge? Probably not. Hey, I got it. Positive fuckin' affirmations, am I right? 'I am thin and my life works on all levels.'" Joe grinned. "Hey, I been meanin' to redecorate, but my designer's on strike."

"Hell, it looks fine to me," Ron replied. "I'm just happy to be able to leave here without having to pay money."

It had been several months since he had seen Joe. The piece on the girl's suicide was based on information the detective had given to him over the phone.

"So anyway," Joe said, "it's good to see you again."

"Yeah, hey, thanks for giving me some time on this." Ron opened his briefcase and pulled out a notebook and a sheaf of faxes. "Here's the stuff you sent me the other day."

"Yeah, here are the files." Joe gestured toward a stack on his desk. "Now, check this out. This morning I get a call from downtown. There's this roving drug squad, sheriff's department. They go on assignment all over the county. Anyway, I get a call from this narco guy, lemme see." Joe reached for a pad on the desk. "Bill Cox is his name. Says he wonders if I can do him a favor. You follow what I'm saying?"

"This ties in to the suicide files?" He was anxious to see the files on Joe's desk and didn't understand this digression.

"Well, stay with me. It seems that this narcotics squad has been after a local dealer—lives out by the beach—name of Jeffrey Fenner. Ring a bell?" Joe grinned.

"No kidding. That's our girl's name—Marilyn Fenner. Ex-husband? Family?" Ron was intrigued.

"He's our jumper's big brother. Anyway, this guy Cox wants the toxicology report on Marilyn. Says if she jumped with drugs in her system maybe we can bring the brother in as accessory to a crime; you know, furnishing contraband."

"I don't get it. What do they want to do?" Ron shifted his weight in the uncomfortable chair.

Joe leaned forward. "Furnishing drugs to someone who commits an act resulting in death can be construed by the courts as murder. They want to scare this guy into cutting a deal and giving up a few of his connections."

"Can they do that?"

Joe shrugged his shoulders. "Sounds pretty farfetched to me. They can give it a shot."

"So, have you got a report from the lab?" Ron asked.

"Yeah, and it seems Marilyn had something in her system, but not a street drug. It's a fairly exotic pharmaceutical, Halcion. Prescription only." Joe shrugged again. "Coincidence. Don't see what damn good it does us." He stood up and patted the stack of files. "So here. Have a seat and rummage through this pile of sad stories. It's my ass if you're seen with these. I got a few things to do. I'll catch you back here in a half hour." He started to leave the cubicle, but then turned back to Ron. "Hey, almost forgot. I know this is kind of gruesome, but I checked out the photos of the dead girls. You know what, I might be a sick puppy, them being dead and all, but I'm damned if they weren't all pretty good looking. I mean like model-type good looking."

CHAPTER 13

H olly was making breakfast when the phone rang. She picked it up and said, "Good morning," assuming that it was Art. He had taken to calling her every morning at 8:30, telling her each time that an attitude adjustment now can change the whole day. She found it flattering, somehow, and would walk around the kitchen making coffee and eggs, talking and sparring with him on her cordless.

"Hey." It was definitely not Art. "You're nice and chirpy this early in the morning. Sounds like you were expecting a call." It was Tony, and Tony was never up this early unless he'd been up all night.

"Hello, how have you been?" It had been less than a week but seemed like months since she had seen him.

"Well, I'm almost on top of the world. I got a label wants to pick us up, do an album. Band's sounding great . . ." There was a pause. "I used to know a girl named Holly that was glad to see me once in a while."

"Are you calling to apologize?" she asked. She realized she didn't even care, didn't want the apology. She just wanted to get off the phone.

"Are you sure I owe you an apology?" Tony's voice wasn't quite right; it was high and hollow. His cocaine voice, she used to call it.

"Oh forget it, Tony. People punch me all the time and then call back like nothing happened. Shit, I think I'll just spend the day looking for someone new to push me around my own goddamned living room and give me another black eye." She hadn't planned to say any of this. In fact, she realized, she had blocked the event and the thought of talking to Tony again.

"Hey," Tony said, "it takes two to tango. You were sneaky. I got mad. I'm over it. Listen,"—and she could tell he was switching subjects on her, like a salesman changing tack—"I'm looking at a truly great opportunity right now and it's gonna sail by me if I don't jump on it, like immediately."

"So what's that got to do with me?" She knew what was coming.

"You know, there's something about your tone that's—naw, forget it. Here's the deal. I need three grand until tomorrow night. It's a done deal. It'll totally solve all my problems."

"Tony, you're out of your fucking mind. Forget it. Go to sleep. Leave me alone." She heard a drawn out inhalation, like someone clearing their sinuses, but longer, and then the clinking of ice. She could picture him snorting the coke and then draining his drink, then giving his head an abrupt shake like a fighter who's just been punched.

"Pay you back thirty-five hundred. That's more than your money's making in your dumb little bank account." Tony was usually very good at getting what he wanted, but at some point of intoxication he totally lost his touch.

"Goodbye, Tony. Don't call again." She heard him yell "Don't you hang up on me, you self-righteous little cunt," and then she put down the phone.

▽

She was still sitting at the kitchen table when the phone rang again. It was ten minutes after the conversation with Tony, and she hadn't moved since she had hung up. She let her answering machine pick up this new call, figuring that Tony might have decided he had more to say.

After listening to her own greeting, though, she was relieved to hear that this time it really was Art. She picked up the line and the answering device cut out.

"Hi." She wondered if she sounded odd.

"Good morning, Holly. Are we screening our calls today?" Somehow it seemed that he always knew what she was doing.

"Tony just called me."

"Oh, your ex. A very decent person, about to become successful, as you once told me. How did his call make you feel?"

"Terrible." She realized that she didn't want to talk about it. "I wish he would disappear."

"Even if he did disappear, don't you know that you're a magnet for the Tonys of this world?"

"What's that supposed to mean?"

"Holly, the Tonys have their radar set to your frequency. Yours just happens to be set to theirs. Until you change your frequency, there will always be another Tony."

She realized Art was right. Nothing ever seemed to change when it came to men. The nice guys were always boring, and the exciting ones were, well, like Tony. "So how do I change frequencies?"

Art replied, "That's exactly what the SOL process is about. We access the child within us, we allow ourselves to be vulnerable, we follow Bobbi's suggestions, and everything changes. Including the people we attract and want to attract."

"All this and more from one fifteen-hundred-dollar seminar." She couldn't keep the sarcasm out of her voice.

"Holly, skepticism is a very good thing. It shows a discriminating mind. Cynicism is a great excuse for staying stuck. Listen . . ." It was that same salesman's technique that Tony had used. "Why do you think people spend the money? You saw the people at Bobbi's talk. They aren't lonely-hearts types looking for a place to be dreary together. They're people committed to changing their lives, transforming themselves. Furthermore, Holly, you're getting this thing for free."

"What do you mean," she asked.

"I mean that I am sponsoring you into the program. Mentoring you—it helps me and it helps you. Now let me ask you this: How much good did therapy ever do you?"

She hadn't told him, but she had been through years of therapy. "It's hard to tell," she said. "I don't know what life would have been without it. Sometimes it seemed pretty useless."

"Right. But you kept on going because you were after something. What was it?"

"I don't know. Happiness?" There was more to it than that, she thought. She needed to change the way she felt.

"You wanted to change the way that you felt, and you always thought that if you could just get down to some bottom line, to some first cause, that you would find the magic key that would open the door to freedom. And then everything would be different. Am I right?"

She turned on the coffee maker. "You make it sound so naive, like it was a dumb thing to hope for."

"Yes, it is naive; no, it's not a dumb thing to hope for. It's naive to think you can just get there passively, expect to get fixed lying on a couch. I used to try to fix it with alcohol. Always looking for that magic key."

She asked, "What happened?" and poured a bowl of granola.

"I went to AA and things got better. But then I found out about regression therapy and inner child work, and I realized alcoholism wasn't my problem—it was my response to my problem."

Holly was curious. "So can you drink like a normal person now?"

Art laughed. "No, if I put alcohol into my system, it would still trigger an alcoholic response."

"What's that?"

"I would keep drinking, and then all that old stuff would come up again and I'd be back to square one." Art was silent for a moment. She put him on speakerphone, got milk from the refrigerator and poured it onto the granola. She removed the coffee pot and poured the steaming black brew into a mug.

Art spoke again. "So, attitude adjustment time. Tony and all the ones like him can be in your past. You didn't step through the doors of SOL by accident—you came looking for something. We began last week at Joanie's house, now let's continue. I'll mentor. You'll be amazed."

She stirred her coffee and spoke into the room, "Why me?"

"Why not?" Art responded, and his chuckle seemed to bounce around Holly's kitchen. "Listen, put down your coffee and try something, okay?"

Had she really made noise sipping her coffee? "What do you mean?" she asked.

"Go over to your doorway," Art's voice said, "and put the backs of your hands up against the frame on either side of you. Keep your arms straight." Art's games were always pretty interesting, so she transferred her cereal and coffee to the kitchen table and then went to the doorway. "Okay, now what?"

"Now," Art said, "press outward like you're trying to make the doorway wider. Are you doing it?"

"Yeah," she replied. "So what's this all about?"

"Push harder. Don't lighten up. Now listen. You are in a box. Just like your life is in a box. No matter how hard you push, the box stays the same. There is no freedom in the box. Are you with me?"

"Yes," she said, "but my arms are getting sore."

"That's right," Art replied. "It's very exhausting spending your life trying to get out of the box. It uses up all your energy so there's none left for the things that really matter."

"Art, I can't do this any more. What's the point?"

"The point?" Art chuckled again. "The point, Holly, is to step out of the box. Just take a step forward."

She stepped forward, and to her amazement her arms floated up entirely of their own accord, like the wings of a wild bird in a sudden breeze.

"You see?" Art's voice filled the room. "Freedom's just a step away. Let's get together."

CHAPTER 14

☟

Ron stared at the pile of folders. Some jobs required stomach and stamina he wasn't sure he had. This was one of them. The simple fact that the eight files each documented a life cut short weighed on him to the point that he wanted to just get up and walk away. After all, there wasn't even a story here, just a hunch, a puzzle he probably couldn't write about even if he solved it.

Suddenly unsure of what to do, he closed his eyes and quieted his mind. He had grown to trust the silence and whatever answers came out of it. After a moment, he opened his eyes and reached for the top file.

There was a case number on the folder's tab. He opened the file and looked at the face page attached to the back cover. It was a standard form, identified at the bottom as SHAD49. The box at the top was titled "Incident," and contained only one word: "suicide." There was the case number again, and the time and date of the "incident," as well as the time of police notification.

This one said "11:50 p.m."—it was a year and a half old. In the box titled "victim's name," he read "Nancy Mills." She had been twenty-four years old. She was from Mar Vista. Wearing jeans, sweater, and a ski parka. Under "synopsis," he read that Nancy Mills had jumped from the palisades in Santa Monica. He had stood at those same cliffs, looking out over the bay; they ran the length of Ocean Avenue, divided from it by a strip of grass and a path. Tourists mingled with strolling locals and a motley collection of homeless people. Only a low fence separated the path from the edge of the cliff, and directly below cars raced by on the Pacific Coast Highway.

Cause of death, the report read, was a broken neck, probably incurred upon striking the cliff side before the completion of her fall. She had landed in some shrubbery only a few feet from the highway.

He flipped the page up. Under it was a transmittal form—a summary that would have been forwarded to a statewide agency to tabulate statistics. This was followed by a page titled "evidence," which referred to items found on the deceased, clothes, contents of purse and pocket, and the notation, "photos."

Next was a full narrative of the event. It detailed the condition of the body, the name of the witness who called the police (a motorist, northbound on the PCH), and concluded with a note that the family of the victim had been notified and "see coroner's report."

He scanned the coroner's report long enough to see the words "No physical evidence indicating second party—death by suicide." Following the report was a Xerox page that showed a driver's license and what appeared to be a nurse's badge from Saint John's Hospital.

He made some entries in his notebook and flipped back to the beginning of the file. Stapled to the inside cover was an envelope. The file was depressing, but his left-brain, analytical mind had taken over.

There were three photos of the girl's body. Two were full body shots taken from different angles. The third was a close-up, head and shoulders. It looked like a photo of a sleeping person. The hair was tousled but still framed the girl's features attractively. She had high cheekbones and nice, clear features, he thought. He remembered Joe's comment about how all the girls were attractive and made a decision.

He rolled his chair back and laid each file on the floor, four to a row, and removed the photographs from each. He laid the photos out on their respective folders and bent over to study the lot of them. Joe was right. Even the grimmer shots revealed a physical attractiveness far beyond any random sample of the population. And, they were consistent in type: blond, tall, slender. This, he thought, was a clear thread connecting all eight incidents. Where there was one, he knew, there would surely be others.

By the time Joe got back, Ron had gathered up the files, replaced the photos, and made notes on each incident. Joe was chewing on a bagel when he came in. "You know," he said, with his mouth full, "if these came glazed it could be a big hit."

Ron glanced up from his notebook. "Right, lox and cream cheese; gimme that on a glazed."

Joe nodded toward the stack of files. "So? Is there a single-bullet theory?" He moved the files over and sat on the desk

Ron leaned back in his chair and flipped a few pages in his notebook. "Okay," he said, "for starters, you noticed what all these girls looked like. Do you think it's just a coincidence?"

Joe said, "In the absence of some other point of commonality, I have to call it random, inconclusive. Weird, but not enough to get a cop excited."

"Okay," Ron replied, "you've got bad guys to chase. But I'm going to follow up on some of this stuff. Call the families, maybe. Did you know that two of the girls had DUIs and had been referred to alcohol counseling?"

"So? That fits—most suicides have histories of depression, substance abuse. What else have you got?"

Ron checked his notes again, running his pencil down a page. "Here, Laura Hunsaker, age twenty-six. Found at the bottom of a ravine in Idyllwild last summer."

"Yeah, what about it?" Joe finished his bagel and wiped his hands together.

"It seems that the Sheriff's department out there investigated it as possible foul play before they sent it over here." Ron checked his notes and pulled the corresponding file. "Here, read the third line from the bottom."

Joe scanned the report. He whistled when he got to the end. "I'll be damned. Halcion. That's what they found in Marilyn

Fenner. Listen, you find a real thread here, I'll take you out to San Nicholas Island. We'll catch the biggest damn fish you ever saw."

"Are you blowing me off?" Ron asked.

"No, hell no." Joe replied. "I think it just got more interesting. I just can't give it any of my time until you bring me something solid."

Ron put his notebook back in his briefcase and stood up. "Joe, thanks for sticking your neck out like this."

"Aw shit, just exposing the department to lawsuits from eight families. That would put me back in uniform, pronto."

They started walking toward the lobby. "I don't see a story here yet, Joe. And if there is one, this conversation won't be in it." They shook hands and Ron stepped out the door into a warm, breezy evening.

CHAPTER 15

Jeff felt weird. It was the kind of weird that usually a drink would fix, or something, but he didn't think so. Not this time. It was like, once he got started, he didn't trust how it would end up. This feeling weird, though, he was getting tired of it. A week now he'd been waiting for it to go away and it just wouldn't lighten up.

"Jeffrey?" Goddammit. Now what?

"Yeah, Mom. I'll be right out." Maybe he was sick. He looked around. He'd grown up in this room, but now it was just "the guest room" and didn't look anything like before. It seemed smaller, too. Now he was a guest, already feeling that he had overstayed his welcome.

"Jeffrey? I'm going to the market—is there anything you want?" His mother was in the hallway, on the other side of the door. He got up and opened it.

"Hi, Mom. You want me to come with you?" She was still pretty, he thought, her hair in a bun and her face smooth except for the lines at her eyes and a pain there that was more pronounced than ever before.

"Are you going to go like that?" With her hint of a German accent and a disapproving glance.

"Jesus, Mom, it's hot out there." He was wearing gray trunks, a tee shirt, and sandals.

"No, it's all right. Fine, fine, come along then." She turned to go. He threw on a pair of slacks and a real shirt and joined her in the kitchen.

There were three huge dogs in the kitchen, jostling each other to be closest to his mother as she walked around the room gathering her keys and purse and shopping list. The dogs were excited because they thought they were going for a walk.

"No, babies, not now. Maybe Jeffrey will be nice and take you for a walk later." It made him crazy, the way she called them her babies, these big dumb strays she kept adopting. Christ, the amount of food they ate. Here he was, thirty-one years old, staying much longer than he intended at his parents' house. Staying in the guest room most of the time. Doing little chores. Walking the idiot dogs. But when he thought about going back to his apartment in the Canyon, he just couldn't see it. He felt too weird.

⍗

The morning after he'd run out of gas coming home from Pop's, he'd finally called his parents. It was Friday and he had slept until ten, then gotten up and straggled to the kitchen. In the cupboard was a can of peaches. He fumbled with a nearly useless can opener for a moment before he finally got the top off and then took the can and a spoon over to his desk. When the peaches were gone, he found some aspirin in his desk drawer and downed them with the heavy syrup. He could already feel the sugar fix coming on.

He had punched the speakerphone button and a dial tone blared out into the room. His parents' number was pre-programmed on his landline. When he heard his father's voice after the first ring, he picked up the handset in such a hurry that it clattered on the desktop.

"Dad. It's me. I've been out of town. I just found out. I'm so sorry—how's Mom?"

"Not so good." It was his father's usual "don't bullshit me" voice. "What's going on with you? Can't you even return a phone call?"

"Hey, I've been screwing up. Things are all screwed up. I'm sorry I was out of touch. In more ways than I can explain." It sounded lame but it was all he had to say.

"Look, Jeff . . ." Calling him Jeff instead of Jeffrey—that was a good sign. It meant that the old guy was lightening up. "Why don't you come stay with us for a few days? I think your mother would appreciate it."

"Okay," he found himself saying, "I think I'll do that. I'll see you soon."

His father said, "Good," and then hung up.

Beach traffic noise came in from the street through the window. He thought about his sister. When they were kids they had been inseparable. Young Jeff and his little sister. She had turned into such a straight arrow, and he had gone the opposite direction. They seemed to have grown apart, but they still talked on the phone occasionally. He had saved her life once, pulled her out of the ocean during a rough summer swell. For a long time after that he was the protective big brother who could do no wrong. He had lost that status some years ago, he realized, and now she was gone. With his elbow on his desk, he rested his forehead in his hand and shook his head back and forth slowly. Christ, he thought, it's all coming apart.

"Jeff. Are you here, or are you flying around in space somewhere?" His mother's voice startled him.

"No, Mom, I was just thinking about Marilyn."

"That's good. I don't want you doing any of your funny stuff here in our house. It's bad enough what your father does." She had that lips-pursed look of disapproval again. Jeff hated that look.

Later, after they unloaded the groceries, he told his mother he was going to run the dogs up at the park. It was late afternoon and all she said was, "Be home for dinner. You know how your father is about that." He rounded up the dogs and their leashes and shepherded the beasts into his mother's station wagon.

An hour later he arrived home just in time to join his parents for dinner. His father was already seated at the end of the dining room table, his hand curled around a snifter of brandy. The man's face was red and he stared down into his dinner as if he had been served a plate of earthworms. Jeff glanced at his mother—her lips were compressed to a pair of thin white lines as she brought his plate and then sat down.

His father took a long draught of the brandy and then resumed staring at his spaghetti, moving his head around as if he were inspecting something for minute flaws. He poked delicately at a meatball and then looked up accusingly at Jeff's mother.

Jeff began eating. He was used to this, but tonight had an extra intensity to it that he was determined to ignore.

"So, Jeff," his mother began, "did you know your sister was going to meetings?"

"Meetings?" he said with his mouth full of pasta. "What kind of meetings?"

"I don't know what kind of meetings." She primly wiped the corners of her mouth.

"Bullshit." His father glared across the table. "Bullshit meetings where everyone sits around and blames their parents for everything." He resumed the inspection of his meal.

Jeff's mother said, "She started going with her friend Kathy. She liked going." She, too, stared down at her food, taking little birdlike nibbles without looking up.

He took a few bites of salad and watched out of the corner of his eye as the old man drained his bourbon. He thought, *The old boy's mean as a snake tonight.*

A string of curses hissed from his father's mouth. "Goddamn fucking son of a bitch." He twirled his fork in the spaghetti. The strands were too short—Jeff's mother always cut them that way.

"After thirty-five years of marriage, you'd think I could get my spaghetti the way I like it." He slurred as he spoke and then slammed his fist on the table. There was a silence. It seemed to last for a long time. Jeff stared off at the wall and thought about how good Janet had looked, and pictured her taillights receding in the night as he pulled the Audi over to the curb, the gas tank empty.

Suddenly there was a motion. His mother picked up her glass and flung iced water across the table. His father flinched as the ice struck him. A slice of lemon bounced off his cheek and landed in the spaghetti. Drenched, the old man scowled for a moment and then started to get up, his open hand raised as if to strike across the table. His chair clattered to the floor behind him.

Jeff jumped up from his position between his parents, one hand out to keep his father at bay. "Oh no, goddammit, not while I'm around." His father looked up at him from a half-standing position, gave a barely perceptible nod, and walked out of the room. "Jesus, Mom." She gave a small shrug and resumed eating. They finished together in silence. Jeff cleared the table. "You okay?" he asked her. She nodded. He said, "Good, 'cause I'm going out for a while."

CHAPTER 16

⏀

He backed the Audi out of his parents' driveway, changed gears and headed toward Crescent Heights Boulevard. A drink sounded like a good idea. No, he thought, a drink is a bad idea. The two things hung in the balance, tilting, for the moment, just slightly in favor of Let's Not Drink. He wondered how long he could keep it that way.

It was past eight but still light out. Daylight savings was a weird thing, Jeff thought. It should work the other way around.

He decided it was time to go to his apartment and headed west on Olympic. He didn't have to stay there, just go check things out. He had left the cash and the gun hidden in the waste basket—that hadn't been such a great idea. Of course, he hadn't meant to stay away for so long. A day or two, maybe, but now it was Friday already, a week later.

It was dark when he reached the Canyon. He parked on the next block over and walked to his place—he didn't really know why. Something didn't seem right but he couldn't put his finger on it.

He climbed the stairs and heard music. It was coming from the apartment across from his. He could see his neighbor, Liz, through the screen door. She had a bathrobe on and a towel around her hair and a glass of wine in her hand.

"Hey, stranger, what's going on?" She came up to the screen door and grinned. Once in a while they would get together late at night, like each was a consolation prize for the other after striking out at the bars.

"Not much, Liz. How're you doing?" Actually, she was a great consolation prize. He wondered why he hadn't tried to spend more time with her. Probably just because they were neighbors. After all, she was right there. Too complicated.

"Missed you lately," she said. The deal was, if he came home at the end of the evening and Liz's door was open, he was welcome to spend the night with her. Which he occasionally did, and they had fun, except it always felt strange leaving.

Strange, like he felt now. He mumbled, "Excuse me," and turned to the door of his apartment. There was a rectangular sign on it, but he couldn't read it because the bulb in his doorway was burned out. When he moved slightly to one side, the light from Liz's apartment illuminated the sign. It was a thirty-day pay-or-quit notice. Great, he thought, just what I need. But he could pay the rent out of the money in the wastebasket, and cover Richard when Gary came through. No problem.

He opened the screen door and put his key in the lock. The door swung inward from the pressure of the key; he heard a snapping sound as a piece of the frame stretched and released. The doorjamb was in splinters. Something white fell to the ground. He picked it up and read, Detective Joe Greiner—Homicide Division, West Los Angeles Police Department. *Holy Christ*, he thought, *the cops have been inside.* He turned around.

"Liz?"

She turned her music down and came to the screen door. "You okay?" She took a sip of her wine.

"Have you noticed anyone around here? Looking for me?" He wondered if how he felt showed in his voice.

"Can't say," she told him. "I just got back from Palm Springs. Why, what's wrong?"

"Oh, nothing. Got a notice for late rent, that's all. Oh well, see ya." He went into his apartment.

He stood in the dark, holding the door shut behind him, trying to picture what he knew he was going to see. As his eyes grew accustomed to the absence of light, he could make out the disarray of things; the mattress half off the bed, desk drawers all pulled open.

He flicked on the light switch but nothing happened. Jesus, another goddamn bill to pay. He shuffled over some debris and into his kitchen. The cupboards were all flung open too. He reached above the fridge and found a flashlight, one of the big, black metal ones like the cops used. Its beam was bright and narrow. He played it around the apartment.

The place was trashed. Across the room in his closet he could see that all his clothes were on the floor. Books and old CDs were strewn about.

He walked around the desk and pointed the beam down to the wastebasket. It was empty, and the garbage that had covered the stash was on the carpet. He turned to the desk. It had been cleared entirely. In its center was his gun, serving as a paperweight for a folded sheet. He slid the note out from under the gun and opened it up.

Jeff. You should have returned my calls. 26 1/2K. Not bad. You still owe me 12. Too bad about your door. Rich.

Okay. Twelve thousand. Rent plus the bills added up to another thousand, and Gary owed him sixteen. So he had three thousand bucks, plus a few hundred in his wallet. Okay, it was still manageable. He wondered how the cop's business card fit into the picture.

He fished his phone out of his pocket and punched in Gary's number. The fucker better answer, he thought. All week long he had tried calling and only succeeded in getting Gary's stupid phone message. It wasn't really even a message, just half a minute of an old fifties tune. After the third ring he heard it again, "What's your name, is it Mary or Sue . . ." and ending with, "Shooby-doop-bop-doowah."

Slamming down the receiver, he put the gun in his pants and walked over to the closet area. He found a sports jacket on the floor and put it on, then flashed the beam around the room one last time and left.

CHAPTER 17

⏀

Referring back to his list, Ron Pool noted that only four of the eight girls had families in the area. Not surprising, he thought. The lifestyle, the sense of possibility, and the allure of Hollywood conspired to attract young women from all parts of the country to this small, quirky area in Southern California.

He picked up his office phone and dialed the first number on the list. On the second ring the other end picked up and a male voice answered, "Yes?"

Ron asked, "Is this Mr. Mills?"

"Who's calling?" the voice was curt and aggressive.

"My name is Ron Pool. I'm with the *Times* and I'm calling to ask a few questions about your daughter."

"Which daughter?"

"Nancy."

There was a long pause. Then the voice at the other end of the line simply said, "Yeah. One thing. No way Nancy jumped. No way. That's all I got. Don't call again." Click. End of first call. And not a very fruitful call at that. He made a notation—"sisters"—next to Nancy Mills' name, and reflected on the father's reaction. He wondered if it was standard fare for parents to deny the possibility of their children being suicide victims. Then he pondered the phrase "suicide victim." Why were they called victims? Why not "suicide perpetrators"?

He cut short the possibility of a prolonged meditation on personal responsibility and dialed the next entry. The first three digits identified it as a Pacific Palisades number. An answering machine picked up—"Hi, you've reached the Fullertons; we're not available right now but please leave a message at the tone." Ron started to leave a message but was interrupted by a woman saying, "Hold on, hold on, just let me turn this damn thing off." There was a small click as the answering device cut out, and then the woman came back on. "Yes, who is it?"

He introduced himself and asked if they could talk briefly about her daughter.

"Well," the woman hesitated, "she was a good girl. She had some problems but I still don't believe she took her own life. Are you writing a story?"

"No," he said, "I'm trying to put together a puzzle."

"What do you mean, a puzzle? And how can I help?" Something in the woman's voice made him decide to be candid with her.

"I think," he told her, "that there's more here than meets the eye."

"So do I," the woman said. "I was very dissatisfied with what the police had to say."

"May I come out and speak to you in person?" He knew from experience that more would be revealed in a face-to-face conversation than over the phone.

She replied, "Yes, by all means," and told him today would be fine and how to get to her house.

One more number to call, then he would drive out to Pacific Palisades. On the way back, he planned to stop at St. John's Hospital in Santa Monica and see if anyone had anything to say about nurse Nancy Mills.

He dialed the last number, the family of Laura Hunsaker in Woodland Hills. She was the one that a hiker had found in a ravine in Idyllwild. The one with the same drug in her system as Marilyn Fenner.

His call went to voice mail. He left his name and number and stated the reason for his call, then hung up and made a note to locate Marilyn Fenner's family.

He had always liked the Palisades. It was neat and clean, with expensive homes and broad, manicured lawns. The streets were wide and lined with trees. Too bad the whole country can't live like this, he thought.

The Fullertons lived in a ranch-style home on a corner lot just off Sunset Boulevard. A new Mercedes was parked in the driveway, which was lined with immaculately kept roses. Mrs. Fullerton came out to greet him as he stepped out of the Land Rover. She was a pretty woman of about fifty, hair pulled straight back in a ponytail, in jeans and a tank top. Her arms were slender and tanned. She pulled off a gardening glove and shook his hand.

"Hi, I'm Ann Fullerton." She led him into the house. Inside, there was a smartness about the decor which matched Ann Fullerton perfectly. In the kitchen, she handed him a tray with a pitcher of ice tea and some cheese and crackers and said, "Let's go out in back."

They sat at a patio table on a huge redwood deck that overlooked a swimming pool and, beyond, a lawn surrounded by fruit trees and a profusion of flowers. Ann Fullerton poured the ice teas and settled back in her chair.

"It's been a year and a half since we lost Linda," she said, "and I still think she's going to pop into the house any time now. Like that creepy old story about the hunting party."

"Did she seem particularly troubled before it happened? Did you keep in touch?" he asked her.

"We were best friends. Like two schoolgirls. She kept me young. She told me everything, or at least that's what I always thought." Mrs. Fullerton looked out over the pool and her eyes narrowed for a moment. Ron just waited.

"You know," she went on, "I think she did have one secret. I think she was seeing someone she didn't want me to know about. I don't know why. It's just a hunch. Never occurred to me before."

"Did she date a lot?"

"Well, she was a beautiful girl, so, yes, there were boyfriends. But not for quite a while. You see, she had had a few experiences that weren't good, so she told me she was taking a time-out from relationships. She started going to these meetings, some self-help kind of thing, where they talked about relationships. Significant others, self-esteem stuff. Psychobabble, I called it."

"Did you go to any of these meetings?" He helped himself to cheese and crackers.

"Yes, I did. It was very entertaining. They had a funny name—SOL, stood for Saving Our Lives. Kind of a sad acronym, isn't it?" She smiled and shook her head. "They were all so serious. But Linda, she was upbeat all the time."

▽

He drove down Chautauqua toward the beach. He and Ann Fullerton had talked for a while, finishing their ice teas and occasionally just listening to the suburban outdoor sounds—birds and insects, children playing in a neighboring yard. She was beautiful, smart, and affluent. He liked her and tried to imagine her carrying the weight of her daughter's death. And the girl had gone to SOL meetings. Now there was a coincidence.

CHAPTER 18

⌄

The view from the restaurant was serene, except for a pack of surfers competing for waves in the August heat. Malibu Beach on a summer Saturday was in overdrive; kids on pointy little boards and middle-aged men on old-style longboards scrambled for wave after wave. The kids zigzagged all over the swells, crashing up into the whitewater and turning back into the green walls with frantic energy, while the older guys were content to move gracefully along the faces, cruising in the pocket where the wave was just about to break.

"I've always loved to watch surfing," Holly told Art.

"Have you ever tried it?" Art looked up as the waitress brought the check for their lunch.

"Yes," she said, reaching for her purse. "I had a boyfriend once who pushed me into some waves on his board. He'd yell 'stand up,' and I would but then I'd fall off right away. Except once, when I rode all the way in to the sand. It was great." She pulled her wallet from the purse.

"Holly, please, I'll take care of this. Don't even consider it." Art laid out a credit card and put it into the little leather folder that the bill had come in.

"Art, we're not on a date," she told him. "I'd feel more comfortable paying my own way."

"Holly, you're my friend. As your friend, I would like to treat you to lunch. I appreciate your company, and this"—he gestured toward the table—"gets charged to my business, so let's just enjoy. Okay?"

She shrugged, thinking it was not okay but not wanting to pursue it any further. "Okay. Well, thank you. It was very good."

The waitress picked up the leather folder and asked if they wanted any more coffee. Holly shook her head, and Art said, "No, thank you. Everything is just fine." He smiled. The waitress was slender and attractive, with long legs and a short skirt. Holly noticed Art watching her as she turned and walked toward the cash register.

They walked out the side exit of the restaurant and onto the pier.

"Let's go out to the end," Art suggested, guiding her by the arm as he spoke. She brought her hand to her hair, as if to smooth it back, using the gesture to disengage herself from him. They walked side by side in silence.

Fishermen stared intently into the water, their lines stretched taut from the ends of fiberglass poles, buckets of bait and chests of tackle on the ground next to them. Children gazed through the slats of the pier railing, impatient for the excitement of the next catch.

"Used to be you could get a good-size halibut off this pier," Art said. "Bonita, perch, the occasional barracuda. Now it's mainly sand sharks and mackerel. Mankind has not been kind to this bay."

They walked on, the smell of fish mingling with the sea breeze, tinged with an aroma of hot dogs from the concession at the end of the pier. Up ahead there was a commotion as a fisherman's pole bent double. The reel clicked loudly, feeding out line as something powerful pulled against it. A crowd of onlookers gathered, children darting in to be close to the action. She caught glimpses of the fisherman as he pulled up on the pole, then let it down and reeled. "Somebody give me a hand," he yelled, and Holly could see that there was a pelican pulling on the line at the end of his pole. It flapped its wings, opening and closing its mouth around the bait it had tried to steal.

The end of the pier was a peaceful scene. An Oriental family fished in silence and stared off into the horizon. She walked over to the north side, looking toward the surfers. The angle was different from here, and sometimes she could only see their heads streaming by over the tops of the waves. She leaned against the railing.

Art moved up behind her.

"That was horrible," she said. "That poor bird."

"Yes, not a pleasant sight, was it? But the bird will go free, and his mind is too small to remember the pain." She felt Art's hands on her shoulders. They moved in toward her neck and began to knead the muscles there, firmly and expertly, knowing just where to dig in to dissolve tension she hadn't even been aware of. She relaxed into it and closed her eyes and felt the afternoon sun as it streamed down onto her face and hair, the sound of the seagulls and distant surf lulling her senses.

He stood close behind her now and massaged her temples in a smooth circular motion. The wind came up for a moment, and she took a deep breath, savoring the freshness of it. "As you progress through the SOL process," Art said, his voice right behind her ear, his face in her hair, "you will no longer create this tension. Instead, you'll awaken to new strengths and insights that you never imagined before." He stopped the rubbing and just applied a light pressure with his fingertips.

"I'm creating tension?" She couldn't see how she could be responsible for a physical condition.

"Oh, yes," Art replied. "You carry your inner conflicts in the muscles of your neck and shoulders. Unresolved, they accumulate and compound. Eventually they will contribute to health problems."

"Does that happen to everyone?"

"Some people carry anger in their gut. It can manifest as digestive problems, ulcers, even cancer. A person's inner condition, the nature of their thinking, will be reflected in the physical dimension." Art stopped the pressure on her temples and let his hands fall back to her shoulders.

"Are you saying that all medical problems are psychosomatic?" she asked. She turned her head to the left and to the right, stretching her neck muscles.

"No," Art replied. "Not psychosomatic. The mind–body connection works at a much deeper level than simple neurosis. The good news is that Bobbi's work can take us to that level, unlock the conflicts, and help us to heal on all levels, intellectually, emotionally, and physically." His hands moved down her arms and came to rest on her hips. He moved even closer and she could feel a new pressure, the pressure of his erection against her.

"I've really come," said Art, "to treasure our little times together."

CHAPTER 19

⏁

The Audi was starting to piss Jeff off. It would feel like it was out of gas and just quit, even though he knew the tank was full. He had driven by Gary's place again, banged on the door and got no response. Gary was really pissing him off. This was Jeff's third try at a face-to-face, since he couldn't get the son of a bitch by phone. Nearly two weeks had passed since they met at Pop's, and something was clearly wrong.

He got out and walked to the front of the car, carrying the wrench that he now kept on the passenger seat. He opened the hood and banged a few times on a little box like thing with some hoses running from it, then got back in the car. It started up again and he drove back to his parents' house.

⏁

"Hey, Mom, how's it going?" His mother was chopping vegetables while the dogs barked in unison.

"You're father is home," was her reply. It was only four o'clock on a Wednesday afternoon.

"Why so early?"

His mother shrugged without looking up. "You got a call from Kathy. She's such a nice girl. Why is she calling you?"

"That's an odd way to put it, Mom. She called because I left a message last night."

"I see. You know she came to the service. Well, how would you know? I forgot; you weren't there." She whittled furiously at a potato.

He started to say something about how he had been out of town that week but thought better of it and just said, "I'll try giving Kathy a call."

He went to the guest bedroom. He was still reluctant to call it his room, even though it looked like he was going to have to give up his apartment. Unless he came up with some bucks, fast.

As he walked into the guest room, he looked around for evidence of tampering. He found that if he kept it reasonably neat his mother would generally stay out, but she still managed to find some reason to come in on occasion.

The gun was in his briefcase, which he kept locked under the bed. It made the briefcase pretty heavy, but surely she wouldn't question that. He had driven back from the Canyon with it last Friday, and was nervous about keeping it here at the house. He sat down on the bed and thumbed Kathy's number. When she answered, he said, "Hey, Kathy, it's me. Jeff," feeling a little bit nervous. He didn't want to hear any more bullshit about "Where were you when your family needed you?"

"Oh, hi Jeff. Glad to hear from you." She sounded pretty nice. "I'm so sorry about Marilyn. How are you?"

He told her he was okay, and they chatted about his sister, about the last time either of them had spoken with her, about old times. Kathy had been a friend of Marilyn's, and of the family, ever since the girls were in their early teens.

"Well, I'd love to see you." He wasn't sure where she was coming from. She had once had a crush on him, but he never allowed it to go anywhere.

"Uh, listen," he said, clearing his throat, "I'm kind of curious about those meetings you used to go to with Marilyn. What are they called?"

"Oh, the SOL meetings?"

"Yeah, that's it. So what goes on there? Do you still go?"

"Well, yes, I do. We talk about ourselves and how we feel. And there's a program for personal growth. You might find it really interesting."

"I might? Like what for?" For some reason he felt offended.

"Well, Jeff, I've seen it help people with all kinds of problems . . ." It seemed she had more to say, but she stopped there. Then she said, "There's a meeting tonight. Would you like to go?"

"You know," he told her, "I think I'd like that. Where is it?"

"I know the way. Why don't I just pick you up at seven-thirty?"

He thought about his car and said, "Okay. I don't have to do anything or talk, do I?"

Kathy laughed and said, "No, silly. Just come check it out. No one will bother you. See ya." And then she hung up.

He put down the phone. He hadn't really had a night out since he had come to his parents' house almost two weeks earlier. He had roamed Hollywood, seen some music, but without drinking he had felt pretty out of it and never spoke to anyone. He didn't want to go to some bullshit group where they worked on their problems, but he was convinced that somewhere in Marilyn's recent past was a clue that would clear up the mystery of her death. Either way, it was too strange. Suicide was out of the question, but any alternative sounded equally crazy.

Dinner was relatively calm. His father drank wine, and wine rarely got the old boy as fired up as the hard stuff did. His conversation centered mainly around the Asshole in the White House and the Morons in Congress, while Jeff and his mother remained silent. When he finished eating Jeff announced that he was going out for a while.

"Oh yeah, where?" His father asked, chewing on a piece of roast.

"Kathy and I are going out." He decided not to antagonize his father by mentioning their destination.

"She's a nice girl." His father looked up. "What's she doing going out with you?"

"Jesus Christ, that's the second time I've heard that tonight, like she's Rebecca from Sunnybrook Farm and I'm fuckin' Charles Manson."

"Don't you talk like that in front of your mother," his father snapped.

"Excuse me," Jeff said, and he got up.

As he picked up his plate from the table, headlights flashed through the dining room window. Kathy's car pulled into the driveway. He had hoped to meet her outside, but now watched as she came to the front door.

"Hi," Kathy said as she stepped into the house. "Did I interrupt dinner?" She looked pretty good, he thought, in a wholesome, cheerleader kind of way.

"No, I was finished anyway." He gave a sideways glance at his father.

"Hi, Mr. and Mrs. Fenner." Kathy walked to the table and bent to give his mother a brief hug. "Smells delicious in here."

"So," his mother inquired, "are you going to a movie?"

"Oh, no, Mrs. Fenner, were going to an SOL meeting," Kathy replied. Jeff looked at her and rolled his eyes.

"Oh, great," his father sneered. "Isn't that lovely. Now you can pick up on the fine tradition of finding your poor mistreated inner child."

"Hey, Dad, lighten up. I'm just going on a hunch. I want to see what Marilyn was into, that's all. It's no big deal." He turned to Kathy and said, "Let's go."

⍅

It was approaching sunset outside as Kathy drove her sporty little two-seater into a church parking lot off Franklin at the foot of the Hollywood Hills. They talked about Marilyn again on the way, though it seemed to Jeff that Kathy kept trying to get him to talk about his own life and how it was going, which was not a subject he was keen to get into. Kathy also put her hand on his leg a lot when she spoke, as if to punctuate what she said. He found it annoying, but couldn't help fantasizing her hand sliding across his pants and landing at his zipper. Now that would put a new spin on the evening, he thought, and wondered if she noticed the bulge in his jeans.

⌀

People filed into the doorway of a small building next to a church. There was a lot of hugging going on, he noticed.

"These people all know each other, right?" he whispered to Kathy as they crossed the parking lot.

"Most of us know each other," she responded. "Don't worry, no one's going to try to hug you."

When he got to the door, a woman simply said, "Welcome," and shook his hand. Inside, he saw a circle of chairs, most of which had keys or business cards on them. He followed as Kathy crossed to the far side of the room and placed her own keys and her purse on two available seats.

Jeff said, "Why don't you say hi to your friends while I sit down and wait for the thing to start, okay?"

"Sure," Kathy said. "Want some coffee? A cookie, maybe?"

He told her, "Yeah, black. A couple of cookies would be nice, thanks," and she went off.

He looked around the room. There were a lot more woman than men. Everyone seemed cheerful enough, clustered in little groups and talking animatedly, like this was their idea of a party. People were starting to settle into their seats. He checked his watch and saw that it was only a few minutes before eight.

When almost everyone was seated, a woman cleared her throat and said, "Greetings, and welcome to the regular Wednesday night meeting of Saving Our Lives." She gave her name and said something about saving her life and suddenly everyone in the room said, "Hi, Janice." He was startled and wanted to laugh, but looked down at his shoes until the impulse passed. The leader was reading some stuff that didn't make much sense, so he scanned the people in the circle. There certainly wasn't anyone that he would normally hang out with, except for the blond girl sitting near the leader.

She was one of the best-looking women he had ever seen. It was funny, the amount of time he had spent in bars looking for someone like this, and here she was at some dopey little meeting. When she glanced in his direction he looked away.

The leader had stopped reading and now talked about herself. Something about how she kept herself fat to build a wall around herself to shield her from intimacy. *What the fuck is she talking about?* he wondered. He looked back at the blond, who was watching the speaker with a puzzled expression. Kathy leaned over and whispered in his ear.

"Stop staring, Jeff. You were cooler than this in high school."

He felt a flush on his neck and cheeks, and a flash of resentment toward Kathy. What in the world did Marilyn come to these things for?

The door opened and he looked up. A man entered, looked around the circle of people, and walked toward him. He looked about fifty, dressed smart but casual, lean like a runner. The man sat in the empty seat next to him and whispered, "Sorry." For coming in late, Jeff assumed. He felt like whispering, "Sorry," and getting up and leaving, but decided to stick around until the meeting was over.

He wondered what it might be like to sleep with Kathy. Maybe if she had a few drinks it would change things. He wouldn't have to have any. But the girl across the way kept invading his thoughts, and he would sweep his eyes around the entire circle just to catch a glance at her without being obvious about it.

The leader wrapped it up. He listened to her talk about how she had always looked for something in her significant other that would help her feel whole, but that now she knew that she needed to embrace herself before she could let down her guard and be available for true intimacy. She said she hugged herself in the mirror every morning and that it was really working for her, thank you for letting me share. Then she announced a five minute coffee break.

Kathy began to talk with the woman seated next to her. Jeff watched the blond get up and walk to the table where the coffee was set up. His own cup was empty. It seemed logical enough to go for a refill. He was about to get up when a voice from his left said, "She looks pretty good, doesn't she?"

Jeff turned toward the voice. It was his new neighbor, the man who had come in late. Not happy about being caught twice now staring at the girl, Jeff merely said, "Yeah, she's okay."

The man grinned and offered his hand. There was something okay about the guy, an air of being sharp and with-it, but relaxed at the same time.

"My name's Ron. You new around here?"

CHAPTER 20

◬

Ron Pool arrived late at the meeting. It looked like any other group he had seen, medium size—about thirty people sitting in a circle. The room was apparently a nursery for the churchgoers' children; he noticed crayon drawings on the walls and toys stacked in the corners. There were meetings all over town, all week long, and this was one he had never been to.

There was only one seat available. He crossed over to it and sat down, whispering an apology as he did so. He looked around the room and noticed a few people he had seen before, among them the attractive blond from Bobbi Bradley's lecture two weeks earlier.

The leader, a plump girl in her twenties, talked about her relationships, or lack of them. She was clearly addicted to the SOL lingo. New Age newspeak, he called it, and found himself unable to pay attention.

After the lecture in Beverly Hills, he had decided that he had seen enough of the SOL phenomenon. His original curiosity had given way to disappointment when he saw there was nothing new here for him. There was a disturbing slant to it all that made him wary of the message. His visit to St. John's Hospital, however, had made it clear to him that he would be revisiting SOL. His motive would be different, but the MO would be the same; show up, listen, meet people, check it out.

He had arrived at St. John's in the late afternoon, after his visit with Ann Fullerton. Looping through the Santa Monica Canyon from Pacific Palisades into the city of Santa Monica, he drove up Wilshire to Twentieth Street and turned into the hospital parking lot.

He walked into the main reception area and decided to bypass the information desk, moving instead past a gift shop to where the elevators were. On instinct, he entered one of the elevators and selected a floor below the one he was on.

He stepped out into a brightly lit hallway. It was empty but, as he walked, he noticed doors open to various rooms. One of these was a nurses' station. There were two nurses inside—one was pouring a cup of coffee.

"Hello," he said. "Could you help me out for a moment?"

The nurse by the coffee machine, a young black woman, put a hand on her hip and gave him a severe look. She said, "Are you absolutely certain you belong down here?" and then broke into a grin.

"I'm looking for someone who knew Nancy Mills," he told her. The two women looked at each other.

"Everyone knew Nancy. She was one of the best people I ever met," said the other nurse, a Hispanic woman with a torrent of black hair spilling from under her cap.

"What happened to Nancy is over a year old," said the first nurse. She stirred her coffee and then asked, "You're not from the police, are you?"

"No. I'm sorry. My name is Ron. Ron Pool—I'm a reporter, actually." He felt slightly awkward, not quite knowing how to explain the reason for his visit.

"Hello, Ron," the black nurse said. "I'm Trina and this is Bianca. What made you come down here?"

"Intuition, I guess," he replied. "Tell me something. You just said, 'What happened to Nancy is over a year old.' What did you mean by that?"

Trina and Bianca exchanged looks again and then Trina asked, "Are you writing a story?"

"I don't know. Not yet."

"Then what are you doing?"

"So far, I'm just trying to sort out a puzzle," he said. "Nancy was a very pretty girl, right?"

"She was beautiful, yes. I think she would have preferred being called a woman." Trina looked directly at him with a trace of humor.

"Okay," he went on, "what would you think if you knew about other beautiful women, all in their twenties and all from the Westside, that shared a similar fate with Nancy Mills?"

"How many other women?" asked Bianca.

"Eight."

Trina raised her eyebrows and looked over to the other nurse. "What do you think?"

"I think I would wonder how many of them went out with the same guy," Bianca responded.

"I would wonder," said Trina, sipping at her coffee, "how many of them went to those meetings Nancy went to."

"What meetings were those?" he asked.

"I don't know—let's see. We used to call it something funny . . ." Trina hesitated.

"Shit-outta-luck," Bianca said.

"Yeah, Shit Outta Luck. SOL," Trina said with a rueful chuckle. "Imagine that. She starts going to something called Saving Our Lives, and within a few months she gets pushed off a cliff."

He was startled. "What makes you say she was pushed off a cliff?"

"Everyone here knows that," Trina told him. "Nancy hated heights and was petrified of falling. If she wanted to kill herself, which I don't believe for a second, the last thing in the world she would have done is jump off a damn cliff."

"Nancy used to talk to the patients," Bianca added. "She had a special talk for the attempted suicides. All about how life was a gift, how it was worth living, right in the moment. How you had to find that special source of courage. Anyway, nurses don't use guns or jump off cliffs. It's too easy to go out with a triple dose of anesthetic cocktail."

When he left the hospital, he called Joe. He was surprised to get right through to the detective. "Hey, guess what?" he said, without any greeting.

"Yeah, what?" Joe was as gruff as ever.

"New thread. I got two of the girls going to these damned SOL meetings." He accelerated through a changing light on Wilshire.

"Isn't that the group you were into?"

"I went a few times. Guess it's time to go back. I mean, what are the odds against that?" He checked his watch—it was almost six.

"Hey," Joe said, "in this town, all the women go to some wacko thing or another. Have you got a real job?"

Ron grinned and said, "Lot of good you've turned out to be." Then he hung up.

⍫

Now, at the SOL meeting, as he listened to this mixed-up girl—woman, he corrected himself—he wondered what his next move should be. The leader droned on, something about hugging herself in the mirror, and then finally announced a coffee break. Some people turned to speak to their neighbors, others left their seats. The attractive blond got up. Ron glanced at the guy sitting next to him and watched him stare at the blond as she walked toward the refreshment table.

"She looks pretty good, doesn't she?"

The guy looked startled, as if he'd been caught doing something illegal, and said, "Yeah, she's okay." He was a younger guy, good looking, maybe thirty. Thin. Something about his eyes. Ron had seen that look before. Hunted, edgy. Dark circles.

Ron introduced himself and offered his hand. "You new around here?"

The guy shook his hand. "I'm Jeff. Yeah, this is my first time at one of these things. Might be my last time, too. How about you?"

Ron laughed. "I come around here once in a while," he said. "What brought you here?"

"Just curious, I guess. My sister used to come here with her friend Kathy—that's who I came with tonight." Jeff gestured over his shoulder.

"Did your sister stop coming?" Ron asked.

"My sister died. The police say she committed suicide, but I think that's a crock."

"Marilyn," Ron said, staring at Jeff.

"Yeah. Did you know her?"

"No. I just heard about her." He paused for a moment. "Marilyn Fenner. And you're her brother, Jeff."

"That's what I said. Why? What's going on?" The kid looked really uncomfortable now.

Ron ignored his questions and asked instead, "You say that your sister used to come here?"

"Yeah. But if you didn't hear about her around here, how come you know about my sister?"

A small bell rang, and the woman who was leading said, "The meeting is about to resume." People returned to their seats.

"Let's talk later. I'd like to ask you a few things." He reached in his pocket and pulled out a card. He gave it to Jeff, who glanced at it, then looked up and said, "You're a reporter?"

"Yeah. I wrote the *Times* piece on your sister."

"So," Jeff asked, "what's a significant other?"

"That's psychobabble for partner. Politically correct for boyfriend, girlfriend, same-sex partner, you name it."

Jeff looked confused. "Psychobabble?"

The leader said, "Would anybody like to share?"

CHAPTER 21

⍟

Driving back from the meeting, Kathy said, "So what did you think?"

Jeff's mind was on the blond and how he hadn't managed to meet her, but he wasn't about to mention that to Kathy. He shrugged.

"I don't know. I mean, most of it sailed right by me, to tell the truth."

"Well, I noticed that you got in quite a conversation with your neighbor. I've seen him around—what's his name again?" Kathy turned to go down Crescent Heights Boulevard.

"Ron. Yeah, we talked about what the girl who spoke said." He decided to keep to himself the fact that he had connected, that he had only come to learn about his sister and that he had hit pay dirt. Or had he? It was quite a coincidence, anyway, and interesting enough to justify sitting through the boring meeting.

"You mean the woman who led the meeting?" Kathy asked.

"Right. The woman who led the meeting. She said some interesting stuff." He hoped Kathy wouldn't ask him what he had found interesting.

"So where did Ron go off to so abruptly? He came in late and left the second it was over," Kathy asked.

He shrugged again. "Damned if I know." *Maybe*, he thought, *I'll call this guy tomorrow.*

"They say that it takes about six meetings before you start getting it." She looked over at him as she changed gears.

"Hey, only five more to go," he said.

"Don't you get smart with me . . ." There went that hand, slap on his leg again, only this time it stayed.

He put his hand on top of hers. Kathy drove in silence.

After a few blocks she said, "Hey, let's go have a drink somewhere. What do you think?"

"Sounds good to me." He wondered what she drank. Well, he could just drink a soda or something. "Let's go to Barney's. Shoot some pool."

"I've never been there. Isn't that place kind of a dive?" They were stopped at a light. When it changed, she took her hand from his leg to shift gears and then replaced it on top of his hand.

"Nah. Scruffy yuppies. Wannabe artistes. Musicians with day jobs and no gigs. It's a good place to shoot pool though."

Kathy turned on Santa Monica Boulevard and then pulled into the parking lot. It was still warm out as they approached the entrance.

Inside, it was crowded at the bar, but the pool tables were in a separate section. Out of eight tables, two were available. He led Kathy to one of them and put a couple of quarters in the slot.

He was racking the balls when a waitress came over.

"Can I get you anything to drink?" The waitress was cheerful enough, but she had a gaunt, hard look, like she had too much history to ever really come back from.

Jeff said, "I'll just have a diet coke. Ice." He looked over at Kathy.

"How about a daiquiri?" she said, chalking the end of her cue stick.

The waitress said, "Wednesday night's Tequila shooter night. Three bucks a shot. Two bucks a beer."

"Perfect." Kathy blew the excess blue chalk off the end of her stick and said, "Let's play."

When the waitress returned with the drinks, Kathy had put six balls in the pockets, to his two. He watched her, tall and big-boned, sizing up her shots and throwing her hair back each time she sank a ball.

Kathy paid for the drinks. He sipped at his coke and watched as she put salt on the back of her hand and licked it, followed with the lime, then, with a flick of her wrist, she downed the tequila. He thought it was a silly ritual, but tonight it seemed like a good omen. Kathy drained half of her beer and set it down, wiped her mouth with the back of her hand, and dropped another ball in the corner pocket.

Three games and four set-ups later, he was still nursing his diet coke. Kathy appeared to get more and more cheerful as she threw back the shooters, and now she came over to him and stood, toe to toe, smiling right in his face. She was almost his height, with a round face and full, rich chestnut hair. Her eyes, he thought, were really quite beautiful.

"So, now what should we do?" Her teeth were perfectly white and straight. He wanted a drink for this, but she was right there, it was only inches, and he bent forward as he closed the space between them.

Their lips touched, and Kathy's mouth opened, soft and moist, their tongues meeting as she moved her mouth against his in a slow side-to-side motion. He felt like he was falling—he reached out to lean the cue stick against the wall and then put his hands around to the small of her back, then moved them down and pulled her body to him. Her hips met his and started moving against him, everything languid, liquid and easy.

Kathy backed off from the embrace and took his hand. As they left there were hoots from one of the tables. A skinny, long-haired old guy with tattoos all over his arms gave Jeff a thumbs-up from the corner of the bar before they stepped out into the night.

Kathy's apartment was in an attractive older fourplex on Sweetzer, about a mile away. During the drive, when she wasn't shifting gears, her hand went to his inner thigh, her fingertips brushing feather-light from his knee up to his belt, which she unbuckled. As she drove up Santa Monica Boulevard at fifty, staying in

second gear, she snapped the button of his jeans. Her hand bur-
rowed under the fabric and grasped him while the speedometer
went up to sixty.

When they were in her flat, Kathy walked to the kitchen and
he followed. It was dark until she opened the freezer section of
her refrigerator and pulled out a bottle. She broke the seal and
placed it on the counter along with two glasses, and told him,
"Take care of these, okay?" before walking into the darkness of
the next room.

Soft piano music came from speakers in the living room. He
stared at the bottle. Tequila. Patron Silver. He poured a glass for
Kathy and put it up to his nose. What the hell, he thought, and
poured a couple inches for himself. Stuff tasted so bad, no way he
was going to drink more than this. He threw back half of it, gave a
brisk shake of his head, and polished the rest.

Kathy appeared, dressed in a long, pale-green satin nightgown open down the front. By the light pouring out from the
open freezer he could see the hard flatness of her stomach, a rich
curve of breasts. She picked up the glass he had poured and drank
until it was empty, then grasped his shirt and pulled him toward
her. They kissed again. She was hungry and aggressive, but soft.

Kathy replaced the bottle in the freezer and shut the door,
then took his hand and led him through the living room, pausing
there to turn up the music, and then into the bedroom.

A candle burned on a nightstand at one side of a king-size bed.
Separate speakers brought the piano into the bedroom. He sat on the
bed and took off his loafers, as Kathy, who towered over him, push
him back gently onto the comforter. She kissed him, her hair falling
onto his face and between their lips, and then finished unzipping his
jeans. He unbuttoned his shirt as she slid his pants and shorts and
socks off. He threw his shirt toward a chair and watched, propped on
his elbows, as Kathy slid out of her nightgown and crawled up and
over him. He would never have guessed her breasts were so large, as
she arched her back and they hung, full and white, just above him.
He reached up and put his lips around an erect nipple. Kathy moaned
and with one hand guided his hand to the soft patch between her

legs. It was warm and wet and slippery, and she moved his hand so that it went into the moist flesh, and then out and up to the firm little button just below her pubic bone. He played his tongue over her nipple while his hand moved and Kathy began a slow circular motion with her hips.

After a moment, she pulled her breast away, kissed him briefly and, grasping his cock, lowered herself onto it just slightly. She bent back down to kiss him again, gently brushing her lips back and forth against his as she moved her hips almost imperceptibly.

The piano music seemed to have taken on a repetitive, almost hypnotic quality. Suddenly Kathy plunged her hips down until he was buried inside her. He could feel her pelvic bone against his, her breasts pressed to his chest. She raised herself up again and resumed the teasing motion, almost entirely disengaged from him. In the candlelight she loomed above him like some conquering goddess, her moving shadow spread across half the ceiling. He tried to push up into her but she wouldn't let him. Then, as he lay there arched upward, she crashed down upon him again.

This time Kathy kissed him once briefly and then slid her parted lips past his face to his ear. She lifted her hips just to the point of losing him and then slammed back down, accelerating her rhythm. He felt her tongue flicking his ear, her breath hot and loud. He started to move against her so that they pounded together with a wild slapping sound. Kathy buried her face in the pillow and groaned at the same instant that he felt himself suddenly go lightheaded; something took over and they moved together, machine-like and effortless as he drained into her.

There was a moment of stillness, and then Kathy's body tensed up briefly and released in a convulsive sob. He smoothed her hair and stared at the circle of light on the ceiling as she cried into the pillow.

⏃

The candle sputtered and the music had stopped. Kathy was asleep. He pulled away from her and sat at the edge of the bed, an idea half formed in his mind as he stared at his shirt on the floor. He stood up, covered Kathy's shoulder with the sheet, and walked into the living room, picking up his clothes as he went.

Dropping the clothes on the sofa, he walked to the refrigerator. He stared at the freezer door for a moment, then opened it and reached for the bottle of Patron.

From the bottle, it didn't have that wicked smell and it went down ice-cold and easy. He took it to the sofa and sat down.

Jesus, he thought. Seduced by my sister's cheerleader chum. They had done it again, Kathy giving him the control this time. It was long and slow, finally heating up until it got as crazy as the first time. When he rolled off Kathy and lay next to her she cupped his face in her hands and said, "I always knew we'd be great together." Then she kissed him and turned around. In less than a minute—he could tell by her breathing—she was asleep.

He took another hit of the tequila and looked at his watch. It was one thirty. Too late to make last call, he thought, and then laughed at the idea.

At one forty-five the bottle was half empty, and he thought about how fucked up everything was. His car was a piece of shit, he was broke, he owed money, and he was losing his apartment. It was all Gary's fault, the miserable little prick; where the fuck was he anyway?

He pulled on his jeans and went to the kitchen. Kathy's purse was on the counter. He went to her room just to check on her—she was out cold. He finished dressing, took the car keys from her purse, and left the apartment, bringing the bottle along.

He went down to the carport and let himself into Kathy's car. The seat was already all the way back—God, she was a big girl. He took another tug at the Patron and drove over to his folks' house.

Letting himself in through the kitchen entrance, he tiptoed back into his room, put on his sports coat and grabbed the briefcase, and stole back out, relieved that the dogs never even woke up.

The two-seater was a blast, he thought, as he jammed through the streets of Hollywood. Too many goddamn red lights, though.

He decided that the ones where there were no cars coming didn't count. Flying through Beverly Hills and past Westwood, he wondered where all the cops were. The little car took the curve by the VA at sixty-five, no problem. He turned on Gorham, then onto Dorothy, and pulled up in front of Gary's apartment.

The door to Gary's place faced the street and was set back slightly from the sidewalk. The windows were dark. He opened his briefcase and took out the gun, then took a long pull at the bottle. The street looked clear. No cars were coming. He got out of the car, tucked the gun in his pants, and walked over to Gary's door. He rang the doorbell. Nothing. He knocked hard and then put his ear to the door—there wasn't a sound from inside.

The street was still clear. He backed up a step and brought his left foot up and smashed it into the door, just below the knob. There was a splintering sound, but the door held. He kicked again and it gave a bit. On the third kick it flew open and he walked into the apartment.

He saw by the light of the street lamps that came through the windows that the place was empty. Trash littered the floor, but Gary was gone. He moved through the apartment and entered the bedroom. It too was empty. A phone started ringing. He followed the sound into the kitchen. It stopped midway through the third ring and he heard Gary's stupid message, "What's your name, is it Mary or Sue?" There on the floor, where the kitchen table used to be, was an answering machine. He brought his foot down on it just as Don and Dewey sang their Shooby-doop-bop-doowah. The gun almost popped out of his belt, so he pushed it back into place as he walked out of the apartment.

An intense light hit his eyes as he stepped outside.

"You! Hands behind your head. Now!" Suddenly he was swept off his feet and found himself lying face down on the concrete.

CHAPTER 22

⬨

I'm feeling very uncomfortable about something." Holly looked at Art as she said this, but then felt compelled to look away.

They were sitting at a table in a coffee bar called the PygmyUp, one of hundreds of similar places with clever names that had recently sprung up throughout the city. Art said, "Facing discomfort is necessary for growth. Can you put it into words?" He sat opposite her, leaning back in his chair, and sipped at his coffee.

"Yes, but I don't really want to. I mean, I'm not sure of my perceptions." She felt awkward now and wished she hadn't brought it up.

"Well, better to go with your feelings. What's going on?" His manner was kind, curious; she had planned what she was going to say, but now it seemed entirely inappropriate.

She shook her head. "I don't know . . ." she began.

"You'll tell me when you're ready." Art smiled and reached across the table to take her hand.

She pulled her hand away and said, "That's just it. You're always so physical. It seems inappropriate. I just want to be really clear with you that we are never going to have sex together."

"Holly, Holly . . ." Art seemed genuinely dismayed. "We have a friendship. A very special friendship. I would never do anything to jeopardize that." He withdrew his hand and drank his coffee, lost in thought for a moment. "Listen," he told her, "we are engaged in a deep process. A process more intimate than sex, and it's bound to bring up resistance. The process is called uncover, discover, and discard. Each time we get together we dig a little deeper."

"So you're telling me I'm entirely off base?" She wasn't convinced of his sincerity, but felt uncomfortable, slightly ridiculous even, in challenging him.

Art put his fingertips together and leaned forward, his elbows on the table. "The reason we get fearful and resistant is because we sense that we are reaching a new threshold of discovery and that something threatening is on the other side."

"What does that have to do with what I said?" she asked.

"Simply that when we are fearful and unwilling to look directly at the thing we fear, we invent bogeymen. I am a convenient bogeyman so that you won't have to look at the truth." Art raised his eyebrows, as if inviting her response.

"And what truth is that?" She was annoyed, but uncomfortable. She didn't know if Art's proposal was an evasion or a real possibility.

"Well, we haven't gotten there yet, have we? Let me ask you this: the other week, at Joanie's, I noticed that you had a bruise over your eye. I'm going to assume that your friend Tony struck you. Now, why do you suppose it's okay for him to hit you?"

"Why would you assume Tony hit me?"

"Holly, let's not play games. Why do you suppose it's okay?"

"I never said it's okay," she retorted. "There's nothing okay about it."

"Right," said Art, "but let's think about what we mean by saying something is okay. It means we are giving it permission. Now, had this ever happened before?"

It infuriated her, the way Art relentlessly dredged up things that he should have no idea about. She wondered again why she continued to meet with him. On the other hand, she thought, the last time they had been together had been quite pleasant.

▽

They had met at his office in Westwood. It was situated in a quaint older building and overlooked a central courtyard and the checkered parasols of a European-style café. She had waited in a wood-paneled reception room while Art finished, she presumed, an appointment with a patient.

The room was pleasant, with hanging plants and meandering New Age music piped in. She read a magazine called *Aquarian Paradigm* while she waited.

At four o'clock sharp, Art appeared. He smoked a pipe, dressed in corduroy slacks and a beige cardigan over a white shirt and tie. He looked like an amiable college professor, smiling down at her as he beckoned her into his office.

"A beautiful day," Art exclaimed. A cool breeze had come up off the Pacific, breaking up the monotony of an endless succession of sweltering days.

"Yes, lovely," she said. She sat down in a deep leather chair. Art sat opposite and gestured to the walls. "Cozy, isn't it?"

She liked the room. It was small but not confining. A bookcase, entirely filled, took up one wall. Another was occupied by a large abstract, warm colors and soft shapes with no angles. An oak desk occupied the corner. To her right was a window that looked out onto the yards and houses of the adjacent residential block.

"It's nice," she told Art. "But what am I doing here?" They usually met in restaurants or coffee shops, sometimes at the museum over by La Brea.

"It's time to take the next step," Art said. "You'll like this. It's fun."

"What are we going to do?"

"I'll show you. By the way, you didn't drink any coffee today, did you?" He had asked her not to, without explaining why.

"No, and I got a slight headache. I never realized that I might be dependent on coffee." He hadn't said anything about aspirin. The headache had subsided around lunchtime.

Art said, "Good. What we're going to do today is take the initial step in regression therapy. To keep the critical mind from interfering with the process, we employ hypnosis." He got up and walked to the desk, returning with a plastic cup in one hand and a pill in the palm of his other.

"This will greatly facilitate our progress." Art handed her the cup of water and the pill. It was a little thing, triangular and orange with some letters on it.

"What will this do?" She was uncomfortable with the idea of taking drugs.

"Virtually nothing, except that you will feel deliciously calm and centered. All those busy thoughts and anxieties will dissolve away, and yet your mind will feel sharp and alert at the same time." When he saw her hesitate, he said, "Really, Holly, you must trust me. I'm a doctor and I'm your friend."

Despite her misgivings, she swallowed the pill with some water and then gave Art the cup. "Now what?" she asked.

"Now we wait about twenty minutes. Actually, I'll be leaving you for a while. Would you like anything?"

"No, thanks. I'll just rest here." The chair was very comfortable. The afternoon sun coming through the window had a lulling effect. She closed her eyes and barely noticed as Art left the room.

She was surprised, when he returned, to realize she had dozed. In her dream, she had skated along the bike path at State Beach, except she didn't have any skates on. She would glide around other skaters, throwing her weight from side to side. It was like doing the bumps on a ski slope, her sandals barely skimming the concrete. The experience seemed so real that it was odd to open her eyes and be back in this room.

Art said, "You may close your eyes again." She did, and found herself right back on the bike path, still skating, only this time she knew she was dreaming and that she really was sitting in a chair in Art's office.

"Imagine," he said, "that you are in a golden space with no boundaries." She stopped skating and, eyes still closed, looked up into the sun. Everything else fell away and she floated in its radiance.

"Now," Art's voice instructed her, directionless, bathing her like the light bathed her, "will yourself to move upward."

She felt the sensation of moving upward, like pushing off the bottom of a pool, but without the resistance of the water. She found that she could control the speed and started laughing as she accelerated.

"Okay, that's very good." Art's voice was with her, even though she had traveled such a long distance. With her fingers she felt the smooth texture of the leather chair.

"Now move to the right . . . good, good, and now to the left." She noticed that whichever way she tilted her head, she could fly through the golden space in that direction.

"Okay, now, Holly, bring yourself to a resting position." Art paused. She waited, suspended in the radiant mist. "Good. Now, the sun is setting. The golden light is streaming outward from you, from your hair and face and fingertips. The sky has become dark. Do you see how many stars there are?"

She nodded. There were millions of them, clouds of stars against the black background. She willed herself to turn—it was the same in every direction.

Art's voice joined her again. "One of those stars is waiting for you. It is your special star, your new home, the place where you will give up your body of light for a while. A great adventure awaits you there. Find the one that is calling you and go to it."

She stretched her arms wide and tilted her head back, felt herself accelerate and saw a milky cluster of stars rush toward her. She coasted through it, turning slowly and opening herself to the possibility of each star. She was about to pass through entirely, set to race through the blackness to the next concentration of fiery pinpoints, when something caught her attention.

Off to her right, and slightly above, a star flashed brighter for an instant. She watched as it did it again, and then again. It was pulsating rhythmically and seemed to loom larger than its neighbors, warmer in its glow, calling to her now as she moved toward it.

Something in the nature of her motion changed. From flying, she was now diving, pulled by the gravity of the sun she approached, joyful as it welcomed her, tearful as a dark gap opened in its center and she entered, now curled up into the smallest ball, floating in the very center of it all. She heard a lazy gurgling and behind it a powerful thrumming, as of the tide racing through a channel. And, over it all, the distant bass sound of a giant echoing drum.

▽

She pinched the bridge of her nose between her eyes, then looked around the coffee house.

Art was watching her, patiently, lines crinkled outward from his eyes as he smiled, his eyes blue against the tan of his face.

"Welcome back," Art said. He seemed amused.

"I'm right here," she retorted, flustered. She wondered how long she had sat there daydreaming. They had been having a conversation.

"I believe we were having a conversation," Art said.

About Tony. That was it, she thought. She brushed at her hair with her fingers. "No, he never beat me up before." Which was basically true. Except for when he would grasp her hair and speak right in her face, saying totally unacceptable things. But only when he had been drinking, she thought. Which was immediately followed by the thought, *When wasn't he drinking?* When had she ever spent time with him that he didn't wind up more or less insanely drunk?

"How about previous boyfriends?" Art persisted.

"Why is this important?" she asked.

"Well, among other things, it would be useful to discover what kind of behavior you accept, and then find out why you think you deserve that behavior. When your concept of what you deserve changes, you will begin to attract a different kind of man."

"How nice for me," she said, but in spite of her sarcasm she wondered if it was really possible that there was a whole world out there, occupying the same space as the one that she knew, but entirely different. Kinder. More truthful. Safe. She thought of her experience in Art's office again, the perfect peace and safety of it, suspended in the liquid darkness, her blood pumping in time to the huge heart above her. If she could have believed that the pill she had taken was responsible for that feeling, she would have signed up for a lifelong prescription.

She picked at the muffin she had ordered. "As long as you don't have any illusions about us having a physical relationship," she said.

"Ah, we're back to that."

"Yes, we're back to that. I'd like to get it settled."

"Holly," Art looked at her intently, "the mind is a very funny thing. Philosophers have been trying to understand it for thousands of years. From Socrates to Kant, and the question still isn't resolved." He waved the waitress away as she offered more coffee. "Huxley said that the mind is a reducing valve, that there is a true world, but that the human mind can only assimilate so much information—the information it thinks it needs to survive and to thrive. So it acts like a filter. He said that the way that each of us reduces and filters reality defines our individual realities, and that each of our realities is by nature skewed. Sometimes our ideas outlive their usefulness. For example, your idea that men are bad may have been an appropriate reaction to something once, but it continues to fulfill itself in your relationships. And, it convinces you that I have ulterior motives. The good news is that sometimes we can take a quantum leap upward, out of the old paradigm, into a new one in which we are freer, more personally powerful."

"Have you ever heard the saying," she asked him, "'If you can't dazzle them with brilliance, baffle them with bullshit'?"

Art put his elbows on the table and rested his chin on his hands. "You're a tough nut to crack," he said. "Listen. There's a story about a man on his deathbed. His wife is sitting next to him, and he tells her, 'Remember before we were married and I got in that accident?' and his wife nodded and said, 'Yes, dear, I remember.' And he said, 'You were there with me.' Then he said, 'Remember when the business failed and I was in despair?' And she said, 'Yes, dear, I remember.' So the husband said, 'You were there with me then, too. And when I got in that auto wreck,

I couldn't walk for a year. Remember that?' The wife shook her head sadly. 'Yes, I remember that too.' Finally, the husband said, 'Now I'm lying here dying, and you're still here with me.' The wife nodded, tears in her eyes, and the husband said, 'You know what I think? I think you're a bloody jinx.' Then he died."

"Is that a joke?" she asked. "Because if it is, it's not very funny."

"No," Art said, "it's a parable about cynicism. The husband reduced the world in such a way that love was impossible. He couldn't help himself."

CHAPTER 23

⊽

By nine Saturday morning, Ron had already finished his run at Griffith Park, returned home, and eaten breakfast. He poured his second cup of coffee at nine and decided it was late enough to call Marilyn Fenner's parents. He wondered about the son, Jeff, as he dialed. The kid looked like he was in trouble—he had that beat-up quality that Ron had seen so many times.

The phone picked up on the first ring. "Hello, what did you find out?" It was a gruff voice, impatient and demanding.

"My name is Ron Pool. I'd like to talk to Mr. or Mrs. Fenner."

"I'm Charles Fenner. Thought you were the goddamned attorney. So who are you?"

Ron explained that he was from the *Times*, that he had written the bit on their daughter, and was wondering if they had a few moments to talk to him.

"It's not a great time for us, Mr. Pool. We're dealing with a problem right now."

He decided to push. "Mr. Fenner, I really only need about ten minutes of your time. I could stop by in the next hour."

"Look," the father said, "my goddamned son is in the county jail and I'm a bit more interested in getting him out than I am in chit-chatting with you."

"He's downtown?"

"Is that where the county jail is? How the hell would I know?"

"Maybe I can help," Ron said. ""What's he in for?"

"Drunk. Something about a goddamn gun. Oh, yeah, and he broke into an empty apartment."

Ron asked, "How much is bail?"

The father said, "Hasn't been set yet. The hearing won't be until Monday. Now I need to clear the line so my lawyer can call me. Goodbye." The phone went dead.

He drained his coffee. Drunk with a gun, lands in the county jail. Maybe it was the end of the line for the guy. It takes what it takes, he thought, wondering once again why problem drinkers are always last to recognize the enormity of their problem.

He dialed the phone again. Time to rearrange his day.

"Joe?" But it was only Joe Greiner's voice mail greeting, the hello sounding like someone was really there. At the tone, Ron identified himself and said, "Listen, I'm going downtown to the county jail. If you get this message, can you help me get quick access to a new guy they got? Our boy Jeff Fenner just got himself busted." The visiting lines at the jail were horrendous, especially on a weekend, when every mother, aunt, wife and girlfriend would come to scold, lament, and weep for their bad boys.

⍍

By the time he arrived at the jail it was 11:00. Joe must have called ahead, because the deputy led him through a maze of hallways to a room full of booths all lined up in a row. Each booth had a telephone on a table, and a chair. Visitors hunched forward, phones to their ears, looking through the wire-reinforced glass partition to the inmate on the other side. Some were arguing, others spoke in hushed tones, looking around to see if they were being overheard.

"Stay here and I'll go get your man," the deputy told him.

He watched the visitors come and go. No one smiled—these were not joyful occasions. A lot of these inmates, he knew, were being processed through this facility on their way to state prison.

The deputy returned. "Okay, you're next."

When the next visitor, a young Hispanic girl with a tiny baby, got up from her booth, he walked over and sat down. He looked through the partition at Jeff Fenner, who seemed somewhat surprised, and picked up the phone.

CHAPTER 24

⏁

J eff was dozing on a bunk when he heard his name on
the loudspeaker. "FENNER. JEFFREY FENNER. Report to
the deputy station at once."

He was led, with no explanation, down a series of hallways
and stairs, and finally to a long, dimly lit room. The deputy
pointed to a booth with an empty seat. Jeff sat down and looked
through the partition.

It was the guy from that SOL meeting, Ron somebody. The
guy had picked up a phone and was gesturing to Jeff to do the
same. What the fuck was he even doing here? He picked up the
phone.

"Hello, Jeff." The guy seemed as cheerful as if they were still
at that goddamned meeting.

"Hello, Ron. What brings you out here?" He wondered if they
tapped the phones. The nearest deputy was out of earshot.

Ron said, "Well, your dad told me what happened, so I
thought I'd come out and say hello. How do you like it in there?"

"What kind of question is that? These fuckin' assholes put
me in here, and I can't get bail set until Monday."

"What fuckin' assholes, Jeff? The fuckin' assholes that found
you drunk with a loaded gun, coming out of an apartment that
you had broken into? Why would they qualify as assholes?"

He couldn't believe it. The guy thought this was funny.

"Okay, so I fucked up. What's that got to do with you?"

"I've sat right there in your seat, is all," Ron said. "Didn't like it a bit."

"You were in here? What for?"

"Which time? Drunk driving, drunk driving, drunk in public, drunk driving," Ron ticked the times off with his fingers. "You'd think I would have learned to equate drinking with jail, wouldn't you?"

"So what are you doing here?" Jeff asked. "Is this something that SOL group does?"

"No." The guy smiled. "I'm here as a member of Alcoholics Anonymous. Let me ask you something. Have you ever tried to not drink?"

Jeff said, "I hadn't had a drink in over a week before this . . ." He gestured vaguely at the walls around him.

"So what happened?"

He considered the question. What happened? Kathy was drinking. He was going to get laid. What did that have to do with anything?

He shrugged his shoulders.

Ron asked, "Is it fair to say that your way isn't working?"

He sat and stared through the partition. His life had been in the toilet even before this happened. Now it seemed like it was spiraling downward toward an even darker place that would be very hard, maybe impossible, to return from.

"Yeah," he said, "it's fair to say that my way isn't working."

"When you get out of here," the guy persisted, "do you really think you can stay away from alcohol? Or just drink moderately?"

He closed his eyes. For some reason tears formed and spilled out. He put his hand up to his face, covering his mouth, and held his breath, but a sob came out anyway and he shook his head.

They sat in silence for a moment. When he opened his eyes Ron was gazing at him, calm, like a doctor with a practiced bedside manner.

"So here's one more question, Jeff. Do you believe in God?"

He shrugged again. "Maybe. Whoever the fuck that is."

"That's good," Ron said. "Here's something you might like to try. 'Dear God, whoever-the-fuck-you-are, I need your help.'"

The line went dead. The deputy came over and told him his time was up. Ron nodded briefly as he rose from his seat. Jeff hung up the phone and looked down at the scratched and mutilated surface of the table, the initials and the gang symbols. Under his breath he said, "Okay, God." He paused and then left out the "whoever" part. "I need your help."

CHAPTER 25

⩔

Holly moved across the darkened stage to join hands with the cast. Her knees felt weak. The theater rang with applause as the curtain went up and the lights hit her full in the face.

They had pulled it off—opening night, the house was packed, and they had it wired. It must feel like that, she thought, being in a really good jazz band, where you know the stuff so well that you can play with it, bend it and stretch it, just for fun.

The curtain went down and the applause continued, so they stayed in place until the curtain went back up again. This time people stood and clapped. It was wonderful. It was better than wonderful. She dropped the others' hands and they all gave a slight bow, still in synch.

Someone whistled. She looked out into the audience and saw Tony in his leather jacket, clapping with his hands above his head. He looked terrific, with a smart new haircut and a broad grin on his face. She had seen him on stage so many times; it was good to have him here seeing her, when it was her night. Like it made them equals. Besides, it would be nice to have someone to be with tonight.

⩔

Earlier in the day, she had been out on her porch reading through her lines and making notes in the margins. The thought that opening night was only hours away was thrilling and frightening; trying to relax was a joke. The director had just called to discuss an idea he had and they had spent twenty minutes hashing it out. At the end, he said he would tell the others and then call her back.

When the phone rang, she picked it up and said, "Hello?"

There was a pause, and then, "Holly, it's me."

Tony—just what she didn't need.

"Tony, hi. Listen, I'm expecting a call back from my director. Can we talk another time?" In another lifetime, she hoped.

"Holly, look, I know you're angry with me, and I owe you a big apology. Can we just talk for a minute?" Tony had never apologized for anything. She said, "Sure."

Tony said, "I was out of line. Totally. I was stressed and crazy, I got too drunk, and I was jealous. I miss you, and I'm sorry."

She didn't know what to say. What could she say? He sounded normal—that was a good sign.

"You sound good, Tony. Are you staying straight?" she asked.

"Absolutely. Life's too good to throw away, you know what I mean?"

She said, "Yes, absolutely," and couldn't think of anything else to say.

"Holly?"

"What?"

"We used to have good times together, didn't we?"

"We've had good times, yeah." She wondered where this was heading.

Tony said, "I made a mistake. Can you forgive me for that?"

She said, "Well, it's hard to forget. But yes, I can forgive you for it." Thinking, what the hell, it can't happen again.

Then Tony said, "Listen, I know what you're thinking, but I'm straight as an arrow. How about having dinner together tonight?"

"Can't," she said. "Tonight's a big night for me."

"Really? What's going on?" He didn't sound suspicious; it was just a question.

She said, "The play starts tonight."

"Jesus, really? That's great. Hey, that's really great—I want to see it. Where?"

"Tony—" she began.

He interrupted. "Listen. I know you must think I'm a complete asshole. I don't blame you. I was one. I just flipped out. I need to see you and apologize in person. Tell you what—have you eaten lunch?"

She hadn't had anything except toast and coffee that morning.

"No, I was going to—"

"Great. Look, just see me for lunch. I've got all kinds of great news. Promise to behave. If I do, maybe you'll let me come tonight. What do you think?"

She hesitated. He really was a great guy when he was straight, which he seemed to be at the moment. And, not only was she hungry, but it would be good to get her mind off the evening ahead, stop obsessing about it and try to have a normal day.

"Where?" she asked.

Tony said, "Let's meet at Factor's like we used to, and split the chef's salad."

That cinched it. Factor's was nearby, and she and Tony had spent a lot of time there back when things were good.

⩇

Now, looking out from the stage, she watched the curtain go down for the last time as the house lights went on. Steve, who had acted in and directed the play, said, "Come on. It's Cinderella time."

CHAPTER 26

☥

Holly woke on Sunday morning feeling like she had just survived a shipwreck. Her head throbbed, her eyes hurt, and her throat was constricted and dry. She put her fingers to her neck and pressed, then swallowed. The whole area was sore and tender; it felt as if she were trying to swallow a peach pit—she couldn't complete the action.

Walking to the bathroom, she staggered as her head suddenly throbbed in pain. Okay, she thought, so I hate drinking, but what's with this sore throat? She had had three glasses of champagne last night, at the party after the show.

When she turned on the bathroom light, the rest of the evening came back to her in a rush. She looked in the mirror at the bruises on her throat and remembered her head slamming into the wall again and again.

She gazed at herself and began to cry, feeling both furious and helpless. *How pathetic I am. How totally pathetic.* She wanted to smash the mirror, kick through the glass shower door, break something, hurt herself. When she realized where her mind was going, she said, "Jesus Christ" and walked out to the kitchen.

Her cell rang. She hesitated, not wanting to deal with Tony. The screen said it was Art calling. She closed her eyes and took the call.

"Holly, top o' the mornin' to ye," he said in a mock Irish brogue. "I let you sleep in for as long as I could, but I've got to know how last night went." He had apologized for not being able to show up for the play, something about a professional obligation.

She tried to say hello. Nothing came out except a dry croaking sound. She forced a cough, which made her wince in pain, but couldn't find her voice.

"Holly? Holly, what's going on?" Art sounded genuinely concerned, but what could she do? She whispered, "Wait a minute" and filled a glass with water from the tap. After she drank it she tried again.

"My voice is gone." It was half whisper, but at least she could talk.

"What happened? Did you get laryngitis overnight?"

"No," she croaked, "that son of a bitch Tony choked me."

"He choked you? Where did this happen? Did he break into your apartment?"

"No, I let him in. I'm such an idiot. I can't believe I let him back in."

"Ah, you let him back in. Why?"

"I don't know," she said. "He called me to apologize and we went to lunch. He was fine. Then he came to the show and we went to a party after that."

"So what happened?" Art asked.

"When we got back here, we put on some music and talked. We got a little, um, intimate. Then Tony went to the bathroom and when he came back it was like Dr. Jekyll and Mr. Hyde. He just flipped on me." Speaking was becoming more painful, so she went back to a whisper.

There was a pause and then Art said, "Holly, it's very important that we get together today. Can you make it to my office at noon?"

She thought about leaving home, about the marks on her throat, and shook her head.

"Holly?"

"No," she whispered. "I can't go anywhere."

"Okay, then I'll pick you up. It's imperative for your recovery. I'll be there at eleven thirty."

"No. I can't. Not today."

"Holly, let me ask you just one thing. Is your life working?"

She thought about it and remembered Tony, charming at lunch, sweet and funny last night, and then shaking her like a rag doll, his huge hands on her throat. She shook her head again.

Out of the silence Art said, "Things will get better. Trust me. Freshen up and then rest. I'll come and get you."

☥

When they got to Art's office, she sank into the leather chair and closed her eyes. She didn't want to be here, but didn't want to be at home either.

Art brought her a cup of water and this time offered her two of the little orange pills. She swallowed them without argument and closed her eyes again. Her headache had gone, but she still felt sore and weary. She heard Art leaving the room and wondered when the pills would take effect, when she could go to that wonderful dreamy zone that Art had taken her to on her last visit.

When she heard the door open again, she realized that she was back in that floating place, where her body was in the chair but her mind could move free as a fish in the ocean. She noticed there was a smile on her face and experimented with it, moving her mouth into a frown, a pout, a grimace. It was all so amusing she wound up with the smile again.

"Holly." Art sounded so gentle and friendly. "Here. I'd like you to take this."

She opened her eyes and saw that he was offering her a teddy bear. She took it and put it on her lap. It was soft and golden with little brown button eyes.

"Now I'd like you to cradle it, that's right, and close your eyes and rock it. That's it."

She held the little bear in her arms and tried to remember being rocked. She could see a rocking chair in her room. Who was in it? She didn't know. She wanted to be held, but there was this noise that wouldn't stop. She was making the noise; why didn't they just pick her up and then she would stop? But now the rocking chair was empty and the light had gone out and there was only the noise and she couldn't turn it off. She rocked the little bear harder and tried to see through the darkness, but there were only blurry shapes around her.

Art's voice broke through and the crying noise stopped.

"Holly, I want you to open and shut your eyes rapidly over and over again." He tapped his fingers rhythmically into his palm. "This fast," he said, "and don't stop. And remember, any time I say, 'Holly, trust me, the doctor needs your help,' any time ever, you will return to this quiet state."

She blinked her eyes open and shut. Art sat across from her, their knees almost touching, and waved his hand back and forth about eighteen inches in front of her face. It was a weird effect, she thought, like strobe lights in a dance club.

"Now, Holly, I'm going to ask you some questions and I want you to go back and find the answers. Don't try to remember. Go back and be there. Do you understand?"

She made herself nod, though the motion made the whole room flicker and strobe.

"That's good, keep blinking your eyes. Okay, did your daddy hit your mommy?"

She watched the hand flicker back and forth in front of her and at the same time saw herself in a kitchen, her kitchen from when she was little. She sat at the breakfast table and her mother moved toward her father, pointing her finger at him, and he was backing away.

"No," she told Art. "He wouldn't dare."

"All right," Art said, "who hit you when you were little?"

She rocked the bear again and tried to see the shapes, but all she saw was that pointing finger and the angry face.

"Nobody *hit* me," she said. She wondered why she said the word "hit" so loudly.

"Holly, close your eyes. That's it. Now, take a deep breath. Very good. Okay, who *hurt* you when you were little?"

She clutched at the bear and looked around in the dark. A shape materialized and approached her. It held her shoulders with huge hands. She tried to turn away but it wouldn't let her. She looked at the shape and tried to see who it was but it was too dark.

"Holly, who hurt you when you were little?" Art's voice was so quiet, it seemed like he was far away. She looked at the shape and saw a face. When she saw who it was she started to shake her head back and forth but the face wouldn't go away. She knew the face but couldn't say the name.

"Holly, who?" Was Art still asking her a question, or was it just an echo of the first time?

She took a deep breath and sat still.

"Uncle Dave hurt me," she whispered.

"What did he do?" Art prodded.

"I . . ." She couldn't find any words so she just shook her head.

"Show me," Art said.

She kept shaking her head. "I can't," she whispered.

"Show me," Art insisted. "I'm Uncle Dave now. Show me. I won't hurt you. Trust me."

She heard the sound of leather sliding through a buckle, the twenty-year-old noise of a zipper, a rustle of fabric. Uncle Dave took her hand and guided it to his lap, pulling her up out of her seat. The bear fell to the ground as she knelt between her uncle's knees and bent forward. She opened her mouth and felt the warm skin thing on her tongue. This was their secret and nobody could ever know. If only Uncle Dave knew how she hated it. If only it wasn't a secret and she could tell her dad and he would tell Uncle Dave to stop.

She felt a hand on the back of her head, pushing her downward now. The thing was huge in her mouth, she backed off so she wouldn't gag but the hand pushed her down again, then it pulled her gently back. The hand pushed her into a slow rhythm. Tears ran down her face; she was wet with them, but nothing mattered. She didn't have to be here. She could skate down the boardwalk at Santa Monica Beach. She could rise up into the night sky and fly anywhere she wanted. She was free now and when the hand pushed her faster and harder she flew faster and higher, until she saw the star that was calling her. She flew toward it until she was falling into it and then it came to her. . . *That's life; that's where the pain is*, and, as her mouth filled with thick warm fluid, she turned away from the sun and flew high into the darkest place between the stars.

CHAPTER 27

⏣

Art looked down at the girl, vacillating between amuse-ment and annoyance. Silly little bitch, he thought. *So beau-tiful. So obedient.* She had passed out just as he had exploded—exquisite, simply exquisite—and slumped, first onto the edge of the chair between his thighs, and then fallen to the floor, hitting her face on the base of his chair on the way. A small dab of blood appeared at the corner of her mouth. He retrieved his phone from his desk and tapped the square icon that would stop recording.

Standing up, he buttoned his pants and fastened his belt. He then knelt by the girl and, first checking the pulse at her neck, pulled up an eyelid. Only white was showing. He stood up and stepped over the girl to walk to his desk, rolling his chair back with him. It could be a petit-mal seizure, he thought. Bloody good thing she didn't bite.

As he sat, he had a premonition that this could take a danger-ous turn for him. From the bottom drawer of his desk he pulled out a small black leather bag. He opened it and peered in at the contents: foil blister packs of pharmaceutical samples, a variety of vials with metal caps that had little rubber dots at their centers, clear tubes of tablets and capsules of all colors, and a pack of dis-posable syringes. *I don't even know her goddamned medical history. Fuck! What a bloody nuisance.*

Anger began to boil up now. The girl on his floor. His wife, trying to run his life. Marilyn Fenner—now her goddamned brother was coming to the meetings. If that asshole remembers me . . . The fool would have to have a drug overdose; that much was obvious.

He took a deep breath. And another. He knew if his mind continued in this direction he would lose control, and when he lost control things always turned out badly.

By the fifth deep breath, he realized that there could be an advantage to the situation. Perhaps she won't remember. She had certainly been out long enough now for that to become increasingly more likely. "How delightful, a repressed memory that's only ten minutes old," he said out loud, in a better humor now.

Searching within the black bag, he found two ampules and a small pack of Kleenex, which he laid out on his desk along with one of the syringes. It's risky, he thought, but what the hell. He pushed the syringe needle into the rubber dot in the middle of the cap on the bottle labeled "Ephedrine," then pulled on the plunger until the bottle was empty. He repeated the procedure with the bottle marked "Valium," then placed the empty bottles in his top drawer. As an afterthought, he reached down and pulled a soda from the small refrigerator on the floor by his desk.

He walked over to where the girl lay, knelt, and chose a spot on her arm for the injection. He pointed the syringe upward and pushed on the plunger just enough so that a small spray of liquid shot out, to ensure that no air would enter the girl's vein, and then slid the needle into the crook of the girl's elbow.

The vein was blue and strong. He pushed the plunger and watched as the syringe emptied—in moments the girl would wake. Or die. Who knows? Jesus, getting her to the car would be awkward.

He pulled the needle out and threw it in the wastebasket. If things went badly he would retrieve it later. During cleanup time. The soda can made a popping sound as he pulled the metal tab.

The girl stirred. He put the soda on the floor, then leaned forward and pulled the girl up and around, arranging her so that they faced each other in a kneeling position. He dabbed at the blood on her lip with a tissue, and then let her fall forward into him so that her cheek was against his chest.

When her eyes opened, she said, "Art?"

"Yes, Holly. Yes, I know," he said, stroking her hair. "Here, have some of this." He offered her the soda, which she drank gratefully.

"What happened?" she asked. "What are we doing on the floor?" She pulled away and looked around the room.

He smiled warmly. "We got in a bit deep for a moment there. Into a place where the emotions are strong, overpowering even, I'm afraid. It was very brave of you to go there."

The girl's eyes fixed on him, clear and unblinking, and she gazed into him for so long he began to wonder if perhaps she had been present to the entire experience. Then she looked down at the floor and said, "I remember about my uncle."

"Yes," he replied. "You were very young. How do you feel about what he did?"

"I can't believe it. It's so disgusting. How can that happen?" She looked up at him, waiting for an answer, hoping he would have one that made sense. Trusting him.

CHAPTER 28

⩒

There was something so refreshing and open about Leanne's face, Ron was happy just to sit and watch her. They were sitting in the back room at Renee's Garden, quiet on a Sunday night.

"I love this place," Leanne said as she forked a piece of chocolate raspberry cake and brought it to her mouth.

"It's wonderful, isn't it?" He dipped his spoon into the coconut sherbet he had ordered. "It's the best kept secret in town. I hope she makes it."

Just then, Renee herself came to their table.

"Hello, darlings. How is everything tonight?" She was a tiny woman, made even smaller by her pronounced stoop. She spoke with a heavy Brooklyn accent.

"Perfect," Leanne said. "This place—" she looked around the room "—it's just so lovely." The restaurant was decorated like a New England country home, with antique prints on the walls and steamer trunks against the walls with colorful quilts draped over them.

Renee put her hands together and nodded, then turned to Ron, raising an eyebrow theatrically.

"Exquisite," he proclaimed. "I'm in love."

Renee looked back at Leanne, her head cocked to one side now, and said, "Yes. If you two don't stay together, I'm going back to being a showgirl in Vegas."

He blushed as he realized how his statement had been interpreted and then decided that maybe Renee wasn't so far off the mark.

"Well, you children come back soon, okay?" She turned and walked away.

"What a character," he said, shaking his head and smiling.

"My God, and that accent. She's too much!" Leanne laughed, white teeth against her tanned face, her shoulders bare in a sleeveless blue silk top. She was beautiful, he thought, but what was more important was how comfortable he felt with her. He had always found her attractive, but until now it hadn't seemed appropriate to ask to see her in the context of a date.

⍢

They had met nearly six years earlier. Ron had been assigned to cover the trial of a prominent West Valley attorney suspected of trying to murder his wife. According to the police testimony, Peter Christensen had beaten his wife, pushed her through a sliding glass door, and then shoved the woman into their pool. Paramedics, responding to a call from the fourteen-year-old daughter, found the woman lying face down in the water in a cloud of blood. The husband had a .21 percent blood-alcohol level. When the police arrived, he told them to mind their own business.

Ron had watched and taken notes throughout the testimony: police, paramedics, the daughter, and then, finally, the victim herself.

Leanne Christensen was a prosecutor's ideal victim—just what the DA needed to counter the fact of her husband's stature as an attorney. She was composed, articulate, and attractive without being cold or unsympathetic. She had been Teacher of the Year two years previous and had since written a book about the education system that had been well received.

During her testimony, Leanne Christensen delivered an unemotional narrative of the events preceding her plunge into the family pool. She maintained her bearing during gentle prodding for details by the assistant DA, and she remained level, if somewhat icy, during most of her husband's defense attorney's questioning. It wasn't until late into the cross-examination, when Harry Wise began to insinuate that she had provoked the fight, that Leanne began to betray any emotion.

Wise spoke, ostensibly to Leanne, while facing the jury.

"Isn't it true, Mrs. Christensen, that after starting an argument in a fit of jealousy over an affair that never happened,"—Wise audibly smacked his left palm with his right fist, punctuating his points—"and after threatening to divorce your husband and 'rake him over the coals' financially"—SMACK!—"and after physically assaulting your husband,"—here a demonstrative and extra-loud smack of the fist for the jury's benefit—"isn't it true that you then, unresponsive to your husband's attempts to calm you down, ran hysterically toward the back yard, at which point you went through the glass door?" Wise turned and faced Leanne, silent, questioning and slightly reproachful in his attitude. To just lay the seed for the possibility of doubt in the mind of one juror, that was his job.

Leanne Christensen had stood up.

"You son of a bitch," she said in a cold, controlled fury. "I've served you dinner." She turned to the jury. "Our children go to school together. Our families have been friends for ten years. We vacation together, for God's sake." She turned back to Wise. "I'm not on trial here. You know me and you know that the way you painted the scene was entirely false." She sat down. After a moment's silence, she leaned toward the microphone and said, "Will there be any more questions?"

The jury deliberated three hours before delivering their verdict: Peter Christensen was found guilty on all counts.

Ron had managed to catch Leanne alone for a brief moment after the trial. He asked her if he could see her briefly, perhaps for lunch, and discuss the case.

They met the next day at a trendy dining spot on Ventura Boulevard called Dominic's. Leanne still wore a stiff, severe look, and lit a cigarette as he approached the table.

"Thank you for meeting with me." He shook Leanne's hand and slid into the booth.

A waiter came. They scanned their menus and ordered.

When the waiter left, Leanne spoke first.

"Jerry Hadfield asked me not to discuss the case." Hadfield was the prosecutor. "He said that on the off chance the motion to appeal was denied, it would cause trouble if I were to talk with you before sentencing." She blew a cloud of smoke into the air and then drummed her fingernails on the polished wood table.

She could have told him this by phone, he thought. He remained silent, hands clasped in front of him.

Leanne put out the cigarette. "Damn these. I quit, until this whole thing happened." She looked up at him. "Anyway, you're probably wondering why we're here, if I can't talk about the case."

He opened his hands and gave a slight nod in a gesture of assent.

"The answer," Leanne continued, "is that I don't know. I just had a feeling I could talk to you." She smiled and softened, vulnerable for a moment.

He made an easy decision. "Okay. I'm not here as a reporter, and whatever we talk about is between you and me, okay?"

Leanne nodded and looked away. When she turned back to face him she said, "Look at me. I'm an intelligent, fairly with-it, relatively successful woman. I marry a guy, we have a beautiful child, we prosper, he tries to kill me. It doesn't make sense. How did this thing happen to me?"

"You want the short, no-bullshit answer?" he asked.

"Be my guest."

"It's clear," he said, "based on the testimony in court, that your husband attacked you in an alcoholic rage."

"I know. He has a problem with drinking. I've been telling him to go to an AA meeting for years."

"The trouble with that," he went on, "is that people don't go to AA until they really want to. Meanwhile, to answer your question, to live with an alcoholic is to participate in the disease of alcoholism."

Leanne's face tightened slightly around her mouth. "What's that supposed to mean?"

"It means that there's such a thing as co-alcoholism. And that, by virtue of living with your husband's drinking and his behavior, even prior to this attack, you qualify as a co-alcoholic. Your daughter too. The question is, do you want to do something about it?"

Leanne stared at him for a moment and then lit another cigarette. "I didn't come here to be given a label. Anyway, I've moved out, with my daughter, and so the problem is removed. Isn't it?" She gestured for the waiter. When he came, she asked for a check. They waited in silence. When the waiter returned, Ron pulled out his wallet. Leanne said, "Forget it. There's no money left anyway, so what's a couple of wasted lunches?" and she offered her credit card.

He reached into a compartment of his wallet and pulled out a business card.

"Here. I have some familiarity with these matters. I didn't mean to offend you. Call me if the going gets rough."

Six months later, he received a call from Leanne. She had moved to Santa Monica with her daughter. She couldn't handle going back to teaching, so she was waitressing at a local restaurant. There really wasn't any money left and that was okay, her husband was in prison, no problem, and her daughter was doing fine in the local school, but something much more basic was wrong. At first she thought it was just shock from the whole episode and then she thought it was depression, but now it wouldn't go away.

"I remember," she said, "that you said there was something I could do about it."

⛢

Renee's was emptying out, the moviegoers checking their watches as they stood up from their tables. Ron and Leanne finished their desserts in silence, looking up at each other and smiling a couple of times, not feeling compelled to make conversation.

Leanne took his hand as they walked out of Renee's.

"You know," Leanne said, "I hated you when you told me that alcoholism was a family disease."

He nodded and laughed. "I remember. You didn't hide it."

"Now I've been in Al-Anon for five years . . ."

"Crazy," he said, "how it goes by."

"Everything about me has changed. The things I value. The way I live. The way I see other people." They had reached the Land Rover. Leanne turned to him, still holding his hand.

"Thank you," she said, looking up at him. "Thank you for caring."

He looked back at her, thinking how his caring had changed. He had cared for her enough, at first, when they were strangers, to tell her the truth about her situation, and she had run from it. Later, when she began to pursue her own recovery, he had cared for her as a companion, responding to her need, talking with her on the phone late into the night. They took up running together on the sand at State Beach.

When, inevitably, Leanne began to take tentative steps into a new social life and began dating, he had stepped aside. For a long while they lost contact.

Now, he thought, he cared in an entirely new way. He found he could only nod his head as she thanked him so earnestly; there was really nothing he could say. Instead, he drew her to him. He touched her hair with his lips, and then her eye as she turned her face up to meet him, and her cheek, then the corner of her mouth. Her mouth opened as she turned slightly and their lips brushed past each other until they found center and fit together. He felt her fingers move up his temples into his hair, up to the top of his head and then sliding down softly to his cheeks as they kissed.

Leanne drew back.

"They say this is the way to ruin a perfectly good friendship."

He opened the door and helped her step up to the seat.

"I don't think so," he said.

CHAPTER 29

⌁

They decided to see some music. Ron liked jazz; Leanne said she liked anything.

". . . except country and opera." She laughed. "But then, I've heard great country—and great opera, come to think of it."

He drove up Wilshire Boulevard toward a club he had in mind.

"There must be something you don't like."

"Well, I'm not real big on Lawrence Welk, and I could do without heavy-metal and rap music."

"Ah," he said, "how could you not like—" he banged a rhythm on the steering wheel—"'It's like a jungle sometimes, it makes me wonder how I keep from goin' under'?'"

Leanne burst out laughing. "Isn't that really old?"

He pulled up in front of the club and peered at the marquee. "Okay, let's do it. This guy's really good."

When they were inside the club, a hostess led them past a long bar to a table against the far wall. When they were seated Leanne asked, "Does that bother you at all?"

"What, walking past a bar? Looking at all those pretty bottles?" He laughed. "I drank for an effect that I don't crave any more. Miraculous, but true."

A few people on the stage were efficiently dismantling some band equipment.

"Our timing is pretty good," he observed. "The headliner starts in about fifteen minutes."

A waitress took their orders for two Perriers. People laughed loudly at a table nearby. The full room buzzed with the chatter of about two hundred people, black, white, students, professionals, some scruffy, some clearly belonging to the Mercedes and BMWs in the lot.

"I think I'm ready to go back to teaching," Leanne said, apropos of nothing.

"I think that's terrific." He looked at Leanne and the din of the club, its entire existence, receded into the background. "I think it'll be great for you."

"You don't think I've been a coward, hiding out all this time?" She looked at him, wide open and vulnerable.

"No, Leanne. For God's sake, you were badly traumatized and you've been focusing entirely on rebuilding your life. You're one of the bravest people I've ever known." He put his hand out on the table and Leanne took it.

"I needed to hear you say that." She looked down at their clasped hands for a moment, then pulled his hand to her mouth and held it there. The waitress came with their drinks. When she left, Leanne said, "So what's this thing you told me about—young beauties jumping out of buildings?"

He squeezed lime into his drink. "I covered a suicide a few weeks back. Pretty gal in her twenties. Somehow, I got a hunch that turned up seven similar suicides in the last couple of years, and enough coincidences between them to convince me that something very odd has been going on—may still be going on, for all I know."

"Like what?"

He shrugged. "Beside their ages and looks?" He leaned forward, elbows on the table. "Well, for starters, they all fell—" he made quote marks in the air with his fingers "—from high places. Two of them had the same drug in their systems—"

Leanne interrupted. "What kind of drug? Coke? Pot?"

"No, that wouldn't mean anything. This one's called Halcion. Prescription. Makes you mellow if you've got anxieties. Good

thing I never knew about them. Oh, and they make you suscepti-
ble to hypnosis."

"So, that's two of them. What else?"

"I got three of them all going to the same self-help meetings.
Not the same meetings, really, but the same deal. Saving Our
Lives—they're all over town."

"So maybe people that go to those meetings are more prone
to taking their lives. Have you checked male suicides to see if they
went to those meetings?" Leanne grinned and brushed her hair
back with her hand.

"Are you making fun of me?" He grinned back, but wondered
if maybe his hunch was wrong, that LA was a big city and that it
contained, among other things, a lot of attractive women, some of
them troubled, some of them fatally so.

"Not really. Well, maybe a little. So, do you think they were
pushed, or deliberately brought to despondency so they jumped?"

"Who could pull that off?" he wondered.

"A therapist," Leanne volunteered.

"Or a psychotic Romeo."

"How about a psychotic Romeo therapist?" Leanne was
enjoying herself now.

"You know about those therapists, don't you?" he asked,
cocking an eyebrow.

"No, what?"

He pulled a pen from his jacket pocket and wrote the word
"therapist" on his paper napkin, then turned it to Leanne.

"Can you divide this into two words?"

Leanne studied it for an instant and then laughed.

"The rapist. I never noticed that. That's truly terrible. I knew
there was a reason I never trusted them."

A deep voice announced over the PA that the band was about
to begin. Applause filled the room as the house lights went off.
Ron and Leanne turned to watch as figures appeared on the darkened stage. When the lights lit up the band and the musicians
launched into their first tune, she took his hand again and there
was nothing but the two of them, immersed in music.

CHAPTER 30

Monday morning at 7 a.m., Jeff found himself in the LA County Sheriff's bus for the second time, only this time it was headed west. There were only four other men in the bus, plus the driver and the guard standing in the enclosure at the front. Nobody spoke. Jeff stared out the window at the gray morning. A marine layer had brought a gloomy fog inland. In a couple hours it would burn off and become one more sizzling summer day.

By 7:40, they were herded out of the bus and into a holding cell adjacent to the West Los Angeles Municipal Courthouse. Because they had missed breakfast at the county jail, they were given sandwiches wrapped in cellophane—stale sourdough rolls with ham and cheese. The guard from the bus unlocked their handcuffs and rolled the cell door shut.

Jeff straddled a wooden bench so that he could rest his back against the wall and unwrapped the sandwich.

"You goin' to trial? Sentencing? What's up, man?" A burly guy that looked like an aging surfer was looking at him from the other end of the bench, about eight feet away. He chewed on his sandwich and appraised Jeff with washed-out blue eyes as he leaned against the opposite wall.

"Bail hearing," Jeff said. The guy had greasy black hair, thick and curly, and a weird little tuft of hair under his lower lip. Jeff didn't want to talk to him.

"Yeah, been there, done that. You know what they want for my fuckin' bail, man? Twenty-five thousand bucks. Twenty-five grand on a fuckin' bogus DUI."

"Yeah? What was bogus about it?" He didn't doubt for a minute that the guy had been caught smashed, snockered, pickled, shitfaced and stumbling out of his pickup truck blowing the cops' Breathalyzer off the scale with Coors and Kamchatka fumes. Just like Jeff himself had been. He had finally come to grips with that, sitting on his bunk, surveying the bustling room full of miscreants in the county jail. Come to realize that the cops weren't full of shit, and that he, Jeff, had gotten laid, had a drink, gotten pissed off, drunk a bottle of tequila, stolen a car, and broken down a door. And that it was the cops' job to bust people like him.

"What d'ya mean, 'what was bogus about it'?" The guy's eyes narrowed, like he had suddenly identified an infiltrator, a spy, something other than the kindred spirit whose agreement he had taken for granted. "Who are you, the fuckin' designated driver?" He spat on the floor of the cell.

Jeff shook his head and took another bite of his sandwich. It seemed like the one thing everyone in the jail system had in common, besides that they were innocent, was that they all got pissed off so easily. Jesus, it was ludicrous.

"No, I'm not the fuckin' designated driver. The fact is, they said I was drunk, and I was drunk. So, the question is, what about you? Were you drunk, or what?"

"So I had a few drinks. So fuckin' what. I was in a bar—what do you think I was doing, eatin' fuckin' dessert?" The guy gave him that hard look now, that don't-fuck-with-me jailhouse scowl, and said, "I got in my truck and drove home. I was fine, man. I was fuckin' fine. Fuckin' pigs got a quota to fill, don't you know that? They get a fuckin' bonus if they fill their quota, so they can buy new boat racks for their RVs, man." He shook his head in contempt. "Fuckin' bogus."

A marshal came and ushered the five men into a hallway and through a door. Jeff was surprised to find himself suddenly in a courtroom: he felt conspicuous in his blue jumpsuit, like in one of those dreams where he'd be in high school with his pajamas on, or on the street with only a gym towel around his waist.

The marshal gestured him toward a bench that lined the wall on one side of the courtroom. A wooden divider topped by a thick panel of clear Plexiglas separated this section from the rest of the room.

He looked out and saw his father in the front of the sparse audience, staring back at him, nodding his head almost imperceptibly, as if in agreement with some inner voice.

When his name was called, he was led by the marshal to a table in front of the judge's bench. A small man with round glasses bent over the table to his right, peering at a file. Beyond him, a tall, gaunt man with crew-cut gray hair sprawled in his chair, gazing up at him with clinical interest.

The judge—a nameplate identified him as the Honorable Timothy Metcalf—peered over his microphone at him and said, "Jeffrey Alan Fenner, you are charged with breaking and entering, carrying a concealed weapon, drunk and disorderly, and drunk driving. How do you plead?"

At this point the small man stood up, adjusted his glasses, and whispered to him, "Just say, 'not guilty, Your Honor.'"

He repeated the words, "Not guilty, Your Honor." So this guy must be Herman Katz, his father's lawyer.

The judge turned his attention to the man sprawled in the chair beyond Katz.

"Mr. Deemer, what have you got?"

Mr. Deemer spread out in his chair like he owned the room and said, "Well, Your Honor, the officers found him exiting the premises. The door had been kicked in. The man had the weapon tucked in his pants, and he blew a 1.6 at the station. He's got no employment of record, so I'd consider him a flight risk. He was inebriated at two in the morning, with a loaded semi-automatic pistol, so that qualifies as a danger to the community in my book. I'm going to recommend bail be set at twenty-five thousand dollars." He looked up at Jeff and smiled cheerfully.

"Mr. Katz?" The Honorable Timothy Metcalf, a jowly black man with a gleaming bald skull, didn't seem too pleased with the prosecuting attorney's nonchalance.

Katz shrugged his shoulders.

"I'd say that's fairly ridiculous. My client has no record. He's living with his family in West Hollywood, a good family who recently endured a tragedy. The police have no evidence that my client damaged the door to the apartment, and it's my understanding that his friend had been living there and that Mr. Fenner didn't know the individual had moved. I say he's no risk to the community, nor is he a flight risk, and I'm asking for him to be released on his own recognizance."

The judge peered down at some papers and nodded wearily, as if it were already the end of the day. Jeff's heart thumped in his chest—his father might not put up bail if the judge went for the DA's recommendation. He'd be stuck in the county jail indefinitely.

"Bail is set at five thousand dollars," the judge proclaimed. He handed a sheaf of papers to his clerk.

Katz took his elbow and whispered up to him, "You'll be out today," then nodded toward the bailiff, who walked Jeff back to the partitioned area and told him to please have a seat, sir.

By four that afternoon, he finally walked out of the county jail. It felt good to be in his own clothes, wearing his watch again, his wallet in his pocket. He looked around the parking area and wondered where his father was.

Half an hour later, a white Land Rover pulled up right next to where he stood. Its driver leaned over and opened the passenger door.

"You ready?" It was the guy who had visited him—Ron somebody. He was grinning cheerfully.

"What are you doing here? Where's my father?" He was baffled that this guy should have shown up.

"Get in. I'll tell you all about it. Unless you'd rather stay here." Another big grin.

He stepped up into the truck. Ron waited until he closed the door and fastened the seat belt before wheeling around and driving out of the lot.

When they pulled into traffic he said, "Okay, what's going on?"

Ron looked over at him and said, "Your folks have had enough. They don't want you in their house anymore."

"What? What do you mean they don't want me in their house anymore? Who told you that?"

"Your father told me. Look in the back."

Jeff looked in the back and saw a suitcase and his briefcase.

"Your clothes and stuff are in the suitcase. I don't know what's in the briefcase, but if there are drugs or another gun, you'd better tell me now."

It was starting to sink in that he wasn't going home. "No, there's no drugs and there's no gun. So where am I supposed to go?"

"Well, that's up to you. From what I understand, you've been evicted from your apartment. Is that right?" Ron pointed the Land Rover up a freeway on-ramp and accelerated.

"Yeah, my apartment is history. I still have to get my stuff somehow." It seemed overwhelming to even think about.

"So the first question is, are you ready to stop drinking?" Ron looked over at him, not grinning now, eyebrows raised in anticipation of an answer.

"I haven't been too good at quitting drinking," he said.

"That's a good answer. But are you willing to go to any lengths to try?"

CHAPTER 31

⩔

By Tuesday, the marks on Holly's throat were no longer visible. She had dreamed that blue handprints were emblazoned on her neck, and that when she awoke something held her by the hair so that she couldn't move her head. The awakening itself had been a dream, but had a quality to it, a texture of realness that she could recall vividly even now, hours later.

She knew it had to do with her session at Art's office. Something had happened there—something frightening, something that hovered on the periphery of her awareness, just slightly out of reach. There was a ponderous feeling to it, a dangerous size and weight, like a large and stupid animal.

She reached for the edge of the pool and turned, concentrating on her swimming. Sometimes she could turn her mind off entirely, tuned only to the reach and pull of each stroke, the quick breath over her shoulder, the clear blue of the water. Twenty laps made a kilometer in her gym's large pool; on a good day she would do twice that. The payoff was always the same—after a light workout and a good swim she would feel refreshed and optimistic, temporarily free from the desolate and oppressive condition that seemed to be her normal state.

Not that anyone knew, except for the doctors and therapists she had seen over the years. She had been told so many different things by so many professionals that she wondered if the mental health field had a scientific basis at all. Depressive with anxiety disorder. That one had come up a few times. Periodic seizure syndrome. One doctor had given her an anti-convulsant, which stopped the seizures but made her feel drowsy. He added a prescription to help her remain alert. When she couldn't sleep, he prescribed a hypnotic that would put her in a dreamless black void until she came to in the morning. Another doctor gave her Ritalin just to shake the groggy feeling that made it impossible to function. Then she would feel slightly edgy—time for a Valium.

The next doctor put her on anti-depressants, without any perceptible improvement. She thought back to the time she had finally weaned herself from all medications. It was at that time, only about four months ago, that she had started going to SOL meetings. Something had started to change for her, though it was hard to put a finger on it. She stopped to adjust her goggles— if she didn't wear them, or if they leaked, the chlorinated water would irritate her eyes—and then resumed swimming.

Whatever it was that was changing seemed to be accelerating now, ever since the night after Bobbi's lecture, when Art and Joanie had taken her on her first strange trip. Now, she thought, it seemed like she was approaching a threshold, a place of danger but also of great possibility. A place that Art had shown her and through which only Art could lead her.

CHAPTER 32

⌁

Jeff showered and picked through the few clothes he had unpacked from the suitcase. It was strange having his pants and shirts hanging in a closet as if he had always lived here. He put on jeans and a dark-blue shirt, slipped on his sandals, and went out to the living room.

It was an old house, probably built in the thirties, with small, boxy rooms, but it was bright and uncluttered. The living room had two walls entirely lined with books, and some bright prints against the other two white walls. He liked the feel of the house and felt secure in the back room that Ron had told him he could use.

"Let's go." Ron had his keys in his hand, ready to leave. A step ahead of him even though Ron had washed the dishes, showered, and made some phone calls. They walked out into the early evening. Santa Ana winds blew through the canyon. The air was dry and hot. He had always loved these conditions—perfect surfing weather when the winds blew the spray off the tops of the swells and held them up so that a surfer could move across the face of a wave for impossibly long distances.

"So where are we headed?" He buckled into the seat of the Rover.

"Good little meeting out in West LA." Ron wheeled out of the driveway and on to the lane that led to Beachwood Canyon.

"What kind of meeting?" He couldn't see going to one of those things Kathy had taken him to. What if she showed up?

"AA, Jeff. We're going to an AA meeting." Ron looked over at him as if he were talking to a dense child.

"If you go to AA, why do you go to those SOL meetings?"

"Curiosity. There's a lot of good information there. The trouble is, they package it up and sell it to you, then they tell you that you won't really 'get it' unless you go recruit other people to come in and buy so that then they can go out and recruit. But the information is good. Most of it, anyway."

They drove in silence for a while. Eventually, they turned onto Highway 10, heading toward the setting sun.

Jeff pulled down the visor to block out the brightness.

"You know, I don't know why you're doing all this, but thanks for giving me a place to stay and everything."

"No problem. Wash your own dishes. Maybe do a few errands."

"Like what?"

"I don't know. Neighbor's got a dog I feed when he's on tour. Musician. You could do that."

"I can't believe how messed up everything got. And how fast." He caught his reflection in a mirror on the visor. The sun had given him some color—he looked pretty good. Not like a guy that just got out of county.

Ron said, "Look how bad things could have gotten."

"What do you mean?"

"Well, given what you were doing . . ."

Jeff cut in, "What do you know about what I was doing?"

Ron explained about Joe Greiner and his call from the Narco Squad.

"You mean they wanted to use my sister's death to set me up?" He was incredulous. "Marilyn didn't take drugs."

"Maybe not," Ron said, "but they found something in her when she died."

"What—Marilyn? That's crazy. What was it?"

Ron told him about the Halcion, and what it was for.

"So they were after me anyway. Unbelievable." He shook his head. "You know what?"

"What?" Ron glanced over.

"You're right. It could have been worse. Much worse." He was silent for a moment and then said, "I still don't get it. How did my name come up in the first place? I mean between you and your cop friend—hey, Joe Greiner, that's the guy that left a card on my door!"

Ron turned onto the San Diego Freeway, heading north, and got off at Santa Monica Boulevard before answering.

"Remember I told you I wrote about your sister?"

Jeff nodded. "Yeah, so?"

"I thought there was something strange about what happened, so I did a little research. Joe helped me."

"What did you come up with?"

"I came up with seven similar cases. Apparent suicides. Young. Attractive. Your name just came up out of the blue."

"Seven. Jesus." He looked out the window. Ron had turned on Westwood Boulevard and they were heading back south.

"I don't know about the others, but I've got this feeling that what happened to my sister has something to do with that SOL group."

"Yeah," Ron nodded. "So do I"

He stopped at a light in the right turn lane. A small crowd stood around the entrance to a church on the corner. Someone noticed Ron's car and waved. Ron drove along the residential block until he found a spot to park. "Try to put all that aside for now," he said as they stepped out of the Rover.

CHAPTER 33

⟡

A freak rain spattered the coast on Wednesday morning—spin-off from a tropical storm battering central
Baja. A cool, damp wind blew in gusts from the south, but by
midday the sky was clear again, the August heat reasserted itself
and the air was sweltering.

The Museum of Natural History is an imposing stone edi-
fice, locked in place between the University of Southern California and the Los Angeles Coliseum. The three institutions share
a space on the map at the uppermost portion of that part of LA
known as South Central, deep in the heart of the city.

Holly was unfamiliar with this part of town. The drive down
Exposition Boulevard got stranger and stranger to her; as she
headed east, the small but respectable middle-class homes gave
way to a grimmer atmosphere, the ironwork on the doors and
windows of the houses betraying a sense of siege on the part of
the inhabitants.

It was with a feeling of relief that she turned onto Menlo and
pulled into the museum parking area. The few cars in the lot were
mainly vans and SUVs—family vehicles nestled in this downtown oasis. She followed a young mother pushing a stroller with a
round-faced baby in the front seat and a pixie-like boy with curly
red hair in the back. The heat, after her air-conditioned ride,
was oppressive. She wondered why Art had been so enthusiastic
about meeting here.

They passed through a gate into an open area with a fountain. A long truck, the size of a large moving van, sat parked in front of the entrance, deep green with dinosaurs and sharks painted in brilliant colors. She went up the stone steps and found Art in the courtyard at the top, straddling a large bronze tortoise in the shade of the building.

He rose, grinning, and came forward to greet her.

"Perfect. It's lovely inside, you'll see." He took her hand and began to lead her to the glass doors of the museum, then stopped and turned toward her again.

"How are you, my dear?" He looked directly into her eyes, his tanned face serious now, the piercing blue eyes unblinking. He wore the cream-colored suit in which she had first seen him. His hand was cool to the touch.

"I'm fine."

She started to look away, but he held her gaze and said, "Really?"

"I don't know" she said. "I've been feeling tired a lot. Coffee just seems to make me feel anxious." Then she told him about the dreams, and the false waking that was still a dream and how something seemed to be floating at the periphery of her attention, something crucial but elusive.

Art pulled her gently toward him and touched her briefly on the forehead with his lips. She could smell his cologne, the scent attractive but subtle. His shirt was brilliant white against a yellow silk tie. She turned her head and rested it against Art's shoulder; a brief tremor ran through her but was replaced by a sense of comfort.

Art patted her back and then kneaded the muscles at her spine with his fingertips. "You've launched into a process of discovery. The subconscious mind is stirring—it doesn't like to be prodded, and now it's making waves in your conscious life."

She disengaged from Art and stepped back. They entered the museum and Art showed an attendant what must have been a member's pass, because they were allowed to proceed without paying.

"So it's normal to feel what I'm feeling?"

"Absolutely. Growth is an awkward thing, and pain is the touchstone of growth. There are no free rides."

"What if I just decided to stop?" she asked.

"Well, that would be like stirring up a hornet's nest and then trying to throw a blanket over it. The hornets get enraged and try to get out so they can do some damage. No, Holly, we must walk steadfastly toward the light." He took her hand again and they walked into the rotunda.

A series of beautiful photographs from China was on display. She marveled at the delicacy and power of each: the pattern of cracking ice in a winter pond, a red bird in a leafless tree against a gray sky, women and children carrying sheaves of wheat along a country path. Her heels clicked against the marble floor and echoed against the high-domed ceiling; the air was delightfully cool. Except for a handful of other visitors, the museum was pleasantly unpopulated.

Art led her into the dinosaur exhibit.

"Look at this," he told her, pointing to a plaque in front of a fearsome recreation of a pre-historic carnivore.

The sign read: Tarbosaurus - late Cretaceous - 90 million years.

"Unbelievable," she said. "Ninety million years ago."

"Yes. It puts our human problems in perspective, doesn't it?"

They entered another room, half of which was dominated by the reassembled skeleton of a *Brontosaurus*. Next, they entered a new chamber; a plaque proclaimed the emergence of early mammals.

"Look at this!" She pointed to a macabre gathering of skeletons, two of which stood about thirty-six inches tall, the other about half that. "It's a family of horses. Thirty million years old."

"Yes. The dinosaurs seem to have disappeared quite suddenly, and then the warm-blooded mammals gained a foothold. Come . . ." He guided her by the elbow toward the next room. "This tells the whole story."

A series of panels, covering three walls, made up a single enormous mural. Holly contemplated the first panel, which described the Big Bang and the early expansion of the universe.

"Now we're fourteen billion years back. So what do they think there was before this big bang. I mean, if everything was condensed into a single point, where was the point?"

Art nodded his head and clapped his hands together.

"Exactly. The point couldn't be in space because all the space was in the point. Fantastic, isn't it?"

The next panel described the cooling and condensing of gases into stars and the eventual formation of galaxies.

Following the progression clockwise, they watched the panorama unfold as the earth was born, cooled, and became covered with water. They walked on to see single-celled life develop, then multiply into more complex combinations and shapes, eventually becoming fish, leaving the water, and transmuting into crawling things. In another thirty steps they had passed through the great eras: Precambrian, Paleozoic, Mesozoic, and into the Cenozoic. She stopped when they reached the panel that showed apes on the left side, dragging their knuckles across the plains. In the center of the panel an almost-human ape stood erect, while increasingly human figures marched toward the next panel; cavemen, gathered around a fire, wielding tools.

"You know," Art said, "there are those who say that this is all a fabrication, a lie inspired by the devil himself to lure man into a false sense of self-sufficiency."

She noticed that, beneath the panels, there was a timeline showing the duration of epochs. The caveman panel to the end of the sequence—the next panel, depicting early civilization giving rise to modern man, the atom bomb, and space exploration—represented a small sliver of the entire timeline.

"Yes," she replied. "I had a college roommate once, a bornagain Christian, who counted the generations of the patriarchs and their ages, added them up, and told me that's how old the universe was. We were theater arts majors together until she dropped out. She told me she had found a new calling." She shook her head. "She wasn't like that when I met her."

They stared up at the final panel, with its depiction of machinery and science, its rocket launch and mushroom cloud.

"Did you know," Art put his hand in the small of her back, "that in Texas there's a place called the Creationist Museum?"

"Does it have dinosaurs?" She laughed.

"It has displays claiming to refute what they call the theories of secular humanism, Darwin in particular. The remarkable thing about it is that the curator and his director are both legitimate scientists. One worked as a geologist and the other was an astrophysicist. They too claimed that the earth was nine thousand years old and that the Biblical account of creation is the only accurate one."

"What about the fossil record, sedimentation, geological strata, carbon-14 and all the rest?"

Art looked at her, his expression one of amused surprise.

"They taught you that in Theater Arts? I'm very impressed."

"My first love was natural history. I can't believe I've never come to this place—it's so wonderful here." She looked around the room. A summer-school class had filed in and now stood in a group in front of the Big Bang illustration. "So how do they explain away all that stuff?"

"No problem," Art replied. His hand moved up her back and to her neck, which he massaged gently with his fingers. "They simply say that God, when he created the earth, created it complete with buried dinosaur bones."

"No, really?"

"Yes, really. In fact, they welcome skepticism and challenges from visitors. I couldn't resist."

"What did you do?"

"Well, I asked if they agreed with modern science about the speed of light, and they said yes. They also agreed when I asked them about the probable size of the universe, and the distance to certain known stars."

"So?"

"So, I pointed out that if they agreed a particular star was more than ten thousand light-years distant, and that if the speed of light is constant, then in order for us to be able to see the star, the light that we're seeing must have originated more than ten thousand years ago. Of course, that would be a thousand years before God created anything."

"Hah. How did they get around that one?"

"Again, no problem. They said, 'If God can create a world complete with living creatures and the bones of monsters that never lived, we have no problem with Him creating light in motion.' In other words, he snapped the photons into existence as if they were en route, nine thousand light years from here."

"That's ridiculous," she exclaimed.

"Ah, but is it any more ridiculous than a single point, existing in no place because by definition no place exists outside it?"

She pondered the question and realized that both propositions were equally bizarre.

"It's a good thing," she said, "that choosing between the two isn't a critical issue for daily living."

She had meant to be sarcastic, but Art took her quite seriously.

"That's just it, you see." There was an intensity now in his manner. "If the Creationists are wrong, and the Big Bang picture"—he gestured at the entire panorama spread around them—"is correct, then where did Spirit come from? Is it just some aspect of psychology—something mundane that evolved out of animal intelligence? Some historical development arising by chance in a series of random mutations? A function of the 'survival of the fittest' process?"

She thought, *When he talks like this you don't know what he's after.* Art dropped his hand from her neck and stepped sideways to the previous panel, gesturing for her to join him.

"Or did it perhaps always exist—before the Big Bang, in another 'place' altogether—a community of spirits, waiting in the wings until the naked ape stood upright"—he pointed at the center illustration—"until his brain evolved to just the right point, and Spirit said, 'It's time,' and volunteered to join us and make us human."

She looked up at the stooped, apelike beings in the left-hand portion of the panel, with their vacant expressions, their brute dumbness as they plodded rightward toward their evolutionary destiny, and then the central figure, looking outward with awareness, a sense of its own presence. She could easily imagine that something had descended from another sphere and inhabited the creature, and that that, much more than the erect posture, was the essence of its humanity.

"So we're really made up of two things, then," she offered.

"Four," Art corrected. "Earth, Water, Air, and Fire . . . Body, Heart, Mind, and Spirit. The trouble is, the first three conspire to shut Spirit out—they establish Ego in its place and relegate Spirit to a subterranean dungeon, where it waits to be awakened."

She turned from the canny stare of the Cro-Magnon on the wall to face Art. "How," she asked, "is it awakened?"

"Ah, now we get to the heart of the matter. When the true self, or the Soul, has finally had enough, when it sees the futility of the domination by Ego, it must make a conscious choice. It begins to listen to new sources of information, as you have done by coming to meetings and engaging with me. It accepts challenges to Ego, as you have done by opening yourself to guided imagery and facilitated awareness. You see, Holly," and here Art reached and touched her gently with his fingers at her left temple, "you are already in the process of awakening Spirit. Now we must dig deeper, and truly examine what Ego has wrought and the powerlessness you feel. In this way it is exposed as the foolish tyrant that it really is and, as it loses its stranglehold on us, new power flows in. This is the essence of Saving Our Lives." He leaned forward and again pressed his lips gently to her forehead.

CHAPTER 34

You think I'm a candidate, don't you?"

"I don't know, Joe. We keep a few seats warm for guys like you."

They were sitting in a booth in the back of a restaurant bar on Wilshire Boulevard. It felt strange, coming from the bright daylight into the dim shadow of the bar's interior. It could have been midnight or four in the morning. Sitting across a booth from the detective, Ron felt as if he were in a stage set from his own past; the smell of old smoke, a bartender wiping down the bar, a few guys in suits sitting solo at the tables, nursing their drinks. Kenny Rogers played "Lady" on the jukebox.

"You know, I went to some meetings once," Joe announced.

"Oh yeah? When was that?" He wasn't surprised. Joe always seemed familiar with the lingo: easy does it, one day at a time, shit happens.

"Back when Janey and I were splitting up. I thought, 'Okay, nothing makes sense. I think I'm the same guy she fell in love with, so what gives?' She was done with me." He shrugged his shoulders and tipped his head to drain his bottle of Heineken. "She used to complain about my drinking, so I figured, I'll do this thing. I'll do the meetings and stop. For her. For Robbie. For Christ's sake, he was only four at the time."

"So that was five years ago." He knew that Robbie was nine now.

"Five years ago. Jesus, you're right. But you know what? She left anyway. Nothin' to do with my drinking. She had another thing going—another cop. Son of a bitch drank twice as much as I did." Joe raised his hand to signal the waitress for a new Heineken. "So you're keepin' a seat warm for me . . . guys like me." He snorted a laugh, but it was a good-humored laugh.

Joe was a big, powerful man. His powder-blue sports coat stretched tight over his shoulders and his hands looked like they could break things better than they could fix them. Ron was fond of the man, glad to think of him as a friend.

"Joe, alcoholism is a self-proclaimed disorder. I honestly don't know if you have a problem with booze. I've never seen you act drunk, behave inappropriately, fall down, any of that stuff. So it's up to you to decide if your life works or not, and if it doesn't, whether alcohol could have anything to do with it. Then—" he sipped at his soda and set the glass down "—the question becomes, can you stop on your own?"

The waitress brought the new bottle, the green glass frosted over.

Joe glanced at it, then made a small smile and spread his hands slightly. He then picked up the bottle by its neck and, push-ing upward with the calloused tip of his thumb, popped off the top and took a swallow.

"One thing does come to mind though," Ron said.

Joe leaned back into the burgundy Naugahyde, cocked his head, and raised an eyebrow.

"When you and Janey were splitting up?"

"Yeah," Joe said. "What about it?"

"If you wanted to prove a point about drinking, why didn't you just stop?"

"What's your point?"

"Just that only a certain kind of drinker makes a connection between quitting drinking and needing help."

"Yeah, well." Joe moved out of the booth. "Gotta hit the john. You know,"—he was standing now—"those were rough times. Haven't felt like that since."

Ron watched Joe walk away toward the rest room at the end of the bar. He turned and nudged open the latticed shutters and watched bars of sunlight slice through and catch the dust swirling lazily in and out of the shadow.

Somewhere out there, up in Petaluma, last he heard, was a seventeen-year-old girl. His ex-wife had never let him see the girl; the last he remembered was a crying two-year-old in Ellen's arms, how the two of them looked so much alike with their alabaster skin and thick red hair. He had tried to make his peace with Ellen, gone to her in the spirit of amends, but forgiveness was not forthcoming, and the girl had remained a stranger.

He had hoped that at some point his daughter would take the lead and call him, if only in an adolescent fit of independence from her mother. Maybe when she was eighteen, he thought. Maybe then it would be time to look her up, make a gentle approach, give her the option to meet him somewhere, to talk. To find out that he was no longer what her mother had told her.

"Hey, be here now, ol' buddy." The detective's voice broke in on his thoughts. He glanced up.

"You looked like you were off in another world." The big man settled himself back into the booth and placed his hands palms down on the table. "So you got Jeff Fenner camped out at your place."

"For the time being. Why, is Narcotics still after him?"

"Naw, the guy's history."

"Yeah," Ron said. "I think he's through."

"So you're going to turn this two-bit dope peddler that couldn't keep his nose out of his own candy into a member of the civilized human race?" Joe picked up his Heineken and tilted it until half the contents disappeared.

"I didn't think you believed there was such a thing, Joe. But no, I'm not going to turn him into anything." He wondered where this conversation was headed. Joe had called him in the morning and arranged this meeting, without saying what for.

The detective shrugged and said, "Okay, okay." Then he pulled a card out of his coat pocket and wrote something on it.

"You might just happen to be around here at ten tonight. You didn't get this from me." He handed the card to Ron.

"What's up?" He took the card and glanced at the address that Joe had scrawled on its back: 1021 Stone Canyon Road.

"Got a break on the A-frame ODs."

CHAPTER 35

༄

The A-frame referred to a group of dedicated swinging couples from the tonier neighborhoods in the Westside and Hollywood. They got their name from the previous decade's locus of formalized upscale swinging, an actual A-frame home in the Hollywood Hills. It had been the site of a continuous, pay-to-play, members-only spouse-swapping party, complete with its own set of rules and formalities.

Ten years later the events had gone almost entirely underground; two of the original couples had regenerated the group—all new recruits—and turned it into a discreet upper-crust pot-luck, sex activities after the chocolate crème brûlée. Once a month, a different couple would host the occasion, and the various record company execs, corporate lawyers, and multi-media entrepreneurs, spouses in tow, would arrive in their German cars as though showing up at just another dinner party. Throw in a judge, an actress and her real-estate-developer husband, and one of the most powerful agents in Hollywood, and you had a heady mix of money, influence, and some stunning physical beauty.

It was an LA kind of thing, Ron mused as he headed down Lincoln Boulevard toward the freeway. He had lived in Los Angeles since he was five years old and was still amazed at some of the city's dirty laundry—not just the tee-shirts-and-sweat-socks variety of Charlie Mansons and kiddie porn hustlers, racist cops, and the chicken hawks at the pier. It was the upper-crust laundry that got hung out to dry once in a while that showed that real human sickness cut across all the social boundaries. Wealth, status, education, political power—none made you exempt.

He had covered the gamut. It was the nature of his job to write unhappy stories, but the A-frame ODs had captured and held the public's imagination for months before the trail went cold and the police back-burnered their investigation. He wrote up the original item for the *Times*. It had been over a year and a half ago, and Joe Greiner had been his conduit for the best police information available. Joe's problem was being a homicide investigator in what everyone, including a grand jury, had declared a non-homicide.

It had been the A-frame group's Valentine's Day gala. For some reason Marty Resnick, the Hollywood agent, was the only one who was allowed to bring partners other than his wife. The rotation put his house in Stone Canyon as the site of the Valentine's get-together.

When the paramedics arrived that night, dessert and coffee had just been consumed, and six people were dead—cardiac arrest and respiratory failure from heroin overdose. Marty and his date, a model from New York, were lying together on the tiled floor of the bathroom adjacent to the den. The actress and her real-estate-developer husband never even made it up from the den sofa, from which they had bent over the marble coffee table to snort the white powder they thought was Molly, the latest designer drug with a reputation for inducing enhanced sexuality. The owner of an independent record company that was in the process of being bought by one of the majors had staggered out the French doors into the cool February night, wife in hand, and together they collapsed at the foot of the brick barbecue.

By the time the police arrived, hot on the heels of the fire department's paramedics, two attorneys from Harry Wise's office were already at the scene, and the dinner guests had been quickly but thoroughly drilled so that their stories fit together as neatly as a jigsaw puzzle.

His cell phone rang just as he got off the Hollywood Freeway.

"Ron, hi. It's six and I'm free." It was Leanne, just off her shift at the Bicycle Café. He was glad to hear her voice; it brought to mind the other night, standing by his car, her face an inch from his, the first kiss out of the way and a new level of trust between them.

"Okay, listen, I'm taking the kid to a meeting at Fairfax and Fountain in an hour. We can get together afterward or, you know, there's an Al-Anon meeting at the same time right next door . . ." He paused.

"We could grab a bite from there," she responded. "I'd like to meet your newcomer."

"Great. We'll be out front at about fifteen before seven. Oh, hey, listen to this . . ." He started to tell her about the A-frame break, but then decided that his cell phone wasn't reliably private.

"I'll fill you in at dinner. See you in forty-five minutes, southeast corner of Fairfax and Fountain."

CHAPTER 36

�

When Jeff turned off the lawn mower, he heard music coming from the house. So, Ron was home; soon they would be off to another meeting. He surveyed the small patch of lawn and the neat stripes that the mower had made. Sweat poured down his back and stomach, dampening the waistband of his shorts.

"Hey, into action. I like it." Ron walked out onto the porch. "What happened? Sleep get too boring?" He grinned.

"It would help if I could get a solid night's sleep. Christ, I lie there sweating like a pig and can't stop my mind." Jeff combed his hair back out of his eyes with his fingers. A salty bead of perspiration ran through his brow and down into his eye.

"Sounds like fun." Ron seemed amused again.

"Yeah, right. Every shitty thing that ever happened to me, every embarrassing little moment gets replayed like some nightmare MTV loop. I mean, what's going on, anyway?"

"I think it's how the mind detoxifies. The body sweats out its poisons, and the mind collects and excretes its own toxic waste. It'll pass. Anyway, nobody ever died from lack of sleep."

"Did you ever feel like this?"

"I can remember like it was just yesterday. It passes." Ron tapped Jeff's shoulder and said, "Let's go. And hey, thanks for doing the lawn."

They stepped into the relative coolness of the house. Saxophone music filled the living room, cheerful in the otherwise gloomy waning of the light.

"Who is that playing?" Jeff asked.

"Lester Young."

"It's pretty cool."

"Glad you like it," Ron said, and turned into the hallway that led to his room.

☖

The evening forgot to cool off. Dressed in baggy shorts, sandals, and a green tee shirt with a snowboard manufacturer's logo on it, Jeff stepped into the Land Rover, still hot after a cold shower. He glanced over at Ron, who looked cool and fresh in his creased tan slacks and a sports shirt. His loafers had tassels and were buffed to a deep oxblood hue.

They drove in silence until Ron turned on Fountain.

His tee shirt clung to the perspiration on his chest. "Man, it's fuckin' hot." He shifted in the seat and realized his back was damp too. "You know, I have to wear a fuckin' suit to court next week. I don't know if I can handle it. Christ, my fuckin' car doesn't even have air conditioning."

Ron looked over at him, his eyebrows slightly raised, then glanced at his rearview before pulling a tight U and turning into a parking spot. They were next to a church, pink in the fading light, with a small group of people gathered at the stairway entrance.

Ron turned off the lights and pulled the key from the ignition.

"You know," he said, "I just heard you say 'fuckin' this and 'fuckin' that' three times in two sentences. You know what that means to me?"

"No, what?" He felt suddenly uncomfortable, defensive.

"It sounds like you don't really know what you feel about anything. Just that it's negative and you've got a vague catch-all word to show that you're generally pissed off." Ron opened the door and started to get out.

"So is Emily Post part of the curriculum here?" he shot back.

"No, Jeff, Emily Post is not part of the curriculum. I'm just trying to help you out. When you talk like that it sounds . . . inarticulate." They stepped out of the car and Ron keyed the lock.

Over the roof Jeff said, "Inarticulate?"

"Sounds like shit, Jeff." Ron headed toward the steps.

Furious at being chastised, he stayed at the curb and watched Ron shake hands, nodding and smiling as he joined the group at the entrance. He leaned against the Land Rover, a headache forming like a storm cloud just behind his temple.

Out of the corner of his eye, he noticed a flash of color approaching from his left. He turned to see an extremely attractive woman in a summer dress the color of the blue hibiscus in Ron's yard, with a deep magenta scarf around her neck. She looked right at him as she approached, stopping right in front of him and smiling as she put out her hand.

"You must be Jeff," she said. Her gray eyes gazed at him levelly as she waited for him to respond. In a curious moment of clarity, he saw himself through her eyes, leaning back against the car, sulking over his wounded pride. It was comical, really, and she was inviting him to step out of it. He grinned and moved away from the Land Rover, shaking her hand.

"I'm Leanne. We're having dinner together, I hear. Let's go see Mr. Popular over there."

After the meeting, they drove down to Melrose Avenue to a place called Nick's Natural Deli. Everything was bright polished blond wood, even the ceiling fans, like someone had outfitted the whole place from one display at Ikea. Ron had ordered from a ponytailed blond waiter named Ben; the guy looked so healthy, Jeff wanted to yank on his earring.

The meal didn't do much to improve his mood. Ron and Leanne attacked their baked vegetable and tofu on rice with gusto, talking cheerfully about their meetings as they chewed, while he picked at the bland carrots and tough, chewy rice in a bored funk.

"Hey, mopey, try some of this to jazz it up." Ron pushed over a bottle of dark brown liquid. Jeff poured it back and forth across his meal as he had seen Ron and Leanne do; anything to add some flavor. He took a bite—it tasted terrific for a second—and looked up in disbelief as a fire spread throughout his mouth, his lips, and down his throat. His face felt hot.

"Jesus, Ron, what is that stuff?" He reached for his glass of water.

Ron speared a cube of shriveled tofu and a broccoli floret covered with the evil sauce and popped it in his mouth.

"That's Nick's Hot Sauce. Place is famous for it. Shoyu with extra garlic and cayenne. You'll get used to it, right Leanne?"

Leanne scooped up a spoonful of rice drenched in the stuff. "It's an acquired taste. Quick, take another bite."

He took another bite. This time the flavor lasted longer, and the burning sensation receded to a background buzz. He ate again—even the tofu tasted pretty good.

"Man," he said, his eyes watering, "this stuff is dangerous." He couldn't help laughing.

They ate in silence for the rest of the meal. He looked up when he was finished, surprised to see the other two watching him affectionately.

"Welcome to the clean plate club," Leanne said, and they all laughed.

They ordered herbal tea as the pony-tailed waiter removed their dishes.

"So," Ron said, "it turns out Jeff here used to be pretty handy with a camera."

"Really?" Leanne turned to Jeff. "Did you work as a photographer?"

He made a self-deprecating gesture. "Years ago. I used to shoot pictures for a surfing magazine. Later I covered events for some of the entertainment weeklies."

"They both sound like fun," Leanne said.

"Yeah, I learned how to shoot from the hip when people didn't want their pictures taken. I'd have a drink in one hand and my Nikon down here . . ." He put his right hand down by his waist and snapped an imaginary photo, making a little clicking sound under his tongue.

"So anyway," Ron continued, "it looks like Jeff has a job offer as an assistant to a friend of mine—a professional photographer."

"Yeah, at nine bucks an hour," he complained.

"Oh, my," Leanne chided. "And how much are you bringing in now?" There was that level stare of intelligent gray eyes again. He looked at Ron, who raised his brows slightly in amusement.

"You can barely eat on that amount, forget about paying rent. I've got two hundred dollars to my name. I'm going to have an attorney bill to pay—I mean, Christ, how am I going to make it all work?" He felt an inward shudder at the impossibility of it all; it came out as a slight twitch, surprising him like an electric shock.

"It seems to me that at this particular moment, you have a place to sleep tonight,"—Ron counted off on his fingers—"your belly is reasonably full, your attorney is willing to accept his pay in the future, and you have a job. So if you can keep your head out of the future—there's nothing there anyway; it hasn't happened yet—then you might find out that things are really pretty good."

Jeff looked back at Leanne, who regarded him sympathetically and said nothing, but nodded slightly.

"Anyway," Ron went on, "there's a camera in my truck, and a nice little telephoto lens that should come in handy."

"Handy for what?" Jeff asked in surprise.

"Well, how would you like to see tomorrow's news happen tonight? Maybe even scoop it from behind the lens?"

"Really? What's the deal?"

"They're bringing in a suspect tonight in the A-frame affair. If we leave here in about—" Ron checked his watch, a stainless steel Heuer "—ten minutes, we should be right on time to catch the arrest."

He rode in the back seat again as Ron drove West on Melrose, onto Santa Monica Boulevard, and then cut up to Sunset. When they turned up the dark entrance to Stone Canyon, Leanne said, "Isn't this the house where those people died?"

"Sure is," Ron replied. He kicked on his high beams; the road seemed to swallow the light.

"Whom would they be arresting up here?" Leanne seemed puzzled. Jeff leaned forward to hear the conversation.

"My guess," Ron answered, "would be Marty Resnick's widow, Joanie. Unless the butler did it." He slowed as they got into the high nine hundreds. They had climbed up into the hills by now and the road had narrowed. Ron took a hard curve to the right and suddenly came upon three four-door sedans, with their parking lights on, edged up against an ivy-covered brick wall. The lead car was pulled partially into a driveway, blocked by a large iron gate.

Ron pulled the Land Rover to the side of the road behind the last of the police cars. The door of the lead car—the one by the gate—opened, and a burly man in a sports coat lumbered toward them out of the darkness. Ron rolled down his window.

"Welcome to the show," the man said. "You're right on time. We're gonna wait out here until the suspect talks to her lawyer. He won't be dumb enough to advise her to hole up in there, so I expect the gate to swing open in a few minutes."

"Joe, Leanne, Jeff." Leanne reached a hand across Ron's chest to shake Joe's hand through the open window. Jeff said, "Hey, Joe," and in his mind thought, *where you goin' with that gun in your hand?* It was fun meeting a cop like this.

"So here's the deal. We go up, you follow. At the top of the driveway, it opens into a big circular area; got a fuckin' fountain all lit up in the middle. You stay on this side of it 'til we bring her out and load her up. Then you follow us down. Okay?"

"Got it," Ron said. "Mind if we happen to get a shot of you escorting her out the door?"

"It's a free country, last time I looked." Joe looked over at the gate—it was barely visible against the blackness behind it, but it clearly hadn't moved yet.

Jeff leaned forward, the camera on his lap, the long lens cold and hard like the barrel of his nine millimeter. He mourned the loss of the gun for an instant and then realized he liked the camera better.

Ron said, "So what broke?" Joanie Resnick had already been questioned half a dozen times. She had been out of town when her husband died, vacationing in Hawaii. Jeff had read about her in *People* magazine or somewhere. For a few months she was a very public Celebrity in Mourning, the grieving widow of Bel Air.

Joe cleared his throat and then turned to spit into the darkness. In the silence there was an audible *plop* from the far side of the road. Jeff saw him turn back and then bend slightly to peer into the car, past Ron to where Leanne sat. After a moment's pause, the detective said, "Excuse me," and then turned back to Ron. "Seems the lady had a boyfriend. Younger guy, Tony Petracca. Calls himself a musician, but Narcotics picked him up for selling an ounce of meth at some nightclub. So guess what he offers up?"

Jeff wondered why the cop wasn't cold out there. A fog had drifted up from the ocean and the air was chilly for the first time in months.

Ron shrugged. "Something pretty good, I imagine."

"Check this. Joanie Resnick finds out her husband's playing spin-the-bottle with the beautiful people, and that it's gonna happen again, this time *in her house.* She knows Marty likes his designer drug 'cause they used to do it together, back when they used to do it together, if you follow what I'm saying." He cleared his throat again, started to turn, but then continued with his story.

"Before she left for her trip, she checked out his stash spot and found a full vial of the stuff. So she goes to her boyfriend and tells him if he gets her a six-hundred-dollar gram of pure china white, she'll give him a new Porsche."

"And then," Ron filled in, "she dumps out the ecstasy and substitutes the heroin. Perfect."

"Hell, I doubt she threw out the sex powder. Probably humped Tony all the way to Maui. Picked up some extra frequent-flyer points in the mile-high club. Anyway, you'll like this part, she strings him out for the Porsche all this time, until a month ago."

A car whispered by, heading up the canyon.

"Then what?" Jeff asked, looking out at the detective from behind Ron's seat.

Jeff saw the cop look back at him in amusement, like he was a six-year-old who hadn't been invited to speak.

"Then she dumped him. Told him to take a hike. Said she had someone new. A broad—Diane Cammell—maybe you'll see her tonight."

"She dumped him for a woman?" Ron chuckled. "And lets him walk? Now that's called leaving a very loose end."

"Yeah, well, go figure. Hey—" There was motion from the driveway. The gate was opening, and one of the other cops flashed his headlights for an instant.

The driveway snaked uphill, flanked by enormous hedges that were black against the darkness. The four cars wound their way up and into the estate single file. Jeff looked out through the rear window and saw the gate slowly swing shut.

At the top of the driveway they broke into a large circular area, fully illuminated, paved in bricks. Water danced in a brightly lit fountain at the center. The house cast a warm glow out onto the drive—it was a large pink two-story affair, lights blazing from every window. To the side he saw two double car garage doors, in front of which several cars were parked haphazardly. A forest green Jaguar sat just beyond the fountain.

Ron turned right onto the brick area and parked against the perimeter so that his—and Jeff's—side faced the house. He had pulled forward just enough that the fountain no longer blocked the view of the front door.

Jeff watched as one of the unmarked cars circled and returned to the driveway beyond the bricked area, pointing his headlights back down toward the gate and stopping there. Joe pulled up just beyond the entrance to the house, while the third car stopped well behind.

Ron switched off the ignition. "Better roll down your window and get a clear view of the front door. Auto focus might not work in this light."

Jeff rolled down the window and pointed the lens at the door, then zoomed in so that the doorway filled the viewfinder vertically. He touched the shutter release gently. The focusing mechanism zeroed in for a clear image and then overshot the mark, making the view blurry. It overcompensated the other way. He flicked a small switch on the barrel of the lens with his thumbnail and manually focused until he got a satisfying, razor-sharp image.

He heard car doors open and then shut. Following the sound, he swung the camera to the left until he saw Joe walking toward the house, accompanied by the cop who had ridden up with him. In the lens the man looked enormous; he peered over the camera and saw that he stood a good six inches taller than Joe. He thought of the huge cop slapping his nightstick in his palm at Lilah's—it seemed like another lifetime ago.

Looking through the lens again, he watched Joe knock on the door. The sound carried in the night air. Only a cop knocked like that—they had a certain touch you could identify, like you could tell a real musician just by the way he tuned his instrument.

The door opened and a pretty blond woman stepped out. She was small, dressed in jeans and a light sweater. He pushed down on the shutter release. The camera made a noticeable sound, but the woman didn't seem to catch it. Behind her, another woman appeared, tall, with closely cropped dark hair. He shot again and kept the button pressed, so that picture after picture was taken. He stopped as the blond woman, now handcuffed, followed Joe to his car, followed by the huge partner. He glanced over the camera again. The tall woman stood in the doorway with her hand covering her mouth. To the left of the entrance, a man peered out through a window. He was backlit, but looked oddly familiar. When he looked through the telephoto, the man had turned away.

CHAPTER 37

꠸

A rt stood at the dining room window, watching as the detective helped Joanie into the unmarked sedan. A conversation from long before replayed in his mind: *Don't you think Tony is somewhat of a future liability?* Cutting right to the chase—Joanie had called him about her husband's murder investigation, telling him she was upset about how unsympathetic the police were being. *What on earth are you talking about, Art?* Joanie stonewalling, not ready to trust him with this.

So the punk had rolled over. It was inevitable, really.

And now, he wondered, how many of his girls had he brought up to Joanie's? Marilyn? Yes, he remembered clearly bringing her to the house. Sandra—yes. And the Hunsaker girl. The nurse. She had been here too.

And Holly.

He looked out across the driveway, past the fountain. A Land Rover was parked there, occupied. He saw the black metal tube of a telephoto lens protruding downward from the back passenger window, clearly visible against the white of the door. When it lifted to point in his direction, he stepped away from the window.

Things were no longer going well. His amusements were becoming too dangerous.

Perhaps it would soon be time to move on. The Carolinas were nice. Or back to Canada, a fresh start. Or, if things really went awry, Australia. But he'd have to round up some cash first. He was broke and, with Joanie in jail, the tap was shut off. His façade was crumbling.

CHAPTER 38

⟟

It was a lovely mixture, Holly thought—the rich scent of leather and the mild spice of cologne that greeted her as she lowered herself into the Jaguar. Art closed the door and walked around the front of the car. He wore a tuxedo, his hair impeccably slicked back, and whistled as he slid into his seat and slid the transmission back toward drive.

He had told her over a week ago to keep this evening free, that something was coming up that would be "quite amusing." Apprehensive at first, she thought that it sounded like a date— she was determined to keep a distinction between what he called "our little times together" and a real date.

She had been flustered when he appeared, punctual to the minute at seven, dressed so formally. Was she underdressed in her slacks and blouse and suede jacket? Art had smiled and assured her everything was fine, she looked lovely, and then, taking her hand, walked her briskly to his car.

"Okay, where in God's name are we going?" She noticed that, even as he whistled, Art's fingers drummed distractedly against the leather cover of his steering wheel, that he seemed agitated, irritable even.

His demeanor changed as he stopped at the light on Olympic. He turned to her as if he had decided to park the car there, in the left lane at the intersection, and put his hand on her shoulder.

"Holly, my dear, this evening is purely about entertainment. We've been entirely too serious for too long. It's my turn on the stage tonight." His hand lingered on her shoulder. The light changed and he didn't move. The cars to their right began rolling forward. A horn blared from behind them. A flicker of annoyance betrayed Art's smile for an instant—the smallest movement of his eyes—before he pressed the accelerator and the Jag's powerful engine pulled them forward. They were heading into town.

They traveled in silence, Art expressionless, moving only to negotiate traffic, his eyes fixed forward, out over the green hood of the Jag. She pushed a button and Miles Davis picked up in the middle of a haunting trumpet solo.

Art turned up Doheny and drove as far as Santa Monica Boulevard, where he turned right. She couldn't imagine where they were heading, nor could she reconcile the odd tension she felt emanating from Art with any possibility of an amusing—as he called it—evening.

Art turned down a side street. They were in West Hollywood now. When Art pulled the Jag into a parking lot adjacent to a large, older wooden building, Holly was surprised. The complex housed a theatre, a dance club, a restaurant, and a supper club, all catering to and dominated by a gay clientele. Ahead of the Jag, a tall woman wearing a man's suit took a ticket from the attendant as she got out of her Mercedes. Her hair was short and dark, combed back—with a moustache, she would have looked like Robert Taylor. A platinum blond in a tight mini-skirt emerged from the passenger side, and the two joined hands as they walked toward the complex.

Art turned down the music and spoke for the first time in ten minutes. "Does that make you uncomfortable?" He pulled up to the parking attendant's booth.

She raised her shoulders in a slight shrug. "Last I heard, we're in the twenty-first century." Tony had brought her here once, to the dance club—she had no idea why—and she remembered feeling distinctly uneasy at the sight of all the same-sex couples dancing.

A valet appeared and opened Art's door, saying, "Good evening, Doctor Bradley." Another attendant appeared at Holly's side and waited as she stepped out onto the pavement. The lot was nearly full and it wasn't even dark yet.

Art took her hand and walked her toward a brick stairway. At the bottom was a courtyard and, beyond it, a doorway set in a white-stone and glass-brick facade to this corner of the complex. Above the door, pink neon letters spelled out "Tulips" in a long-hand script.

Inside, Tulips was an Art Deco affair, everything black lacquer on white with chrome and smoked glass. Small round tables with white tablecloths, each with its own black salt-and-pepper shaker and a red rose in a slender black vase, filled most of the room and surrounded a stage that was elevated about two feet off the floor.

A few people occupied the tables nearest the stage; she recognized them from the meetings. Ted turned and waved, motioning for them to come to his table. Art led her to the group, saying, "Thank you for coming. I have to go take care of some details," and then walked up onto the stage and through the curtains at its rear.

Cynthia—the woman who had led the meeting several weeks before—sat across from Holly. Her dark hair was swept straight back and fastened with a clip. She leaned toward Holly and said, "Everyone else will be here in the next half hour. The whole place will be full."

Holly looked at the stage, the single microphone on a stand, a row of six chairs facing the audience, and, beyond these, a drum kit flanked by keyboard and bass equipment. Turning back to Cynthia, she said, "What in the world is going on here?"

"You really don't know?" Cynthia sipped at a martini glass. "Art worked his way through medical school as a performer. He hypnotizes people."

"Yes, but now he just does it for fun," Ted added. He wore an Argyle vest that stretched tight over the huge mound of his belly. Perspiration glistened on his soft pink features. "I plan to volunteer to be in the act."

The room began to fill up. A waiter arrived at their table, a beautiful man with a pageboy haircut. He asked them, with exaggerated politeness, what they wanted. Cynthia ordered another martini. Ted and Holly asked for ice teas. As the waiter was about to leave, Holly asked, "Why is this place called Tulips?" The waiter placed a forefinger against his cheek and cocked his head slightly, looking down at her with a smirk. He said, "The owner had a friend who could do wonderful things with tulips," and then turned to the next table.

The room was full when the lights dimmed at eight. The musicians took their places on the stage and began a light, jazzy shuffle. A spotlight circled the floor where the microphone stood, and a disembodied voice came over the house speakers, announcing "LA's fabulous Art Bradley, the hip hypnotist." The room broke into applause as Art stepped onto the stage and walked to the mike.

"Good evening, ladies and gentlemen, my friends. In fact many of you I think of as my family." He was the epitome of charm: poised, confident, a hint of humor in the glint of his eye.

"Thank you for your kindness in joining me for our little show tonight. I want you to know, first of all, that the proceeds from the ticket sales will go entirely to the SOL general fund—" applause "—where a portion of it will be used for sponsoring those who cannot otherwise afford to attend a Weekend Intensive at our Idyllwild workshop." More applause.

"Now I'd like to tell you about our little time together." He paused, clasping his hands together and surveying the room with a satisfied air. "The American Heritage Dictionary defines hypnosis as 'A sleeplike state usually induced by another person in which the subject may experience forgotten or suppressed memories, hallucinations, and heightened suggestibility.'" Another pause, a benevolent smile, and he continued. "We all know that, in the hands of a qualified professional, the reclaiming of 'forgotten or suppressed memories' can be essential to recovery from a broad array of psychological and emotional disorders. Tonight, however, we're going to have some fun with the 'heightened

'suggestibility' part. Oh, and forget about the hallucinations."
Laughter from the audience. Cynthia tilted her martini glass, set
it down, and raised her hand for the waiter.

Holly watched, fascinated, as Art introduced his show. He
had a patter, a shtick. It was almost grotesque, except that he
pulled it off with such ease and charm.

"Okay, now I'm going to need six people up here"—hands
shot up throughout the room—"and I guarantee that by the end
of the session you'll feel terrific, refreshed and full of energy like
you've just had a great night's sleep." More hands were raised. Art
started pointing to people, saying, "Okay, you, wonderful, come
on up," searching the room as though for the perfect candidates.
The band struck up "When the Saints Come Marching In" as
the volunteers made their way to the stage. When he had chosen
five people, Art came to the edge of the stage and looked down
at Holly, Ted, and Cynthia. For a moment Holly was afraid Art
was about to recruit her, but both her table companions had their
hands up and Art magnanimously selected Ted, who eagerly
lumbered up onto the stage. Cynthia made a little spiral in the
air with her index finger and rolled her eyes, obviously feeling her
martinis.

Art had the volunteers line up in two rows, Ted and the other
two men standing behind the three women. He told the women to
close their eyes and breathe deeply, to relax and trust the process.
He carried the mike with him now, and walked from one woman
to the next, reassuring them. He told them to start swaying back
and forth, to keep their eyes closed, to notice the tranquility
within them. As he continued to soothe the women, he moved
to the one on the right, a large-boned blond in a short skirt, and
gave her a gentle push backward. She slumped into the arms of
the man behind her, who helped her back into a standing position. Art directed them to sit in the chairs on the stage, and then
he pushed the next woman as she swayed. Eyes still closed, she
too fell back and was caught, and she and the man who caught
her seated themselves. Art stepped over to the remaining woman.
She swayed slightly, but held herself rigid with her arms out for

balance. Art tapped her on the shoulder and her arms rotated wildly as she tried to keep from falling backward into Ted, who stood behind her.

Art lowered the mike, but Holly heard him say to the woman, "I'm sorry, you're too tense. Maybe some other time." The woman left the stage and Art asked for another volunteer.

When all six of the volunteers were seated on the stage, Art told them to close their eyes and then led them in a deep-breathing routine. "Okay, we're feeling very relaxed. There's a sense of heaviness in our arms and legs, a wonderful heavy feeling, your hands, your head . . . You're in a hammock. There are thick white clouds in the sky. Follow them . . . We're friends now. When I touch your forehead you will fall into a deep sleep." The keyboardist played an eerie sustained chord that shimmered while Art spoke.

"A magnet is pulling your hands downward. Now we're going to go deeper than any sounds you might hear . . . Only my voice will matter. Nod your heads."

Holly watched as the six on stage slowly nodded their heads. Art walked by each of them and touched their foreheads, saying, "Go to sleep." Immediately, the volunteers' heads slumped forward, chins to their chests, arms dangling at their sides. It was spooky, she thought, that they should have relinquished their consciousness so easily, so completely.

"Now," Art continued, "we're on a bus. It's very warm. In fact it's downright hot and humid—it's okay, go ahead and fan yourselves." The blond fanned herself vigorously, an annoyed expression on her face, as though the heat were an annoying imposition. The others waved their hands languidly, as if overcome with lethargy.

"Okay, well, it's cooling off. Someone opened a window and now the cold air is rushing in. My God, it's freezing out and we're in shorts and tee shirts. Brrrr . . ." The people on stage shivered and held themselves against invisible winds.

Art put the group through a series of scenarios: a tragic movie that brought them to tears, a clown that had them slapping their knees and laughing, a scolding schoolmaster that made them twist in their chairs, cringing. He told them they were jockeys at the Kentucky Derby and they slapped their sides and bounced as though riding invisible horses. They became secretaries, typing on invisible keyboards.

Holly laughed with the rest of the audience—it was amazing, really, how completely immersed the six were, how totally in Art's command. But she was uneasy at the same time. It made her uncomfortable to see grown people manipulated like this—they were automatons, not even in their bodies. She wondered what, if anything, they were thinking while they followed Art's increasingly ridiculous suggestions.

Art surveyed the audience, winking at Holly as his gaze swept around the room.

"We're going to wake up now," he said into the microphone. "And when we wake up, after I count to five, we're going to feel terrific, but—" he paused "—when I touch your foreheads you will go back into a deep sleep." He counted to five and the people seated on the stage awakened. "That's it. Stretch a little. Don't you feel wonderful? You—" he approached a well-dressed bearded man at the end of the row "—how do you feel?" He touched the man's forehead and said, "Sleep." The man's eyes closed and his chin fell back to his chest. Art went to the next person, a young Asian woman in a tight miniskirt. "Wasn't that wild?" The woman smiled and began to nod, but slumped back into a slumber when Art touched her forehead and told her to sleep.

When the six were all back to sleep, Art told them they were members of an orchestra, that each was playing his or her favorite instrument. The band began to play "I Got Rhythm" and the six sleeping people on stage sat up in their seats and mimed playing instruments with total involvement.

Holly couldn't help laughing. Ted played an invisible drum kit with intense concentration, an ear cocked toward the band while he nodded his head to the beat. Occasionally he snapped his right hand out with a flourish to hit a phantom cymbal. To his right, a plump, middle-aged woman sawed away at an invisible cello—oblivious to the band, she swayed to her own rhythm with a look of sublime rapture on her face.

Cynthia leaned across the table and said, "Isn't it just amazing?" Her clip had dislodged and sat askew at the side of her head while a mass of loose hair fell over her face. Holly looked at her dubiously and replied, "Right, amazing." She looked around the room; people were laughing, enjoying the show, and yet she, Holly, was finding it increasingly disturbing.

Cynthia leaned even farther toward her. "You know, I used to go to AA meetings, until I found SOL. Now I can drink and have fun again!" She giggled and lurched back to an upright position, bringing what was left of her newest drink with her as she dragged her hand across the table. It splashed on her lap, then the glass rolled off and fell to the floor. Cynthia looked at Holly and gave an exaggerated shrug, then raised her hand for the waiter.

Onstage, Art gleefully conducted his absurd orchestra. Suddenly he commanded, "Stop!" and the band snapped off. The six in their chairs trailed off in their group pantomime and resumed their sleeping postures.

"Okay, when I count to five we're going to wake up feeling great, only this time we're embarrassed to find that we're not wearing any clothes; one . . . two . . . "

When the women awoke they immediately crossed their legs and folded their arms across their chests. The men clasped their hands together and covered their genital areas. All six looked out at the audience and then at each other with a mixture of embarrassment and suspicion. Art walked up to the bearded man and offered to shake his hand. The man fidgeted and brought one hand up; Art touched his forehead and said, "Sleep," and the man was gone.

In the next hour, Art put the volunteers to sleep, suggested a scenario, and woke them at least a dozen times. They tap danced, bowed, dribbled and shot invisible basketballs, and ate non-existent food. They flexed muscles in a bodybuilding contest and snapped their fingers in a Flamenco dance. All the while Art kept his patter going, looking out to the audience with a sympathetic grin and the occasional shrug, as if to say even he wasn't quite sure what was really going on.

The show ended with a particularly absurd mock striptease by a large Hispanic man. He strutted all over the stage while the band played "Stripper," flinging his jacket out to the audience and unbuttoning his shirt before Art called for applause and sent him back to his chair. Art thanked all six of the volunteers and put them back to sleep, telling two of them they would be stuck to their seats when the others returned to their tables. Then he whispered something in Ted's ear and told the lot of them to wake up and go back and join their companions in the audience.

Ted climbed off the stage grinning, and returned to his seat between Holly and Cynthia. Three of the others also returned to their tables, but the Hispanic man and the blond remained onstage, trying without success to stand up. They looked down helplessly at their chairs, as if the secret to their problem was to be found there, and then stared up at Art. The blond shrugged her shoulders and said, "I can't do it." Art snapped his fingers and told them to get up, then urged the audience to applaud.

The band struck up its opening theme as the remaining two volunteers left the stage. The audience clapped and Art returned the mike to its stand and clapped along with them.

"I want to thank you all for coming and a special thanks to Maria, Ted . . ." As Art named off the people who had participated onstage, Ted grinned and said to Holly, "Wow. Was that wild, or what?" He was still grinning and shaking his head, clapping along with the others, when Art said, "And when I'm at the top of that ski slope and give that final push over the edge, I always like to say, 'Geronimo'," and the band segued into an Indian war dance. A strange faraway look came to Ted's face and he jumped up and started whooping, patting his hand to his lips as he hopped around on one foot between the tables.

CHAPTER 39

⟳

A rt's mood was upbeat as they drove back to Holly's
place. There was no trace of the irritability he had displayed
earlier. Now he was positively expansive, carrying on about spiritual growth and the nurturing of the wounded inner child, exor-
cising the demons of one's childhood, and the incredible potential of hypnosis as a tool. It was at this point that he reached in his
pocket and pulled out an envelope, from which he removed two
of the little triangular pills.

"Tonight, my dear, is breakthrough night." Art passed the
pills to Holly as he drove back down Doheny, conjuring from the
console next to his seat a can of diet soda. "Time to pierce the
veil of mystery and get to the heart of the matter, to uncover and
discover so that we may discard, finally and for good, the dark
secrets that cast their shadow on your spirit."

After what she had just witnessed onstage at Tulips, she had
no intention of submitting to hypnosis tonight, if ever again. It
was too creepy. And yet, it seemed like she stood at a threshold,
just a step away from a kind of freedom she could barely imagine—it was just a feeling, really. Or hope, or grasping at a deadly
straw.

She shuddered at a sudden, unformed premonition and
decided to play for time.

She turned on the Jag's overhead light and examined the
pills. They were identical to the ones she had taken before except
that they were yellow.

"What are these, anyway, and why are they a different color than last time?" she asked.

Art popped the top from the soda can and handed it to her.

"They're called Halcion. We're adjusting the dosage slightly upward. A wonderful tool, as valuable in therapy as a scalpel in surgery."

The comparison was rather grim, but she didn't comment. Instead, she turned off the light, took the soda from Art, and put her right hand—the one with the pills—to her mouth. She opened her mouth and tilted her head back, taking a large swallow of the soda. Her right hand fell to her side and she deposited the pills in her jacket pocket.

▽

When they got to her place, Art led her to the sofa and suggested she close her eyes and relax. He then went to the kitchen to dial his cell—ostensibly to retrieve messages, but in fact, she presumed, to allow enough time for the pills to take effect.

Leaning back against the cushions and closing her eyes, she pondered her situation. She could simply tell Art she didn't feel well, that he should go, that they could resume some other time. Or, she could pretend to sleep; that would be the way of least resistance. But what she wanted most was to know what he was really after, and tonight she had an opportunity, such as it was, to spy on him. To be fully present while she allowed him to think he was effecting the displacement of her volitional self.

Why, she wondered, did she need so badly to do this, to set him up? The answer came as she heard her refrigerator open and then shut: because if she knew beyond a shadow of a doubt that she could trust him, only then could she allow him to lead her to the freedom he promised. It was a bit like spying on your own funeral to see who your friends were.

She heard footsteps and kept her eyes closed as Art settled into the chair on the other side of the coffee table.

"When I tell you to sleep, you will fall into a state where there is nothing at all. No feeling, no sight, not even darkness, just the sound of my voice. Now, keeping your eyes closed, rise up out of your body, leaving it here in this room. There is a hole in the ceiling, and as you pass through it into the night sky, you look down and see us sitting here and we become smaller as you drift upward." His voice had a calm, compelling quality. She followed it with her imagination, she could see the house receding below her, but still she remained firmly conscious of herself seated in the sofa, of Art's presence across the table, of the trace of his scent even from this distance, of the memory of the people on stage and their absurd willingness to follow his every direction.

"Now you have left everything behind and, as a fog obscures the sky, even the stars disappear, and you are warm and comfortable and it is time to sleep."

She allowed her head to fall slightly to the right and let her face go slack, mouth slightly opened. She thought of the moments in Art's performance where Ted, seemingly fully awake, insisted that two and two added up to five. Where was Ted when his body was laughingly demonstrating on his fingers that two plus two obviously made five? If even such a small piece of his critical thinking ability was gone, could Ted really have been present? Could he have made the same decisions, felt the same feelings, come to the same conclusions as in his normal state?

"When you wake . . ." She pictured Art seated in the deep easy chair, his feet up on the ottoman, hands lightly folded at his stomach. She wanted to open her eyes. "When you wake, you will be very glad to see me—you want so badly to talk, to tell your secrets. Every secret is like a heavy stone in the sack that you carry, and as you pull each stone from the sack and hand it to me it disappears and your spirit grows lighter, more free. When I touch you and say 'sleep,' you will return to sleep. Now, awaken . . ."

She opened her eyes and sat up, looking around her and then at Art as she had seen the volunteers on stage do.

He sat just as she had pictured him, elegant in his outfit, a hint of a smile on his lips, his head cast slightly downward as he peered, unblinking, upward though his brows. "We have much to talk about, wouldn't you say?"

She wasn't sure of the appropriate response. Was she expected to suddenly begin spouting repressed memories?

"I don't know . . . I guess so," was the best she could come up with.

Art pressed on. "The bruise above your eye. Who did it?"

"Tony. He hit me." That was no secret; Art knew that Tony had tried to strangle her last week.

"He struck you on other occasions, didn't he?"

"Yes."

"And he isn't the first boyfriend who has done this to you. Am I right?"

It was something she had tried to deny even to herself—she certainly didn't feel like talking about it but, short of dropping the charade, there was no avoiding it.

"Yes. It happened before."

"Holly, what did Uncle Dave do?"

Suddenly, as if looking at a long-lost photograph, or turning a corner and seeing a part of the city she had forgotten she had visited before, the memory was clear as day.

"He penetrated me." The words just came out. She was sure she wasn't hypnotized, yet there it was, the thing remembered, the thing said.

"How often?"

"Whenever he stayed with us. When my parents went out. A lot." She held this new realization in a dazed wonderment. A sob welled up, unbidden. The previous revelation about her uncle had left her furious, sometimes depressed, sometimes manic with a desire to call him, or fly up to Seattle and confront him. But this, this left her with a cold, focused fury. She thought of the little girl she had been.

"Did you tell anyone?" Art stared at her thoughtfully, patient, uncritical.

"Yes." Another revelation.

"Who?"

"My mother." How could she have forgotten all this?

"And?"

"She told me I was lying."

"It must have made it difficult for you to trust anyone after that."

What's to trust, she thought. People do what they're going to do.

"Do you trust me?" Art inquired.

She faltered. Was this a setup? He seemed to be asking all the right questions. They were engaged in a process, and he was staying true to it, wasn't he?

"Yes," she replied. Firmly.

Art stood and walked over to where she sat.

"That's good. I'm so very glad." He reached out and touched her forehead gently. "Now sleep."

She closed her eyes and sagged back into the sofa. A feeling of dread came over her as she heard the sound of a zipper, the rustle of fabric—but no, there was no sound, nor movement, just the strange sense of Art poised over her. Expecting her to be asleep. Why had she heard that sound so distinctly?

"When you wake up, Holly, you will be so glad to see me—nothing else matters anymore. Together we have overcome the enemy, banished the demons. And you have missed me, missed having our bodies together"—oh boy, here it was, big time—"missed having me inside you."

To her relief, Art moved away from her, back to the other side of the table. She had the feeling that comes when slamming the brakes brings you right up on the tail of the car in front of you. Like something had just been shot into her veins.

"When you hear me knocking at the door"—his voice was coming from over by the stereo—"you'll wake up, and you'll be so happy I'm home, you'll want to put on our favorite song—I'm leaving it right here. And then you're going to come to the front door and lead me back here to the sofa and we'll undress each other." She heard him set something on the shelf by the stereo receiver and then walk around the room. He was turning out lights, first the two big lamps on the end tables flanking the sofa, then over to the kitchen.

When his footsteps receded in the hallway, she opened her eyes. The only light came from the little bronze cat with the imitation candle-flame bulb on the dining room table.

Christ, what a raging asshole! She had no idea what she was going to do. She listened to see if Art would close the door—the easiest thing would be to just lock the man out, deal with it later. But there was no click, no door shutting ahead of the three firm knocks that rang back down the hallway, her signal to wake up and play out his sick script.

She went to the baker's rack where the stereo was. The CD well in the player was open; right on top of it was the Miles Davis CD.

Three more knocks, slightly louder than before. "I'll be right there," she called out, and then spotted Tony's CD, sitting on the glass shelf next to the amplifier. She popped it in the deck and pushed "play" and "pause," turned the volume way up, and went to the door.

It was open, Art standing there with a big smile on his face. *And I'm so happy to see you,* she thought bitterly. She smiled and held out her hand, guiding him back to the living room. As they passed the baker's rack, she reached out and tapped the "pause" button and Tony's band shattered the silence, his voice singing, "You cheated, you lied, you made me cry, so fuck you," in an insolent, hoarse bluesy shout. A piercing guitar made something vibrate in the kitchen; the bass was palpable through the floor.

She turned to watch Art, dropping his hand and folding her arms as he slapped at the CD player and stopped the blaring music.

"Isn't that our favorite song?" She was having fun now; his game was over and she felt a defiant elation, a new freedom in her anger.

Art stood there, his hand still on the CD player. "I have only your best interests at heart." Straight-faced, like nothing was different.

"You manipulative son of a bitch." She realized that a switch had gone off in her mind, that Art was in fact irredeemably repulsive, standing there in his ridiculous outfit, and that she couldn't imagine what she had ever found attractive about him.

"Holly . . ." Art took a step toward her.

She held his gaze for a moment, then reached into her pocket and handed him the pills.

"You make Uncle Dave look like a boy scout. Now get out of here."

Art stared at her, silent. A muscle twitched in his jaw. His mouth opened as if he were about to speak—a small whitish gob stretched at the corner of his lips—then he shook his head and turned, walking down the hallway and out the door without a word.

CHAPTER 40

It was a hot and crowded day at Venice beach. Jeff cut through the river of people milling on the boardwalk and passed the park where the rollerbladers skated to music blasting from a portable PA system and skateboarders performed tricks on a wooden ramp. Out onto the blazing sand, where he had to jog toward the shore to keep his feet from burning.

Out in the water, a wave reared up and broke, easily six feet high, followed by another. By the time he got to the shoreline, five more had lined up and peeled perfectly to the left, directly in front of the lifeguard tower.

Children waded in the shallow water. A fat man in flowered trunks stood knee-deep in the water; when the white foam hit him, he remained motionless as it came up to his waist. Jeff moved out past the fat man and put the fins on. A few boogie boarders hovered outside the impact zone—the size of the surf seemed to be keeping the swimmers inside.

The ocean was cool and refreshing. It felt good to be in the water, healthy and clear headed. It felt good to be sober. He pushed through the light chop, kicking his fins and moving briskly toward the outside. When he got to the spot where the larger waves had begun breaking, he turned and looked back at the beach, using the fins to stay afloat in the deep water.

The black and yellow flag flew over the lifeguard tower—no board surfing allowed. The entire beach was strewn with towels and umbrellas and people, mostly concentrated on the gentle rise from the tide line to the tower. Behind that, a stretch of flat beach extended about fifty yards wide before you got to the boardwalk. A red jeep with a long yellow paddleboard on its roof was parked next to the tower. A lifeguard stood at the jeep's open door, pointing out toward the horizon.

He turned around. A green wall loomed ahead of him, advancing and steepening rapidly. He swam up to meet it, getting lifted by the swell as it passed, turning at the crest to look down the face. It was a long drop to the bottom. He had to swim farther out to meet the larger wave that followed. When it passed, he turned to watch from behind as it crashed with a roar.

It was the third wave that set up just right, peaking in front of him with a promise of an unbroken shoulder to the left. He kicked hard with his fins and felt the wave pick him up, thrusting him toward the beach as it threatened to break. He extended his left arm and leaned toward it, moving down and across the face of the wave as it came down behind him. Drawing a straight line along the vertical green surface, Jeff sped, weightless, the churning curl right at his heels.

The wave finally closed out, breaking in front of him and pitching him out into the flat water ahead, then catching up with him and pushing him under, spinning and bouncing off the sandy bottom, before finally releasing him and passing him by.

Standing in waist high water, he saw the fat man forty yards down the beach. It had been years since he had ridden a wave so well. The thought came to him that it was crazy to have lived by the beach for so long and never gone in the water. Too involved in the nightmare of getting loaded.

Half an hour and six memorable rides later, he walked up the rise of the beach, fins in his hand. The lifeguard, standing on the platform outside the tower enclosure, said, "Nice riding."

Jeff looked up and grinned. "Yeah. It's fun out there. Where's this swell coming from, anyway?"

The lifeguard shaded his eyes and looked out at the ocean, scanning up and down the surf line. "There's a big hurricane about five hundred miles off the tip of Baja, moving this way. Plus a new swell coming in from somewhere near Australia."

"So it's going to get bigger?"

"Huge." The lifeguard pointed toward the horizon. "Look at this."

Distant lines approached, evenly spaced. The nearest formed a distinct swell, becoming steeper as it advanced toward the shore. It was bigger than the ones he had seen so far, and when it broke it crashed all at once, too big to contour itself to the shifting sandbars below.

He sat on his towel next to the tower and watched. Overhead, a news helicopter passed by. A small plane pulled a banner advertising beer. The west wind came up, offsetting the heat from the sun. He turned as he heard the lifeguard step off the ramp and watched him go to the shoreline, using a loudspeaker to clear people out of the ocean. There was a large triangular patch of brown water—an undertow—forming where his last ride had ended. The fat man turned and lumbered back into ankle-deep water.

CHAPTER 41

⌁

Unbelievable. Art had called, saying he had a video of their session in his office, things Holly had said while in "a highly lucid moment of connection" to her "wounded inner child." He told her it was important—critical even—for her psychological well-being and spiritual health that she watch it. He was texting her a link as they were speaking. She hung up without responding.

Too agitated to sit, Holly paced around her kitchen, feeling a tremor in her hands and the old familiar lightheadedness that preceded a seizure. She reached in her purse and fished out a Xanax and chewed it into a foul-tasting, crumbly paste. The act itself, with its promise of relief, calmed her enough to make a decision.

She watched, first with dread, then in horror as the events at the session in Art's office unfolded on the small screen of her phone. At first, the camera had just been pointed at the wall and there was only audio. She gasped when the angle abruptly changed. No detail was spared in the close-up: Art in her mouth, his hand behind her head, his naked hips moving.

Her cell phone trilled in her hand. She stabbed at the screen and said, "You creepy little prick. What do you want?" She put him on speakerphone and held it at arm's length, as if to distance herself as much as possible.

His voice blared from the device. "Actually, I'm a bit short on funds, Holly my dear. Round up what you can and meet me at the Malibu Beach Inn. You should be able to get there in an hour."

"Are you out of your fucking mind?" She was shouting at the phone. "What if I don't?"

"Holly, one tap on my phone and the video goes online. Who knows? It might go viral and you'll finally be a star."

⩛

And now here he was, saying, "Let's go have tea and dessert at the restaurant on the pier," as if nothing had changed. They were in the lot just north of the hotel, her BMW parked next to Art's Jag. A wave smashed down in the shore break as Art got out of his car.

"Come now, Holly, last time. No tricks, I promise. It's just that—" he paused as he locked the Jag "—there are a few things you should know before we part. And you'll never have to worry about what I sent you."

Christ. Okay, she thought, decaf and a piece of pie, she would listen to what the asshole had to say, and that would be the end of it.

But then they got to the entrance to the pier and Art said, "The ocean tonight is truly magnificent. You really must see this," and he led her by the elbow, past the restaurant to where they could look north toward the point. A wave exploded against the pilings underneath them, and the entire pier shuddered.

A long dark wall approached Malibu Point three hundred yards to the north and, far out from the shore, broke with a sharp crack, the whitewater churning toward the beach as the wave peeled southward in obedience to the contour of the rocky bottom. The entire wall of water finally collapsed thunderously beneath their feet. Another one was already forming on the moonless horizon.

Art guided her forcefully now toward the end of the pier, where the bait house and coffee shop loomed in the darkness. There was so much power in this place—there, another crash, bigger than before—she would ignore this man, let him say his bullshit, give him whatever he wanted, and the hell with him.

"You're angry with me." How very astute. So the man had earned his PhD.

"At least it's nice to know what's what, have all our cards on the table."

Art said, "What's what . . . isn't that a lovely idea?"

"At least we've finally arrived at the truth."

"Ha! The truth. Is that with a capital T? What if I told you nobody knows what's what?" He walked behind her now. "Did you ever see a movie called *An Occurrence at Owl Creek Bridge?*" She had, in fact—it was required material in the Film School at UCLA. A Confederate soldier on a bridge gets hung, the rope breaks and he swims down the river in the night, away from the rifle shots and the baying hounds—he runs down a road toward safety, toward a house he knows. A beautiful woman floats down the steps from the veranda, her hand stretched forth to greet him. When their fingers touch the rope snaps taut and the soldier is hanging from the bridge.

"What about it?"

"Kazantzakis, Borges, the storytellers of India with their endless nested dreams; they all have the same theme." He caught up with her now; they were more than halfway to the bait shop. The ocean had been calm for a moment.

"So?" His bullshit seemed so dreary now; how could she ever have found him interesting?

"The point, my dear, is that there is no 'what's what.' We have no way of proving 'what is.' You see, I can't even prove that I am really here."

There was a light fog, not the thick kind that begins in wisps and then rolls in billows over the surface of the ocean, but the kind that hangs evenly in the air, adding a chill to the night.

Art droned on. "At the very best I can only assume I'm here, talking to you, and not lying in a dentist's chair somewhere, under the influence of too much nitrous oxide, having a fabulous hallucination." He took her elbow again; she pulled away and walked ahead. "Or pinned under a wrecked auto, bleeding to death and in shock, in total denial of what is happening to me, inventing this here instead. But 'here' is only in my head."

The sea was black, the horizon invisible. They had come to the end of the pier; the lights from the restaurant were blocked by the bait shop and the darkness was nearly complete. Holly turned to the right and walked to the north side of the pier. She stepped past a bench and looked out over the railing toward the point. What was the man carrying on about?

"Jesus, Art, what's your point? I have the money you wanted." She reached into her purse. She looked back and saw that Art stood on the other side of the bench, his hands in his pockets, peering up into the night sky. "Do you even have a point?"

"So what do you do?" he asked, as though she hadn't said anything. "How do you feel when everything you think you know loses its solidity? When all your nice, taken-for-granted beliefs become wispy, smoky, phantom ideas that you can no longer connect to? Where the simple facts of God and good, of moral principal and right living are not only called into question but suddenly seem naive, ridiculous, unacceptable to the intelligence? When a termite colony seems the only apt metaphor for human behavior, what do you do? To what or whom do you turn for comfort? What is left to guide your actions?"

Crazy, she thought, how his voice was hypnotic even now, relentless, as though he could engulf her in his bullshit just by the force of its delivery. A wave formed, farther out than the previous set, and rushed forward, suspended vertically for an endless moment before collapsing in a sustained roar. An even larger one reared behind it.

A point of light flicked on in the path of the outer wave, then seemed to submerge, casting a greenish glow that rose as the swell lifted it. Near the top, the glow emerged from the water and became a narrow beam pointing down into the trough of the wave. In the dim glow from the pier, she could see that a surfer was hurtling down the face of the beast, a flashlight attached to his forearm and a white trail flaring off the board behind him. He hit the flat water of the trough at the same time as the lip of the wave hit—he was just ahead of it, banking hard and accelerating into the steep rushing wall, his left arm extended forward, the radiant beam shooting out in front of him.

She exclaimed, "Incredible!" and stepped up to the railing, absorbed in the spectacle. The first wave was just now looming at the end of the pier, its crest reaching to touch the underside of the wooden slats of the deck. There was a sucking sound as the water pulled away from the pilings; she looked down and saw their gray shapes like bones in a bone yard.

The surfer had climbed to the top of the wave and then turned back to race downward, banking hard to avoid the lip smashing behind him, flying up into the middle of the wave as the curl caught up and buried him. For seconds only the shaft of light was visible.

The first wave finally shattered right under where she and Art stood. Spray flew up over their heads and the deck trembled. Halfway to the point, the flashlight emerged from the hollow of the second wave. An entire section of the wall broke in front of the surfer—he turned his board toward shore and lay down as the whitewater exploded around him.

She felt a hand on the seat of her jeans.

"Holly, my dear—"

"Art, why don't you shut up and go home. I don't even care what you do."

The wave rose up at the end of the pier now, larger than the last, another monster already behind it, the sucking sound below even louder.

He said, "Holly . . ." in that same calm, persistent voice. "There is no home. No truth, no God, and nowhere left to go." She felt his hands lift and push, felt herself pitch forward, felt the pain as her ankles slammed against the railing, saw the gray bones of the pilings as she fell.

CHAPTER 42

⊽

It was interesting, sitting at a bar and not having a drink. Jeff looked around; the place was packed. There were bottles of beer, snifters of brandy, shots of tequila, mixed drinks, drinks on ice, and coffee drinks all around him. The smell of cognac wafted over from his left—across the bar a couple drank with two straws from a concoction served in a coconut shell. The amazing thing about it, he thought, was that he didn't care, didn't need a drink, didn't even want one.

He and Ron, along with half a dozen others from the meeting that had just ended, were waiting for a table to be cleared so they could all sit together. It seemed like a long way to drive just for an AA meeting—"Is this what they mean by any lengths?" he had asked Ron, who just chuckled—but it was a good, friendly group and he had enjoyed himself.

Every five or six minutes since they had arrived, the floor shook and dishes rattled as huge waves pounded the pier. He was about to excuse himself so he could go out and watch the surf—there was a view through the restaurant windows, but it was difficult to really see—when he saw a familiar figure outside on the pier.

Jeff was sitting on a barstool, facing Ron, with the bar to his left. To his right were a window and a side exit that let out onto the pier. A couple walked by, and out of the corner of his eye he saw the man, dressed in dark slacks and a windbreaker, take his companion by the elbow as if guiding her toward the end of the pier. In fact, he thought, he had seen her before too. But he couldn't connect the two of them. There was no way that the man, whom he hadn't seen in years, could be with the blond from that SOL meeting. No way.

"Excuse me?" he asked. Ron had been talking about something that had been said earlier, at the meeting, calling it psychobabble. Said it sound like some of that SOL bullshit.

"What's up? You look like the liberty bell just went off behind your eyes." Ron glanced out the window at the couple, now receding into the darkness. Then he looked back at Jeff with that patient look, like Jeff had a slow processor upstairs but would eventually come up with a response.

"Hey, I'm fine. I'm just gonna hit the men's room for a minute and then maybe step outside and watch the surf." Ron looked at him with interest and gave a small smile. Jeff left the bar and walked through the main restaurant, past the restrooms, and out the main entrance, and then looped around through the huge doors at the pier's entrance. The two were barely visible now. He waited for a moment while the pier trembled like an aftershock from an earthquake.

He followed, keeping to the right side of the pier, walking between the benches and the railing, moving fast enough that he could gain some ground on the couple. He saw the girl disengage herself from the man. Now, as he followed, she walked ahead of the man by several feet. What was going on?

As they approached the bait shop, the man caught up with the girl. In a moment of silence, between the sets of crashing waves, he heard the man talking. Pieces of sentences floated on the mist. Silence from the girl.

He looked back. The restaurant was far behind him, cheerfully lit, seeming almost unreal against the backdrop of low hills across the Pacific Coast Highway. He wondered what Ron would think of what he was doing, following some couple in the dark. Stalking. He brushed the doubt aside; something odd was going on here.

When he turned again, he saw that the two were in the even darker shadow by the south side of the bait shop. He took the opportunity to catch up and obscure himself against the shore-ward side of the structure and then peered out to find that they had disappeared. He followed and then came to a stop at the next corner of the bait shop.

They had turned to the right and walked a short distance to the corner of the pier. The girl stood at the railing, facing north, on the other side of a bench from the man. Jeff was sure of who he was now—sure about both of them.

From his place by the building, he could hear the blond, only about fifteen feet away, ask the guy, "What's your point?" Half a beat later: "Do you even have a point?" The guy droned on about Christian beliefs and God, about principals and human behavior and metaphors—*What the hell was happening?*

An enormous wave reared up on the point and began peeling off with impeccable form, thunderously, but with an eerie pre-cision. A second, even larger, wave towered behind it and sud-denly—he couldn't believe it—some maniac with a flashlight attached to his arm took three strokes on a longboard and pow-ered down the face, then made a radical bottom turn, using all its torque for the speed he needed to move forward.

The girl leaned on the railing and made an exclamation that was drowned by the roar of the surf. The guy on the wave pointed his light down the line, poised in maximum trim, and proceeded to get eaten alive as the curl caught up with, enveloped, and then passed him. He thought the surfer had bought it—what a spooky tumble he was headed for—when he noticed the light moving in a line through the glass top of the tunnel. Suddenly the flashlight reappeared and the guy was in the clear.

A larger wave was already building behind this one. Perhaps the guy on the board knew it, because he chose to straighten out and ride the churning white soup toward shore, whereas kicking out over the top of the wave would have put him in the path of the monster outside.

He saw the man walk around the bench and place his hand on the seat of the blond's pants. He heard her say, "Shut up," and then the guy said something he couldn't hear. There was a sucking sound as the water rushed toward the wave that the surfer had ridden—he was bouncing toward shore fifty yards to the north, but now the swell was approaching the pier and about to thump down on the pilings.

There was a quick motion of the man's arm and shoulder, and the blond went over the railing.

CHAPTER 43

~V~

It was a good thing, the water being so warm. Jeff had run straight into the man from behind, knocking him aside, and gone over the rail without even thinking it through. He had landed feet first in the blackness, shot down to the bottom, and pushed up through the surface right next to the blond.

The thing was to get her away from the pilings. The wave was going to break right in front of them, and the nearest piling, encrusted with razor-edged barnacles, was only about six feet away. The only way to go was down. He wondered if she could swim.

When she saw him, an involuntary little shriek came out of her, but she wasn't flailing, didn't seem to be panicking. He just yelled, "The bottom—away from the pier." Then, with a black wall of water the size of a house ready to crash right on top of them, he grabbed the fabric of the girl's sweatshirt with his left hand, heard her take a breath as he did, and pushed her under the surface.

Her hand hit his ear when she took her first stroke, but it helped propel them downward and away from the pier. He kicked hard and stroked with his right hand, aiming for the bottom, out of the wave's grip.

It was peaceful for a moment. He had a flash of an old familiar revulsion: he had always loved the ocean, and sandy bottoms or coral reefs in clear tropical water, but rocky bottoms that he couldn't see had always spooked him. He had fished from this pier when he was a kid, and knew what lived down here. Crabs the size of dinner plates, sand sharks, stingrays, God knew what else . . .

Suddenly there was a sickening lurch as a current, unstoppable as a freight train, picked them up and whipped them, first out to sea, then sideways for a terrifying moment, before pulling them toward shore. The handful of sweatshirt was ripped out of his grip as he was catapulted into a somersault. For an instant he was out ahead of the soup, long enough to catch a breath before being pummeled under and thrust face first against the girl. He felt himself get driven down until his back hit the rocks on the bottom, the girl on top of him. His hand shot out and grabbed her arm—there was a brief tug as the wave tried to reclaim her, and then they were out of its grip. He kicked off the bottom, pushing the girl up ahead of him until they popped up through the surface and into the air.

He heard her gasping for breath—she probably didn't get that extra lungful that he got. They were still close to the pier, but maybe twenty feet toward shore from where they had started.

"Can you swim?" he asked her.

"Yes."

"Then swim fast, straight out, go under before you meet the wave."

The next wave was already drawing water, pulling them outward, sucking against the barnacles and the pilings. They swam with the outflow, straight toward the towering face, bigger than the last wave, and when they met it dove hard for the bottom. They had momentum this time: he reached out and felt the smooth, slimy surface of a rock and waited for the iron grip of the wave to take him, but felt only a passing tug and then it was over.

This time when they came up, the sea was calm. He figured they had about two to three minutes before the next set hit; the main thing now was to get inside, out of the impact zone. If they could move away from the pier, then even if another set came they could just let it push them in toward shore.

He explained it to the girl and she just said, "Let's go," and broke into a steady stroke toward the beach.

CHAPTER 44

☥

Ron told the others from the meeting he would join them in a few minutes. Sam, an old-timer he had known ever since coming into the rooms of AA fourteen years ago, came up to him and said, "What happened to your new guy?" Sam had bushy white hair and wild scraggly eyebrows. He stood about five foot six and seemed to find an element of humor in almost everything that happened around him.

"I don't know," Ron said. "He mentioned something about going out on the pier and watching the surf."

"Well, I was just out there, saw some guy on a wave with a goddamn flashlight. Nobody on the pier though. Hope your kid's not getting squirrelly on you." Sam laughed and went over to the corner where the tables had been pushed together to accommodate the group from the meeting.

Too squirrelly. Actually, Ron thought, the kid was doing pretty well. Suited up, showed up, kept his attitude in pretty good check. Doing fine at his new job.

So, squirrelly didn't fit, but where the hell was he? He had an odd feeling about it now—ten minutes had gone by. Sam said there was no one out on the pier. So now he could forget about it and go join the others, or he could take a walk, have a little look around outside.

There had been times, he thought as he stepped out onto the pier, when he hadn't listened to his intuition, and each time there had been a price to pay. The AA book told him that, after taking certain actions, his thinking would function on the intuitive plane, and that he could rely upon it.

Now, his intuition told him to find Jeff.

He stepped out of the restaurant and begun walking toward the end of the pier when a huge wave broke. A solitary figure approached from the end of the pier; it was dark, but even at this distance he knew it wasn't Jeff. He had seen the couple that had grabbed Jeff's attention, barely catching a glance of them as they walked by. Where was the woman?

He broke into a jog down the middle of the pier. The man coming toward him moved to the south rail, walking briskly toward the shore. He had his hands in his pockets and was hunched forward, shoulders up, looking southward, as if he didn't want to be seen.

Ron slowed to a walk and veered to his left, cutting the man off. He looked, in surprise, into the face of Art Bradley, co-founder of the SOL movement.

The man said, "Hurry, there's been an accident," then brushed by him and continued toward the entrance to the pier.

Another wave exploded as Ron took off at a run toward the end of the pier. Spray flew up over the railing. In the silence that followed, he thought he heard voices from somewhere ahead, hard to place in the misty darkness.

There was no one in sight. He walked around the gift shop on the one side, then the bait shop on the other—still nobody. It didn't make sense: even if Jeff never came out here, where was the girl that had walked out with Art?

It wasn't until he was halfway back, moving toward the entrance, that he heard rhythmic splashing noises and looked over the railing again. There they were, both of them, for Christ's sake, Jeff and the girl, taking long, slow strokes, heading shoreward about ten feet from the pilings.

He leaned over the railing and yelled down at them. "Hey!"

Jeff stopped and looked up, treading water.

Ron called out, "You need help?"

"No. Meet us on the beach." He sounded pretty good, like they were just down there goofing off or something. Like, no big deal.

What the hell was going on?

CHAPTER 45

N o, I don't want the police," the blond girl said. She shuddered and then, as if by marshaling a huge reserve of will, she assumed a look and posture of self-assurance and composure, her eyes daring Ron to protest.

Her name was Holly. She looked good, even soaking wet, sitting there in the driver's seat of the Land Rover, the door open and the water dripping off her into the car. "I've seen you before."

"SOL, Franklin Street. And I saw you at the Beverly Hills seminar the other week."

"That man's insane, you know." She hugged herself, trying to get warm.

"We know that." Ron was putting it all together. It made sense, in the big picture, but it was still hard to accept. "So Art pushed you?" It was unbelievable, and yet so obvious at the same time.

"Yeah. I was standing on the pier, watching this guy surf with a flashlight. It was incredible! I wasn't even thinking about Art. I had tuned him out, he was so full of shit, and then, boom! I'm over the railing—I'm flying. And then I'm in the water, like a bad dream."

"I saw it happen," Jeff said.

"You were watching us?" The blond—Holly—looked at him, eyes narrowed. "What were you doing out there?"

Jeff shrugged. "I don't know. I saw Jack walk by the restaurant with you. It was so weird, I had to check it out."

Ron asked, "Who's Jack?"

"Jack's the guy that pushed her," Jeff said. "Who's Art?"

Ron started laughing. "You got rescued," he said to Holly, "because he thought he saw someone he knew."

Holly turned to Jeff. "I guess you did rescue me," she said. Jeff shrugged.

Ron watched the two of them: Jeff simple and open, casual even while he stood dripping wet next to the car; Holly pressing her index finger from the top of her jaw toward her ear, then shaking her head, saying, "It sounds like I'm still under water."

There was a moment's silence.

"You know, I wasn't so worried about the swim, but that wave—and the pilings—good God." Holly yawned, then pressed once more at her ear. "There, that's better."

Jeff said, "You have to get to the bottom, where the wave can't get you."

"How did you know that?"

"I used to surf a lot. You get a sense for the ocean."

"Why did you quit?" Holly asked.

"You have to get up early in the morning." Jeff bent down and took off a tennis shoe. When he turned it over salt water poured out.

"So?"

"So, I was busy doing other things." Jeff shook out his other shoe and then removed his socks. "Look, that guy that pushed you, I'm not mixing him up with anyone else. He might be calling himself Art, but his real name is Jack Stanley."

Ron said, "Art Bradley's been around here for a while. When did you know him?"

"I haven't seen him in at least five years. He disappeared from the scene."

"What scene?" If Jeff was right, Ron was curious what Joe could pull up on the man. How far back his history as Dr. Art Bradley went.

"The rock and roll dope scene," Jeff said. "He was the rock doc up in San Francisco. Xanax, Valium, Dexedrine, Oxy, you name it and he would write a scrip for it. For a price."

Holly combed back her hair with her fingers. Ron watched her shudder for an instant, shake her head, look down at the ground.

"You know what he always talked about?" she said. "How people needed to have faith in each other. 'Trust me,' he was always saying. God!" She stepped down from the driver's seat and stood on the pavement in her bare feet. "I lost something out there."

Ron wondered what it could have been. Her faith in a rational world? Her belief that people really are what they appear to be? He looked at her with sympathy, unable to formulate a useful response.

"What did you lose?" Jeff asked.

"My purse. And my keys."

CHAPTER 46

Sitting in the back seat of the Land Rover, heading south on the Pacific Coast Highway, Holly said, "You're telling me Art is a serial killer?"

Ron, the older man, flicked his brights at an oncoming car driving with its lights off, and said over his shoulder, "It fits the puzzle pretty neatly."

"That's insane."

"Insanity does come to mind." Ron moved a switch on the dashboard and warm air started blowing from a vent. She was grateful. She was cold to the point of shivering and it intensified her feeling of anxiety. She wondered how the other guy, Jeff, felt.

"How many people? And what ties them all together, or to Art?"

"Eight that I know of," Ron said. "All attractive, women in their mid twenties. All appeared to have taken their own lives by jumping from high places. At night."

"Over what period of time?" she asked.

"About two years."

"Couldn't it be a coincidence? I mean, a lot more than eight people killed themselves in the last two years. You could probably arrange them into all kinds of little groups."

Ron stopped for the light at Topanga Canyon. "At least three of them went to SOL meetings."

Jeff turned and said, "Including my sister."

She looked at him, shocked by the revelation. "I'm sorry to hear that," was all she could come up with.

"You know what I think is strange?" Jeff asked. Then, without waiting for an answer, he said, "What I think is strange is that you just got pushed off a pier by a maniac, and you're trying to dismiss what we're saying as a bunch of coincidences."

"Is that what I'm doing?" It dawned on her that at some basic level she still wasn't accepting the fact that Art had tried to kill her.

"Listen, there's no way my sister killed herself. Or that she was taking drugs." Jeff turned to Ron. "What was that stuff called?"

"Halcion."

"Yeah, no way." Jeff shook his head in disbelief.

She couldn't breathe. The sensation of being cold returned, more intense than before, even though the car's heater had warmed the air. Drawing into herself, she could hear the pulse drumming in her ears. As if from a distance, Jeff's voice continued, but she could not make out what he was saying. She held her arms crossing her chest and found that she was inhaling and exhaling rapidly through her mouth.

"Hey. HEY!" Jeff was yelling now. She saw him, turned around in his seat, a look of alarmed concern on his face. She felt the car pull over and stop.

"Are you okay?" Jeff asked. She still couldn't answer. She heard Ron say something about shock and shook her head.

"I'll be all right—" there, she had found her voice "—in a minute."

"Christ," Jeff said. "You scared me there. What happened?"

"It felt like I was falling again," she said. She took a deep breath, then another. The icy feeling inside was subsiding. "Halcion—that's not a very common drug, is it?"

"Why?" asked Ron.

"That's what Art gave me during our sessions. He said it made me more receptive to hypnosis."

"He hypnotized you?" Jeff seemed astonished.

"Twice. The third time I pretended to go along with it, but I didn't take the pills."

"Why not?" Jeff asked.

"I just had a feeling about it. On some level, I didn't trust him." It was crazy, she thought, how the whole picture was so clear now. After Art had left her place last Thursday night, she had been too furious at his betrayal to see beyond her anger. Even after he had thrown her into the water, the surprise and shock of it had clouded her thinking. But now it was perfectly obvious: that Art was a predator and she had been the prey since the beginning. That her caution, her protestations, and his reassurances had all been part of his game, a game he enjoyed. A game he had played before.

"I just want to go home now."

CHAPTER 47

▽

They drove in silence, down the Coast Highway to the tunnel, east on the Interstate 10 to Centinela. Jeff watched as headlights approached and passed, the dreary LA landscape always the same, the warm air from the heater lulling him into a comfortable stupor. He felt sore and battered; his back, he had discovered, was bleeding where it had been scraped by the rocks.

They were on Olympic Boulevard now, past Century City, when Holly said, "This is it, turn right." Half a block later she said, "That's where I live," and Ron pulled into a driveway that led to the back of the building. He stopped where the driveway met a path to the front entrance.

Opening the door for Holly, Ron asked, "How are you going to get in?"

"I have a key hidden outside," Holly told him. She stepped out of the Land Rover. Jeff got out, too, and the three of them stood awkwardly by the car.

Holly said, "Thank you for your help," and put out her hand. It was slender and cold to his touch, the fingers stiff and unyielding. When she turned and extended her hand to Ron, he said, "We should probably come in with you. It might not be a good time to be alone."

She withdrew her hand and said, "I'd rather be by myself right now. We can get together tomorrow or something, okay?"

She gave her phone number, which Ron wrote on a pad he kept on his dashboard.

"We'll stay here for a few minutes. In case you can't get in, or you change your mind." He gave her a business card. Jeff watched as she walked to the apartment entrance, wondering if he would ever see her again. How could you go through what they had just experienced and then never have contact? He wanted to say something, but nothing came to mind.

They stood in silence for a moment. He pictured Holly walking down a hallway, her hair plastered flat against her head, clothes still damp and sticking to her body. His own jeans and shirt were stiff with salt now and he noticed a briny odor in the still air.

"Don't you think it's a bit strange that she's not reacting to what just happened?" He had been wondering about this ever since they left Malibu.

"Very strange," Ron said. "Shock could explain it. In which case, it's totally irresponsible of us to let her go home alone. Not to mention the fact that we just broke several laws."

"What do you mean?"

"Failure to report a felony assault. You witnessed an attempted murder—we should have taken this directly to the police." Ron remained standing by the car door, as if anticipating Holly's return.

"So she didn't want to do that. What's wrong with that?" He could just see it: sitting in the goddamned Malibu Sheriff's station, filling out forms and answering the same questions over and over. Forget about it. "Anyway, why didn't you force the issue? You usually play it by the book, don't you?"

"Well," Ron said, "I've been thinking about that. Maybe it fits my purpose to take this to Joe Greiner and let him run with it."

"What is your purpose?"

"To solve this thing and put an end to it."

The door at the apartment entrance opened and Holly stepped back out onto the path, still in her wet clothes, carrying an overnight bag with her right hand. In her left hand she held a Barbie doll with a nail pinning a square of paper to its forehead. Her lips were compressed to a thin line, her face white as she said, "I can't stay here."

CHAPTER 48

⩘

O n Sunday morning, Ron woke up earlier than usual.
The sky was deep blue with a rose tint to the east. A breeze
flowed through the canyon, and an owl that lived under a neighbor's eaves called out into the silence.

It was a fine time to go for a run, but he decided to stay at
home until the others woke up. Holly was asleep on the sofa in the
living room, so he took care to move silently. In the kitchen, he sat
down at the table with a glass of orange juice and considered the
evening before, the day ahead.

They had offered to go back up to her apartment with her,
give her time to shower and gather some things, but she had said,
"Forget it. I've got what I need." She made a feeble pitch for him
to drive her to a hotel, but put up no resistance when he offered
his place for the evening.

In the car, Jeff had asked Holly how she knew that Art had
been to her place. She had read from the note that had been nailed
to the doll. "'Surf's up,' it says, and there's a little smiley face."

Now it was eight o'clock the following morning and Ron
was reading the Sunday paper when he heard the sound of tires
crunching gravel in his driveway. Since his guests were still sleeping, he went through the garage and stepped out onto the gravel.

"Good morning." He walked up to where Joe Greiner sat in
his beat-up Taurus.

"What's good about it?" Joe seemed especially surly and made no move to get out of the car. "I got to pick up Robbie in fuckin' Simi Valley in two hours . . ."

"Why Simi Valley?" He was puzzled. Joe loved being with his boy.

"Because Janie just moved out there to live with Dan the fuckin' man, that's why."

"Who's that?"

"Dan Glodin. Get this, he's a fuckin' Chippie." Joe shook his head and opened the door of the station wagon. He was clean-shaven, dressed in khaki pants and a madras shirt, but had a weary, haunted look that Ron remembered from his own image in the mirror years before.

"So this better be good. What have you got?" Joe was squinting even though the sun was behind him.

"What I told you. Remember the profile on the girls in the files?"

"Yeah, mid twenties, they all looked good. What else?"

"And I traced at least three of them to that SOL group."

Joe lit a cigarette. "Did you tell me that?"

Ron watched Joe's hands as he lit the cigarette. No telltale tremor, just a nervous, burnt-out intensity. "You weren't very impressed."

"So why am I here?"

Ron told him about the events of the previous evening, about how Jeff had witnessed the act. About running into Art Bradley on the pier, and how Jeff had identified Art Bradley as a shrink from the Bay Area with an entirely different name.

"And you say that the Sheriff's office wasn't informed?" Joe dropped the butt of the cigarette and ground it into the gravel.

"The girl didn't want to talk to them. I thought it over and decided to bring it to you. This is our guy; there's no doubt in my mind about it." He turned to go back into the house.

When they got to the kitchen, Holly was making coffee. She wore sandals and green shorts with a brown tank top. From the other room Jeff shouted, "Black, with one of those yellow packets."

At the kitchen table, over coffee, Joe questioned Jeff and Holly as Ron listened and occasionally added to the story. Holly was angry when she found out that Joe was a cop, but backed off when Ron qualified him as a friend.

Joe asked her, "Why didn't you want the police involved? Don't you want to see this man put away?"

Holly gazed at him for a moment, as if gauging his intelligence, or at least his receptivity to new ideas, and then said, "Do you really think I want to be a witness against my therapist? The same man who knows that I've attempted suicide in the past? That I've been treated for seizures and depression? That I've been visiting shrinks since I was fifteen?" She picked up her cup and drank from it. "I can see it now. 'She was distraught. Suicidal. I didn't see it coming, but I tried to stop her when she jumped.'"

"But I saw the whole thing. He can't do that," Jeff protested.

"It was dark. There was a fog that night. You were far away." Ron had been tossing this around in his mind earlier in the morning, trying to come to terms with his failure to take the matter to the Malibu Sheriff.

"Okay, I hear you," Joe said. "But what do you want to do, pretend it never happened?"

"I haven't thought it through yet." Holly shrugged her shoulders. "But I'm not going to let him change my whole life."

"I think we can put him together with the other girls that died," Ron said.

"I don't know how," Joe said. "Without Holly, we don't even have a case open to bring him in for questioning." He pulled a pad out of his back pocket and turned to Jeff. "What did you say his name used to be?"

CHAPTER 49

⌖

On Monday morning, Jeff raced down the canyon, hopped Sunset Boulevard over to Crescent Heights, and continued speeding after he turned west on Olympic. At 8:40, he couldn't risk the downtown freeway traffic. If he didn't jam, he'd be late. If he got pulled over, same deal. *That's just the way it goes*, he thought, sweating now as the traffic backed up at Beverly Drive.

His court appearance was scheduled at 9:00, but Herman Katz, his attorney, told him to be there early. He said there were some things they had to discuss.

Worse, Ron had taken part of his workday off in order to support him in court, and was probably there waiting for him.

When he finally pulled into the West LA Court parking lot, it was 9:05. A clerk directed him to a hearing room on the second floor. The hallway was empty, but Room 206 was nearly full. He saw Ron in the second row with a seat next to him. When Jeff sat down, Ron looked at him and gave a thumbs-up sign, whispering, "Way to go." Jeff shrugged and looked around. Herman Katz was leaning back in his chair, making notes on a yellow pad, seated at one of two tables in front of the judge's bench, while he watched a man at the other table stand and pick up a shotgun with a red tag hanging from it.

There was a noticeable tension in the courtroom.

The man with the shotgun—the same prosecutor who had argued for high bail on Jeff the week before—held the weapon up and directed his attention toward a woman seated at the witness stand to the judge's left.

"Mrs. DeTemple, have you ever seen this gun before?"

The woman stared at the gun without blinking, then shifted her gaze to the prosecutor and said, "Yes."

"Who was in possession of the weapon at that time?"

"He was." She pointed to a heavyset, crew-cut man in his mid forties who was seated next to Herman Katz.

"And what was your husband doing with the weapon at that time?" The prosecutor put the gun down.

The woman sat rigid. Jeff could see her head was shaking in a barely controlled tremor. She said, "He was pointing it at me."

In the next hour, he listened as the story unfolded. The husband had been molesting his older daughter for the past three years, since the girl was ten, and the mother had remained silent. But when the younger daughter turned ten and the father began with her, the woman had threatened to go to the police. That's when he put the shotgun in her face.

By the time the older daughter finished her testimony—at the prosecutor's direction, it was brutally explicit—there was a palpable hostility in the room. Jeff watched in a daze as Herman Katz asked a few perfunctory questions without even standing up.

"How can you defend a guy like that?" he whispered to Ron. The judge looked up sharply and scowled.

When the court broke for recess, he went out to the hallway with Ron. Other people filtered out, subdued, some speaking in low voices. Finally, Katz emerged.

"We're going to ask for a continuance," he said, not even bothering to offer his hand. "That judge wants to put someone away, and he won't get a shot at that sick son of a bitch today."

"Are you sure he'll give me one?" He felt panic, as though the whole process were disintegrating right in front of him, sabotaged by the act of a random pervert.

"Can't be sure of anything," Katz said. "Anyway, you were late this morning. Don't do that again. Now, what have you got for me?"

Jeff reached in his pocket and pulled out his wallet. "This is all I've got right now." He handed Katz four hundreds.

"That's not enough. Your dad gave me three thousand to get started—I need sixteen hundred more from you." Katz, who couldn't have been more than five foot six, peered up through his rimless round glasses at him with a look of contempt.

"I just started a job," Jeff said. "I get paid on Friday, and I've got a check coming for a photo I took." Ron had taken his shots of the bust in Stone Canyon to the paper and one of them had been printed in the Metro section. It felt good, doing something like that.

Katz turned to Ron. "Have you got what we talked about?"

"Yes, three copies." Ron reached in his coat pocket and pulled out three envelopes.

"Don't worry about it," Katz said to Jeff. "Just remember when you're in the court room to keep your mouth shut."

When he was called to appear, Jeff stood and walked through the low swinging gate to stand before Judge Metcalf. Katz cleared his throat and said, "Your Honor, we request a continuance."

"On what basis?" The judge looked down at them in annoyance, as though they had just performed a gross breach of protocol.

"On the basis that I have not had time to review the facts of this case and prepare an adequate defense, Your Honor." Katz looked up, adjusted his glasses, and then made a small, helpless gesture with his hands.

"Motion denied." Then, nodding to the prosecutor, Judge Metcalf said, "Mr. Deemer, get on with your case."

Jeff noticed a shallow cardboard box with his gun in a plastic bag on the prosecution table. Mr. Deemer got up, read the charges, and then said, "The officers are available to testify, sir."

Katz bent to his briefcase and picked up two of the envelopes Ron had given him. "May I make a submission for the record, sir?"

The judge said, "What have you got?" and leaned forward to accept an envelope. Deemer took the other one. Jeff wondered what was going on as the two men opened the envelopes and read the single sheet each extracted.

When the judge finished, he put the letter down. "Well, Mr. Deemer?"

Deemer studied his copy for an extra moment and then looked up. "We'll accept a year probation and time served for a change of plea."

"Is that acceptable to your client, Mr. Katz?" The Honorable Timothy Metcalf, his bald, dark head shiny above his black robe, had changed his demeanor; he looked weary now, unable to sustain the crisp, hang-em-high attitude he had carried this far.

"Say yes," Katz hissed.

"Yes. Yes, sir," he stammered.

The judge read a minute's worth of legal gibberish, then peered down at him and said, "Do you understand?" To which he said, "Yes, sir," again, and the judge said, "Good," and slammed his hammer down. "Case closed."

"Jesus," Jeff said as he walked down the hall with Ron. "What just happened?"

"How about grace?" Ron said.

"I don't know what that means."

When they got to the elevator, Ron pushed the button and then turned to face him. "An unearned gift."

Leaving the elevator, he asked, "But what was in that letter?"

"I told the judge and the prosecutor that we were a pair of drunks."

"What?"

"I said I used to be an idiot when I drank, but since I stopped fourteen years ago I haven't wound up in jail once."

"What's that got to do with my case?"

"I said that I've seen the same thing happen for a lot of other people, and that you had a good chance at being one of them."

"Is that all?" Jeff was astonished.

"Pretty much."

"Amazing!"

"Yeah . . . and the jails are overcrowded."

CHAPTER 50

༤

They crossed Purdue and headed for the West Los Angeles Police station. Inside, they waited as the desk sergeant went to get Joe Greiner.

"He seems like a pretty decent guy," Jeff said.

"Who, the sergeant?"

"Yeah."

"Why shouldn't he be?"

"I don't know. I'm just used to thinking of cops as assholes."

"Most of the cops I know," Ron said, "are pretty decent guys."

Sitting in Joe Greiner's cramped cubicle, Jeff looked around at the bulletins, sticky-notes, mug shots, and general clutter that covered every available surface. Next to the computer screen was a picture of a pudgy boy of about ten, he guessed, with the same big nose that Joe had.

"So how was your visit with his honor Tim Metcalf today?" Greiner was as gruff as the last time Jeff had met him, but with a trace of humor this time, like he was ready to lighten up some.

"Unreal," Jeff said.

"Yeah, you can never tell whether he's gonna hang 'em or hug 'em. What did you get, probation?"

"One year."

"Santa came early for you this year." Joe bent over from his seat with a grunt and picked a folder from a briefcase lying open on the floor. "Let's get down to business. Hey, what happened to the girl?"

Ron explained that they had driven her back to her car in Malibu late Sunday morning and had followed her back to her apartment. "She invited us up to her place. Everything seemed okay there. We had some coffee and then left. Oh, and we swapped out her lock on the front door."

Joe opened the folder he had picked up. "Our man has an interesting background. Two of them, in fact." He picked a sheet from the folder. "Art Bradley. Never had a brush with the authorities, not even a traffic ticket. Has a California driver's license, five years old. Prior to that, he doesn't exist." He threw the sheet on the desk. "Probably picked the name from hospital records, infant that died at birth around the same year Art was born."

"And prior to five years ago?" Ron asked.

"Well, then we get a much more colorful personality." He picked the next page from the file and waved it briefly. "Jack Stanley, a psychiatrist, Canadian citizen. Five drunk driving arrests in six years, all up in the Bay area. Must have had a pretty good lawyer—he never did any time. He did, however, lose his license to practice. Here . . ." He pulled a computer printed mug shot from the folder and handed it to Ron.

"That's him all right. He's looking pretty ragged here."

"Yeah," Joe said. "They probably booked him the morning after. Now, check this: he was wanted as a witness—not a suspect—in the disappearance of two students from the art school up there. Both female. Still unresolved, and that's when Jack Stanley dropped off the planet."

"And Art Bradley began to create a life for himself in Los Angeles." Ron studied the mug shot and then handed it back to Joe.

"What a coincidence." Joe turned to Jeff. "So you knew him in his previous incarnation. What do you remember about him? Anything that pops into your mind, even trivial details, might help."

Jeff thought back to the days when he had a business relationship with one of San Francisco's major rock promoters. His job was to deliver a pound of coke a week. The promoter never sold any of it; he snorted enough to kill an elephant and gave the rest away to grease the wheels of the music business. Dr. Jack Stanley was part of the inner circle, along with the upper-echelon musicians, groupies, and a few outsiders: attorneys, financial backers, even a city councilman.

"They used to call him Doctor Jack," he began and then hesitated.

"Go on," Joe said. "I don't give a shit about what you were doing up there."

"Yeah, well . . . He was always a snappy dresser. And he knew all the party girls, the bimbos and the pros. Shep Donahue, the guy I worked for, used to call Doctor Jack if some big shot came into town and wanted a certain kind of girl."

"What do you mean, 'a certain kind of girl'?" Joe asked.

"Something other than the groupie trash that anyone could have. Sometimes he'd get requests, like for twins or for special talent. There was this one from Nicaragua, Anna Banana, the Mouth from the South, they used to call her. Or maybe someone wanted a real clean-cut college type. Doctor Jack would always come through."

Joe pulled out a note pad and a pen. "Okay, get into it. Details, whatever comes to your mind."

He thought about the old times. Back when everything worked. He would take the money from the coke and buy pounds of top-grade weed from his connection in Humboldt, then take it down to LA.

"He wasn't into drugs. He always had some coke—mine, but he got it through Mark, this promoter—" He stopped, reddening in sudden discomfort.

"I'm telling you, for Christ's sake, don't worry about it." Joe laughed and shook his head.

"Okay," Jeff said. "Anyway, Doctor Jack kept the coke for the girls. Plus, he was everyone's pill connection. But he only drank booze. Lots of it." He could picture the man in his impeccable Italian suits, drinking 'round the clock with the rest of the gang, still the life of the party the next day when all the druggies were burnt out and fading. "He liked Moosehead beer and Bushmills. The beer was his daytime drink."

The cop seemed to be writing down more than Jeff was telling. When he stopped, he tapped his pen twice on the pad and looked up. "Did the guy have a real practice? You know, as a therapist?"

"Oh yeah," Jeff said. "He had an office over by Union Square. Very upscale."

"Anything else?" Joe reached for a half donut that was perched amid the clutter on his desk.

"Not much comes to mind. Oh . . . he did introduce me to Lilah."

"Who's Lilah?" Joe jotted down the name.

He shrugged. "Some wacko party girl." He decided to leave it at that.

The cop wasn't going for it. "I'm supposed to write that down? I mean, you singled her out like her name should mean something. What's up?"

Jeff looked over at Ron, who knew some of his history with Lilah. "Well, we, um, hung out a lot."

"That's informative," Ron said. "Was she your girlfriend?"

Jeff thought of Lilah, her wild hair and ridiculous mannerisms. The way her lips stuck to her teeth when she was high. The paradox of her softness and toughness when she was straight.

"She was everybody's girlfriend."

"Where is she now?" Joe prodded.

He told the detective Lilah's address, adding, "I don't think he even knows she's down here, so I doubt she'll help us."

There was a pause where no one spoke. Finally Ron stood up and said, "Are you going to bring him in?"

"Not yet," Joe said. "Without Holly, there's not enough to go with. But you've my attention at last—something's got to come up that will tie this all together."

"I've got some ideas to follow up," Ron said. "Let's talk tomorrow."

As they crossed the street to get to Ron's car, Jeff heard Joe's voice.

"Hey, Jeff!"

He turned around. The detective was standing at the top step by the station entrance.

"You take it easy now."

No cop had ever told him to take it easy.

CHAPTER 51

⏃

Holly woke to a sense of dread. She felt as if she were in a strange place, somewhere she had never been, rather than her own bed. She wondered why she had been so adamant about going home despite Ron and Jeff's misgivings.

The day before, when Jeff and Ron were leaving, she had thanked them again, then closed the door and turned the new lock, a deadbolt with a smooth, well-oiled action and a satisfyingly solid feel to it. She had looked through the fisheye lens in the door, peering out at a distorted view of the landing, the few steps to her doorway, the brick courtyard and the hedge beyond. Nobody coming.

She had then walked quietly, carefully, around every room, along every wall, of her apartment, studying, trying to feel what was wrong. She had even checked out the closets—nothing seemed to have been disturbed, yet something was very disturbing, and the new lock did very little to reassure her.

So now it was Monday. Other than dread, she felt numb. Funny, she thought, how near the word dread was to dead.

She stared out the kitchen window at a cloudless blue early-September sky, finishing her cereal and coffee without even noticing the process. When she was done, she put the dishes in the sink and went back to the table.

She tapped a key on her phone and watched the screen come to life. Shaking her head, hating what she was doing, she selected the link that Art had sent.

Holly, it's important—critical even—for your psychological well-being and spiritual health

What a load of crap. The guy was a nut, a psychopath. What did he know about psychological well-being and spiritual health?

The key to your re-integration with the inner child . . .

Bullshit.

There was something new.

"Dear, dear Holly." That voice, patient, chiding. "I never took you for a leaper. Pills maybe. Possibly even a wrist slasher, but never a leaper." In the background, she could hear the sounds of cars passing, the Miles Davis CD playing in the background. She pictured Art, driving the Jag down the Coast Highway, speaking into his phone.

"And now you are born again. Really, what you have is much like a new life. With new people. And we . . . Well, Holly, we are moving apart. For the time being. It reminds me of two people dancing who have changed partners. Now I am moving across the floor and away from you. In a short while, the dance will bring us together. It's too bad, really. You remind me so much of someone I once loved."

His voice had that same smooth, self-assured quality that he had always carried. What did he mean, the dance will bring us together? She imagined herself waving her hands in his face, saying, *Hello, guess what? I'm awake now, what are you going to do, shoot me from a distance, you moron?*

"I'm thinking of going away for a while. I have some matters to clean up, so to speak. Loose ends, as it were."

Staring at the phone, she imagined herself hitting Art, striking him again and again. She pictured him shrinking as she flailed at him, becoming insubstantial, like tissue paper, and drifting away on the breeze. Mechanically, against her best resistance, she kept watching.

The session began.

"Holly." Art's voice, gentle, and friendly. "Here. I'd like you to take this."

She remembered the teddy bear.

"Now I'd like you to cradle it. That's right; and close your eyes and rock it. That's it."

There was silence, and then the sound of her crying softly.

"Holly, I want you to open and shut your eyes rapidly over and over again." There was a tapping, rhythmic sound. "This fast, and don't stop."

More silence. She remembered the effect of blinking her eyes, the two little orange pills, the heat of the sunlight coming in the window.

"Now, Holly, I'm going to ask you some questions and I want you to go back and find the answers. Don't try to remember. Go back and be there. Do you understand?"

Art's voice was saying, ". . . take a deep breath. Very good. Okay, who *hurt* you when you were little?"

Nothing. Then, quietly: "Holly, who hurt you when you were little?"

"Uncle Dave hurt me." It was a whisper.

"What did he do?" Art prodded.

"I . . ."

"Show me," Art said.

"I can't," Holly heard herself say.

"Show me," Art insisted. "I'm Uncle Dave now. Show me. I won't hurt you. Trust me."

And then she heard that sound. She turned away, unable to watch what she knew was coming.

The sound of leather sliding through a buckle, the twenty-year-old noise of a zipper, a rustle of fabric.

She remembered Uncle Dave's hand on the back of her head. Art's hand.

Her left hand twitched slightly and then jumped with a strange will of its own. She knew what this was and moved toward the telephone but never got there. A power greater than herself had taken over; it would have its way with her, as it always had, until it was done, and she would wake up in a hospital, or on a restaurant floor, or in the aisle of an airplane, or safe in her bed, grateful, if the last, to be unbloodied and unbruised.

CHAPTER 52

On Tuesday, Ron sat at his desk at work, finishing up a piece on telemarketing scammers that were ripping off elderly citizens. There was the Nigerian government refund charade, FCC wireless-license lottery general partnerships, and the usual oil and gas "investments," all preying on retirees, trying to separate them from the savings they lived on. He was listing tactics for defending against these callers—"Tell them you just need to switch phones, then put the receiver down, off the hook, and leave it there for twenty minutes"—when Peter Riddle, one of the whiz kids from the research department, set a computer printout in front of him. He looked up and saw that the kid was grinning. "That was fast. What did you find?"

Peter was about twenty-two, an intern, probably still in college. "I started with all the Stanleys in the Vancouver area and struck out, so I backtracked from the San Francisco Board of Licensing and found out that Jack Stanley was credentialed out of the University of Washington. I called the university and they pulled records tracing him to a Valley High School in Vancouver, BC."

"Wonderful." He could have done the work, but the interns upstairs were faster and seemed to enjoy the thrill of the hunt. "So who is—" he picked up the print-out "—Phyllis Stanley?"

Andrew beamed. "Jack Stanley's sister. According to city records, she was his legal guardian after their mother died. Father's whereabouts unknown. Jack was eleven, the sister seventeen."

"No kidding." The sister's current address was in Escondido, an inland city in what they called North County in San Diego County. He looked up. "Thanks, Peter. Good work."

It was 10:30. In another half hour he could turn in the scam-artist piece, and nothing else on his desk was on fire. It was stacking up but could wait another day. He hadn't seen Leanne for what seemed like too long—and he knew she had this Tuesday off. Hoping that she would be home, he dialed her number.

"Hello?" It was odd: hearing her voice, he could smell her hair.

"Hi there. This is Sal Monella from Oil and Gas Technology Investors. How are you today, Ma'am?"

There was a pause. "Sal Monella?" And a slight laugh. "Pretty well, thanks. How can I help you?" She seemed uncertain.

He hadn't expected to fool her, just to make her laugh with the silly name. "We're looking for experienced investors who can handle some degree of risk in order to participate in an extremely high-yield investment opportunity. Do you fit that profile?"

He was sure Leanne would recognize his voice. Instead, she said, "Just a minute, let me switch phones." He heard her put down the receiver. A Mary Black song was playing in the background. Vague clattering noises would accompany the music now and then, as though Leanne were picking up around the house. The song ended and a new one started; the commotion in the background continued. When a vacuum cleaner switched on, he hung up and went back to finishing his piece.

Twenty minutes later, the phone on his desk rang.

"Hi." It was Leanne. "Am I interrupting your work?"

"No, I just wrapped it up. How's it going?"

"I just got this ridiculous call."

"Really?"

Leanne sounded amused. "Yeah. One of those scam-artist calls." Was she putting him on? "Hey, aren't you doing a piece on telemarketing hustles?"

"As we speak."

"Gee, I should have kept the guy on the phone longer and told you what the whole pitch was." *Gee.*

"Did you get his name?"

"Um, let me see . . . Sal something-or-other." Sticking to her guns.

"How did you get rid of him?" What the hell.

"I put him on hold." She giggled. "Anyway, when do I get to see you?"

"How about lunch?" He told her about Phyllis Stanley and suggested that Leanne join him on the drive to Escondido. "There's a good Mexican restaurant in Carlsbad. We can stop there for lunch."

He scanned the telemarketing piece and had just hit the print command on the PC, anxious to get in his car and pick up Leanne in Santa Monica, when his phone rang again.

"Ron?" It was Jeff.

"Hey, how are you doing?" Part of the deal with Jeff was that he check in on a daily basis. Ron's portion of these conversations often seemed to consist entirely of "Hmmm . . . really? . . . gee, that's too bad," while Jeff went through his litany of woes. Finally, Ron would tell him to cut the crap, make a few suggestions, and they would hang up. Right now, he wasn't feeling up to it.

"I got a call from Holly." He sounded agitated.

"Okay. How is she?"

"Not so good. She told me she had some kind of seizure yesterday. Now she says that someone's watching her."

"Watching her? Where is she?" He checked his watch: it was ten past eleven.

"She's in her apartment. She says she woke up last night and someone was in her closet." Jeff gave a nervous laugh. "In her closet, can you believe it?"

"Did she check to see if anyone was there?" Poor girl. It would be terrifying, he imagined, opening a closet when you were convinced someone was inside.

"She says she talked to him first. Told him what an asshole he was, and that she was calling the police."

He asked, "Who does she think it was?"

Jeff said, "Art—Jack Stanley. She says she got a kitchen knife and watched the door all night. Then when she opened it in the morning he was gone."

"How does she explain that?"

"She wants me to come over tonight so she can show me. What do you think?"

He couldn't come up with an answer. The kid sure didn't need a weird scene like this right now. But hell, he was already in it. "Doesn't she have any friends? Or family nearby?"

"I don't know," Jeff said. "She called me."

⛛

When Ron pulled up in front of Leanne's apartment, she was just opening the door at the front entrance. He got out of the Land Rover and watched her as she walked down the few stairs and along the brick pathway that led through a well-kept lawn and neat garden to a wrought-iron gate that let out onto the sidewalk. She smiled as she saw him and, closing the gate behind her, walked up to him, kissed his lips briefly, then pressed her lips to the V of his chest exposed by his open shirt collar. The noon sun glinted off her hair, and he breathed in a subtle scent of rose as he held her.

Heading south on the 405, he told Leanne the little he knew about Art Bradley/Jack Stanley's sister.

"Did she ask what you wanted to talk about?" Leanne asked.

"She doesn't know we're coming." He had made that decision pretty easily. The door is too easy to close over the phone. If Phyllis Stanley had refused to see him, it would be unlikely that a follow-up visit would change anything.

"So we're winging it, then." She smiled as she said it.

Later, as they approached Long Beach and had finally passed the dense knot of noon traffic, he remembered his conversation with Jeff. Leanne sat sideways in her seat, one leg tucked under her as she faced him and listened while he recounted the story.

When he was done, she nodded thoughtfully and said nothing. He switched to the diamond lane, picked up some speed, and then asked, "Well, what do you think?"

"It's a very sad story," Leanne said. She wasn't analyzing the facts of the story, he realized, but instead was feeling the plight of the girl.

"Remember what I told you about how she behaved after the murder attempt? How she sat there conversing as though she had just come in from a casual swim?"

"Yes," Leanne said. "She's learned not to feel her feelings. No wonder she has seizures."

"And instead of experiencing her justifiable fear—what she's just gone through—she's manifesting paranoid delusions." He turned up the air conditioning a notch.

"With Art as the logical candidate for a bogeyman." Leanne reached out and put her hand on his thigh. "Your guy Jeff is in an interesting position. What did you tell him to do?"

He shrugged. "What could I say? He works 'til six. He's got a commitment at a seven-thirty meeting—I told him he can't duck out on that—and then he'll head over to the girl's place. If his car will get him that far."

They drove in silence for a while, Ron content just to have Leanne close by, this old friendship with its brand new dimension, so full of promise and so natural in its unfolding. After a while he put an old Yusef Latif CD on and the hypnotic lines of the sax took them through Irvine and Laguna Niguel, past San Clemente and down into the clear open land of Camp Pendleton.

"Everything seems to change right through here," Leanne said over the music.

"I know," he replied. "The sky seems bigger."

"And bluer. I like it."

He left the freeway at Carlsbad Village Drive and drove west almost to the coast before turning into a parking area that serviced some attractive shops, a small resort, and a Mexican restaurant with a sign that said, "Welcome to Fidel's."

They both ordered chicken tostadas and ice tea. When the waitress left Leanne said, "I hope they cook their chicken properly here." There was a twinkle in her eye.

"What's that supposed to mean?" Fidel's was an attractive place and a very good restaurant, and he was surprised that Leanne would question it.

"Well," Leanne said, dipping a chip into the guacamole they had been served, "I just saw an article on contaminated chicken. You can get food poisoning from some kind of bacteria . . ."

"Salmonella," he said, and then saw that Leanne was looking down at the table in front of her, her long hair almost hiding the expression on her face. She was barely suppressing a laugh.

▽

It took another twenty minutes to get from Fidel's to Escondido. Heading inland, the scenery went from coastal eclectic to a uniformity of pink houses with rust-colored tile roofs and then became suddenly rural where the development stopped and the original flavor of San Diego County had been left intact. Then, as they got farther east, a new flavor, city-in-the-desert, took over.

"Do you know where you're going?" Leanne asked, after he had made several seemingly random turns and they wound up back on the main road they had come in on. She seemed amused.

He looked at his notes, which were scrawled on a pad that extended from a suction cup that adhered to the dash panel. "McAllister Road was supposed to run into Old Grove, but it didn't. Or at least, I didn't see it." He turned the car around and backtracked to McAllister. This time, by going straight instead of following the curve of the road, they wound up on Old Grove, winding uphill with a ravine to their right. A sudden left turn took them away from the ravine and into a private drive. Next to an open gate a sign said, "Welcome to the VALLEY VIEW RETIREMENT COMMUNITY."

"How old is this woman?" Leanne asked.

He slowed the Land Rover. The road had narrowed and now curved sharply uphill. "Our therapist friend's records show him to be fifty-five, and she's six years older, so . . ."

They pulled over a rise and suddenly came out on a plateau. To the left was a spectacular view of the lower hills and, beyond that, the sprawling valley city of Escondido. To the right was a long row of mobile homes, though mobility was not one of their features. Each qualified as a small house, with a patch of lawn and a garden or shrubbery separating it from the drive. Beyond the first row stretched other rows of identical homes.

A sign on the front door of the first structure said "MAN-AGER." He pulled up to the empty carport next to it. A long ramp gently inclined up to the door. He had just stepped on the ramp, Leanne behind him, when a voice came from behind a screen door.

"Can I help you?" It was an unfriendly voice, not very convincing in its offer to help. The screen door remained closed.

"Yes," he said. "We're looking for Phyllis Stanley. I understand she lives here."

"What do you want?" He could make out the outline of a person on the other side of the screen. A person sitting at the doorway.

"I'd like to ask her a few questions, that's all." He had the feeling that if this guardian of the community wanted to, she could prevent them from finding Art's sister, and that their whole trip would be in vain. He wondered if phoning ahead would have been the better way to go.

"What kind of questions?" The voice maintained its suspicious tone; the figure behind the screen didn't move.

"I'd rather take that up with Ms. Stanley."

The voice said, "She's not talking to anyone. Goodbye."

It was hot in the mid-afternoon sun. A faint tang of sage wafted in on the breeze off the hillside. He looked down the row of mobile homes. A large American flag stuck out from the roof of the fourth home, and a thin old man with a powder-blue hat and gardening gloves pruned a rosebush below the trellised porch. Maybe, he thought, the old man will help us.

As Ron turned, Leanne called out, "We're worried about her brother. We thought maybe she could help."

There was a silence that seemed almost universal. Even the old man had stopped moving. Then the screen door slowly opened.

"Who are you?" The woman sat in a wheelchair, an expensive motorized one with a small tray in front of her like the kind that folds out from an airline seat. Her left hand operated the controls on the armrest. There was a cigarette in her right hand and a large glass half full of amber liquid on the tray.

Ron introduced himself and Leanne. He didn't mention working for the *Times*.

"How do you know my brother?"

He had interviewed thousands of people in his career. Death row inmates, police, politicians, athletes, astronauts, and children, but somehow found himself unprepared for the question. As he searched for a response, Leanne said, "Your brother Jack tried to kill someone." Well, there it was.

"Take it to the police." The woman sat there, unmoving, her chair half in and half out of the doorway, the screen door propped open behind her by one of the large wheels. Her hair was steel-gray, swept back from her forehead and fastened severely in the back. Her features were well defined, eyes the same piercing blue that he remembered from seeing Art at the SOL meetings. Once, he thought, she might have been an attractive woman. Now she looked hardened by smoke and alcohol, by life and the desert; her skin was parched and dark, lined like a dry creek bed. A delicate gold crucifix hung from her neck.

Leanne said, "He pushed a young woman off a pier. At night."

Phyllis Stanley flinched, but contained it, tried to stop it, as though struck and too proud to acknowledge the insult. She reached for the glass and he saw, as she lifted it, that her hand shook. He wondered if it had been like that before Leanne had spoken.

The woman took her time draining the glass, staring out at him over the rim as she drank. When she was done, she took a long drag on the cigarette and then blew the smoke out so that it went upward and sideways from the corner of her mouth. "What do you want from me?"

"We'd like," he said, "to understand him. We think that he has harmed others. He needs to be stopped."

"I am not my brother's keeper." The woman sat erect in her chair, as unmoving and unblinking as a lizard on a hot rock.

"Maybe not now, but you certainly were back in North Vancouver." He watched the woman's eyes as they registered suspicion and flicked to Leanne, then back to him.

"So, you're police."

"No, but they're right behind us." He held her gaze.

The woman's hand went to her crucifix and caressed it. There was another long silence. It seemed as though measurements were being taken, history reviewed, values and costs weighed, all behind that penetrating stare, before everything seemed to click into place like a lock on a safe and a surrender was made. Phyllis Stanley breathed deeply, then looked down at the gold cross. "All right." She looked back up, then pushed a button on the console with her left hand and maneuvered the wheelchair down the ramp.

CHAPTER 53

⏁

Phyllis Stanley's wheelchair hummed slightly as it led the way across the gravel drive to a ten-foot-wide strip of lawn. Ron and Leanne followed until the woman stopped at the far edge of the grass strip; from here the hillside of scrub brush and mesquite dropped off steeply and the view looked out on a panorama of the valley.

"I have always feared this moment." The woman's hand, Ron noticed, still rested on the control console of the wheelchair, her finger poised over the forward button, as if on a whim she might launch herself over the edge and down into the gully below. Her fingers were long and slender, her hands surprisingly attractive. "Even God couldn't ease the fear."

"What have you been afraid of?" Leanne asked. She held Ron's hand as they stood at the woman's side.

"That my brother would finally cause trouble. Real trouble. Followed the Devil's path, I would have called it—" she paused "—when I had faith."

"What happened?" He felt the softness of Leanne's skin, the welcome kiss of a gusting breeze, and wondered if Phyllis Stanley had any people in her life, friendships, a partner.

"To my faith?" She reached down by her side and produced a pint bottle of Seagram's 7 and poured decisively into her cup. "I have faith in this now. It gives me solace, while it lasts, where otherwise there is none."

A hawk circled against the stark desert sky, drifting with a predatory economy of motion. It rose effortlessly on a thermal and then hung, suspended, before spiraling down into the gully. Leanne reached out and touched the woman's shoulder. "Tell us about your brother."

"Yes . . . my little brother." Phyllis Stanley nodded thoughtfully, and then went on. "You know, I tried to offer Jackie a good life, but too much had already happened. God knows, the boy never really had a chance. I couldn't help him, and he wouldn't seek salvation in the Church. He was too damaged by then."

Leanne pressed on. "How was he damaged?"

"Hah!" It was a bitter snort of a laugh. "When Jackie was first learning to walk, I remember our father slapping the back of his head. Knocked him down face first on the concrete driveway. He didn't stop doing that until he disappeared three years later."

"Disappeared?" He remembered Peter's report: "Father's whereabouts unknown."

"That's what he did." The woman took a deep draught of her whiskey. "He left the house drunk one night and never came back. We lived in fear of the day of his return for a year, and then our mother gave his clothes to charity. We had two glorious years after that. Best years of my life."

"He came back?" Leanne said. She would, he thought, have been a good interviewer, the way she could draw a story out of a reluctant witness.

"No. Much worse. Mother brought Harold home . . ." The woman drank again, then lit a cigarette. He noticed that her hands were steady as she lit the match and brought it to the tobacco. "And from then on, Harold ran that house like Stalin ran Russia."

"And he beat Jack?" Ron asked.

"Oh, no. He had a special fondness for little Jackie. A very special fondness."

He had a feeling about where this was going. "How did he show that fondness?"

"Oh, well, I didn't see it now, did I? But little Jackie always threw up after he came out of the room they were in, so you use your imagination." She cocked her head and squinted at them, the first time she had looked up since beginning her story.

"Where," Leanne asked, "was your mother while this was happening?"

"She was working. Somebody had to, and Harold wasn't about to any more than good old Dad ever had."

"Didn't your brother say anything to her?"

The woman looked back out at the valley. The gully below was already in shadow as the sun moved toward the sea behind them. "Oh, he tried, but she wouldn't have any of it. Told him he was a liar, that he was living in a fantasy world, and anyway, didn't he see he was better off not getting beat all the time." She shook her head, almost imperceptibly, as if inwardly facing something she refused to accept.

"How long did this go on?" Leanne asked.

"Almost two years." Phyllis Stanley pushed a button on her console and the wheelchair turned so that she faced him and Leanne. She picked up her glass, which was half full, and drained it quickly, then brushed at her upper lip with the tips of her fingers. "One day we took a day trip to Vancouver Island. A picnic at the park, looking out over the bay. Pretending to be a nice little family. Hah!" Another bitter snort, followed by a fit of coughing. "Mother and Harold were standing at the cliff, watching the boats. Jackie was . . . I don't know. He must have been nearby. I was reading a book. That's what I did. I read anything I could find that would take me away."

In the distance, a pair of military helicopters crossed the sky, heading north. Probably, he thought, to Camp Pendleton, just past Oceanside. He wondered why he had come, how this pathetic story was going to help him, what his motives had been. And why should Leanne be part of this? What had he expected to hear about a psychopath's childhood?

No one spoke for several minutes. The woman finished her cigarette and stubbed it out in a shot glass that served as an ashtray. Then she resumed her story. "I heard my mother shout, 'Hey!' and then scream, but when I looked up she wasn't there . . ." She stopped again.

"Yes . . .?" Leanne prompted.

"I heard Harold call Jackie a crazy little son of a bitch and start beating on him. I looked around, but mother had disappeared. I got up and walked over to where Jackie was lying on the ground and saw Harold go to the edge of the cliff and look down. He was shaking his head and looking all around. Then he just took off. He must have run all the way back to the ferry landing and caught the first boat back."

"Where was your mother?" he asked, even though he already knew the answer.

"She was on the rocks far below, half in the water. The Harbor Patrol took us home. A week later the RCMP picked up Harold trying to cross into Washington state. He tried to convince them that Jackie had pushed our mother, but they weren't having any of it."

"What happened to him?" he asked.

"He went to prison. They gave him twenty-five years, but he got killed after two. Someone stabbed him in the neck with a homemade knife."

Leanne said, "So then it was just the two of you."

"That's right." The woman wheeled the chair around and headed back toward her home. As they crossed the drive she said, "I gave the next five years of my life trying to make it right for that boy, but it wasn't enough." When she reached the bottom of the ramp leading to her front door, she turned to face them. "That's all. I haven't seen him in years. He used to visit, send money once in a while. It helped." She nodded, as if in dismissal, and turned to negotiate the ramp.

"Do you know where he is now?" He had a feeling she had left something out.

Phyllis Stanley pressed the button that took her wheelchair to the doorway of her mobile home and then turned so she could back in through the threshold. She disappeared into the mobile home for a moment. When she returned she leaned down and passed him a photograph and a folded piece of paper.

Ron looked at the photo and showed it to Leanne. It was a faded black-and-white of two children, a boy and a girl in what looked to be a backyard. Between them stood a woman in her mid twenties. Tall, slender, attractive, and blond.

Leanne studied the photograph and handed it back to the older woman.

"He's staying with some people in Brentwood. That's the number he left." She guided the wheelchair backward again, pushing the door open behind her.

"Miss Stanley?" Leanne called out.

"Yes?"

"I don't mean to get too personal, but would you tell us how you came to be . . . um . . . how you hurt yourself?"

She looked down at them, harsh and distant as when their visit had begun, and said, "I fell."

CHAPTER 54

When Jeff arrived at Holly's around ten that evening, his first thought was that she looked pretty frayed at the edges. The first time he had seen her, that night at the SOL meeting, Holly, dressed in faded blue jeans and a simple white sleeveless blouse, had looked terrific. Beautiful, unattainable, the kind of girl he could only think about and desire from a distance. The next time, she had been dripping wet in her clothes, fresh from the Malibu surf, grim and pale, although on the following day she had put it back together and looked great again.

This time, Holly had that look he knew so well; he had seen it too many times before in the mirror—the no-sleep, running on coffee and nerves and whatever-else-it-takes look. When she answered the door, wearing cutoff jeans and an Elton John tee shirt, she didn't even say hello; she motioned him in, leaned out the doorway and looked up the stairway immediately on the right and down the hallway beyond it. Then she ducked back in and locked the deadbolt that he had put in a few days before.

"Look at this. You won't believe it," Holly said. There were clothes all over the floor of the hallway, mainly coats and jackets. The hall closet, just to the right of the front door, was open, a bare bulb illuminating its interior. The closet ceiling sloped up from left to right, conforming to the stairway outside. On the floor inside the closet, the carpet had been ripped up and peeled back, exposing a trap door.

"Pull it up," Holly said.

He looked at her questioningly, uncomfortable with her intensity, the nervous edge to her command. He squatted at the entrance to the closet and lifted the loose plywood square from the floor.

About two and a half feet down was hard-packed dirt. He saw footprints in the dusty surface immediately below. To the right, leading into the darkness of the crawlspace, were other marks, like tracks—the kind, he thought, that someone would make if they were crawling on hands and knees.

He glanced over his shoulder at Holly. "What does this mean to you?"

"This is how he gets in," she said.

"Who?"

"Art. How many psychotics do you think I know?"

He stifled a grin as he realized that he didn't have an answer for that question. For all he knew, she was a living magnet for pathological nut cases. "Did you rip up the carpeting, or was it already loose?" He indicated the row of carpet tacks sticking out of the bottom of the fabric where it lay peeled back from the hatch.

"I had to pull it up," Holly admitted.

"Why did you do that?"

"Because, goddammit, he was in there half the night and then disappeared. I told you, when I opened the door he was gone. What do you think we've got here, fucking Houdini?" She almost shrieked this last, on the cusp between anger and hysteria.

"Let's go sit down and talk about this calmly, can we?" He didn't wait for an answer; he took Holly's hand and led her to the living room. She followed docilely and sat on the sofa. There was a flashlight on the coffee table.

She seemed subdued for the moment. He went to the kitchen and brought back two glasses of soda. "Look," he said, sitting down next to Holly, "you've got to admit that this is pretty far-fetched. I mean, even if there's a way into the crawlspace from outside, it's not very likely that anyone, even Jack Stanley, would be—" he groped for words "—*stalking* you, for Christ's sake."

"Listen to this." Holly turned and knocked on the living room wall behind her. It produced a hollow sound. "What do you suppose is on the other side?"

"I have no idea," he said. He pictured the configuration of the building; half of the wall behind the sofa was also the right-hand wall of the hall closet. She had knocked beyond the end of the closet. Holly's kitchen extended from the far end of the living room, and the two bedrooms were beyond the opposite living room wall. "Maybe it's part of your neighbor's apartment."

"No," Holly said. "I've been over there. When they knock on the wall facing this direction, you can't hear it from here. There's something in between. It's where he stays and listens to me."

"Really!" Christ, she was over the edge. He remembered looking out his apartment window once at five in the morning, all the lights turned off, staring into the parking lot across the street at what he was convinced were two people having sex on the ground. When the sun came up all that was there were two parallel concrete tire stops, painted white. In the dark he had been convinced of what they were, that they were moving, writhing, passionate and insane in their indifference to their exposure. "Excuse me," he said, and he got up to go to the bathroom.

He looked into the mirror for a moment and then rubbed the heels of his hands against his eyes and the bridge of his nose. What was going on here? This girl had flipped—what did she want from him? Looking again at his reflection, he combed his hair back with his fingers. His glance fell to the counter.

An array of small orange plastic containers lined the tile where it met the wall. He picked up the nearest one and read the label. Tegretol. There were only a few tablets left. The next vial was half full and read, "Lunesta. Take one tablet at bedtime." He checked the other two bottles. One contained Xanax. Hard to get, but better than Valium. The last vial was marked "Adderall" and was nearly full. Something he had read about but never tried. It was meant to calm down hyperactive children, but was supposed to have an opposite, stimulant effect on non-afflicted adults. He wondered how many Holly had taken. Depending on when she had started, it could definitely account for her behavior now.

He replaced the bottles and returned to the living room. Holly was still sitting on the sofa, staring out across the room, alert, as though listening for a sound she was expecting to hear repeated.

"Holly—" She turned and focused on him, surprised. "How long since the last time you slept?"

"I don't know. Sunday night, I slept at Ron's house."

"That was Saturday. Three nights ago."

"I know. I slept here Sunday night. Then Monday morning . . ." She hesitated, then continued. "You know, I told you, I had a seizure. I woke up from that in the middle of the afternoon."

"Yesterday?"

"Yeah, yesterday. Why?"

"You're taking drugs." He watched her face, feeling sorry for her, the way the chemicals were affecting her.

"What's that got to do with anything?"

"It could have a lot to do with the way you're seeing things."

"You think I'm seeing things?" She said this defiantly, almost amused, as if she had some proof to show him that would validate her whole paranoid theory.

"I didn't mean that," he said, exasperated. "I'm talking about the way you're seeing . . . Oh, the hell with it. Look, why are you taking all that stuff?"

Holly looked down at her hands in her lap. Her nails, he noticed, were bitten short. She took a deep breath, which turned into a yawn, then placed her hand over her eyes for a moment. When she looked at him again, she seemed suddenly exhausted.

"The Tegretol keeps me from having seizures. I stopped taking it when I met Art. That's one of the reasons I kept listening to him; I didn't have any seizures during the time I knew him."

"What about the other stuff?"

"The anti-convulsant acts as a depressant. It makes me so lethargic, I can't do anything. So one doctor prescribed the Adderall—it's a stimulant mixed. It worked pretty well but sometimes it would last too long and I couldn't get to sleep."

"So you got the Lunesta." He could understand the logic of it perfectly. Juggling chemicals, just trying to feel normal.

"Right. They would knock me out. Then I told another doctor what I was doing. He was shocked, and told me to throw away the uppers and downers. He prescribed the Xanax for anxiety."

"So which of these have you been taking?" he asked.

"All of them." He could see the desperation in her eyes. "I couldn't just go to sleep. I tried, but God! He was listening to me. Watching me, for all I know." She stood, picking up the flashlight from the table. "Come with me. I've got something else to show you."

He followed her down the hallway and out the front door. They turned right and walked through the outside hall, past the neighbor's apartment and the one beyond that, then down a few stairs.

The stairs led out to the carport. Holly turned right and walked the width of one of the parking slots and then led him through an open door. They were in a laundry room; he could tell by the smell and the boxlike outlines of the machines. Holly turned on the light and guided him diagonally across the room to the far corner where two large dryers were stacked.

"Look." She pointed at the cinderblock wall behind the dryers. The machines were set so that their backs were close to the wall, but were offset by several feet from the corner.

Holly pointed the beam from the flashlight into the recess and played it across a large rectangle of particleboard set against the wall, extending from the corner to somewhere behind the lower dryer. "Move that aside."

He slid the particleboard to the right and looked down at a hole in the wall where six cinderblocks were missing. At his feet, the dirt floor of the crawlspace met the concrete floor of the laundry room. In the circle of the flashlight beam, a footprint, and beyond, the same impressions as in Holly's closet.

"I know how crazy it sounds," Holly said from behind him. "But how does it look?"

"It's pretty spooky, I'll give you that." Still, the crawl space, and the access, had been there since the place was built—probably fifty years ago—and the marks could have been left by anyone. An exterminator looking for termites, maybe. *Yeah, right*, he thought.

"Where are you going?" Holly asked, following him around to the driveway and out toward the street.

"I want to get something from my car."

At the curb, he opened the Audi and groped in the glove compartment. He felt the familiar handle of a Buck knife, pulled it out, and locked the car.

Back in the apartment, he stepped into the closet and down into the crawl space. The floor was now level with his thighs. Turning to his right, he pulled out the Buck knife and stabbed it into the wall. The hard steel point bit deeply into the soft material.

"What in God's name are you doing?" Holly asked.

"Well—" he yanked down on the knife handle and then sawed briefly. "Now you've got me curious about what's behind your living room. Don't you want to know?"

She didn't say anything. He stabbed the knife into the wall again, this time about two inches to the left of the first cut, and again sawed downward. Finally, connecting the tops and bottoms of the incisions, he gouged out a square of the drywall.

"Pass me the flashlight, would you?" Holly handed it down to him. He pointed the beam into the opening, but could see nothing. Putting the flashlight down, he made another hole about four inches below the first one.

Now he put the flashlight flush to the wall against the lower hole and his eye to the upper one. About seven feet away he saw two-by-four framing outlining large areas of unfinished particleboard; it was the back of the living room wall Holly had knocked on earlier. He pointed the flashlight to the left. About ten feet away he could see another wall.

"What do you see? There's a space behind the wall, isn't there?" Holly knelt on the floor next to the hatch.

"You're right. There's a whole goddamn room there. It's wasted space under the stairway and the upper landing." He pointed the flashlight downward. The wooden framework extended down into the ground, while the particleboard ended flush with the flooring. Below it, the dirt surface extended far beyond the flashlight's reach.

He handed Holly the flashlight and said, "Shine this down through the hatch in the direction I'm facing."

Looking downward through the lower hole, he saw the beam cross the space and disappear into the gloom. "Point it downward," he said, his forehead to the wall.

"Stop! Back up a little." He couldn't believe what he saw. "Now sweep slowly to my left."

Dazed, he stared at the dirt. Beer bottles littered the ground. A larger bottle stood upright, still partially full.

"What is it? What do you see?" The beam wavered as Holly's hand shook.

"Give me back the flashlight." He took it and ducked down under the floor, crawled through a narrow space between two-by-fours, and stood up in the room that Holly had predicted, that he had so confidently denied. There was still a chance, he thought, to disprove the whole fantasy, to find a reasonable explanation—that the bottles were left over from contractors doing structural repair, something that made sense.

He bent down and aimed the light at one of the beer bottles, unsurprised to read the familiar Moosehead label. With resignation, he swung the beam around to illuminate the distinctive square body and gold label of the Bushmills bottle.

CHAPTER 55

�◇

The place was on fire.

Tony looked out into the audience, grinning, his Fender Precision bass hanging low over his belt, hands in the air as the crowd cheered and whistled. People were screaming, "More!" but the manager had told them to cut it at one o'clock and their second encore had already taken them ten minutes past that.

Thursday night at the Roxy, midnight show, and a crowd that knew how to party: rock critics that knew the night was young, record company guys that liked to burn it until dawn, dealers and dealmakers and other musicians, checking out what's hot. No lames like at the early shows, the ones where the wannabees and the hasbeens cranked out their over-rehearsed noise.

Tonight it was Tony that was hot. Tony and his band had just ripped through the best set of their lives and now, staring into the spotlights, he was searching for the payoff.

It was the women that made the evening interesting. Especially the women at the Roxy on a late Thursday night. The models, the party girls, the coke whores, the waitresses from the restaurants, the hot ones that the house let in free.

Later, after packing their gear into the truck and getting their share of the draw from the club manager, the band went next door to the Rainbow for pizza and whiskey and beer and whatever else presented itself. They scored a booth in the far corner of the back room, where it was dark and private but not so dark and private that they couldn't be noticed.

By the time their pizza arrived, at least a dozen people had stopped by the table to tell him and the band how good the show had been. Three of them, party girls from the Valley, he figured, were now wedged into the booth, picking at the pizza and ordering drinks as though they were intimates of the band members. He wasn't interested; there was too much possibility in the air.

It was on the way up the narrow stairs to the restroom that he saw what he wanted to see. A wild tangle of dark hair, high, sharp cheekbones under brown eyes that laughed all by themselves, the almost boyish body with the round little ass that he had watched from the Roxy stage. She hadn't cared about anything or anybody. Just the dancing, the music—his music. She had danced in the aisles, danced on her chair, danced on a table and clapped her hands to the beat high above her head, tossing her crazy hair out of her face, completely on fire.

Now she was coming down the stairs, swiping the back of her hand across one nostril and then the other.

"Hey!" she said, and she put her hand on his wrist. "You were fucking great." And then just looked at him, her mouth curved with a sly humor. Standing two steps above him, she was eye to eye with him. That's fine, he thought. He liked them small.

A vial materialized in her hand; she tapped it twice on his wrist and motioned with her head toward the top landing. There was something aggressive, almost pugnacious, in the set of her jaw. Her nose was slightly off, perhaps broken and never set properly.

In the men's room, he set his back to the door so they could be alone, and opened the vial. He poked into it with the key to his van and put the white powder to his lips, inhaling gently through his mouth. A subtle medicinal aroma filled his mouth as the powder dissolved instantly. He knew that flavor. In a city of rip-offs and ridiculously diluted street drugs, this girl had the best coke he had seen in years. She smiled up at him with perfect white teeth. Using the key again, he helped himself to a couple of healthy snorts, then capped the vial and held it out to the girl.

"I'm Lilah." She took the vial and then let her hand fall to the buckle of his belt, which she hooked with her index finger.

She gave a couple of little tugs and, with the coke just freezing the back of his head, he thought, *Yeah, cool, I'll go for some right here.* But instead, she said, "Let's go," and tugged his belt again, this time pulling him away from the door, which opened behind him. He realized he had heard knocking without even registering it.

▽

They stopped at the market for some Wild Turkey and ice cream. The place was so bright he put on his sunglasses, but Lilah careened around the place like a child at a playground. She wore skintight pants in a leopard-skin print and a halter top and pointy silver flats.

When they met at the check stand, he put his bottle of Wild Turkey on the counter and watched as Lilah removed items from the basket she had filled. Espresso ice cream, lemon sherbet, two six-packs of cherry soda, a pack of scouring pads, a can of butane cigarette-lighter refill, baking soda, and a bottle of Courvoisier.

Starting up the van, he said, "What's all that stuff about?"

"Oh, it's stuff for Richard, so he doesn't run out."

"Who's Richard?" The whole way from Hollywood, there hadn't been any mention of a Richard, or anyone else for that matter, that might turn up at her place.

"Oh, Richard's great. You'll like him." She waved her hand in the air, vague and dismissive. She tipped some powder from the vial onto her hand and it placed it under his nose. "This came from Richard."

He decided that Richard's presence might not be such a bad thing after all. He inhaled sharply and turned out of the market parking lot and up Montana to where Lilah said she lived.

He stood in the hallway as Lilah unlocked the door to her apartment. She opened it and then, holding the bag of groceries, she turned and pushed the door hard with her ass. It had a large crack emanating from an indentation at about hip level—right where a foot would go if you were pissed off enough, he thought. There were cracks in the doorjamb as well, and the door popped open on Lilah's third try.

From the hallway, he saw a perfectly normal, orderly living room. A sofa, a couple of chairs, a television set in a console. Windows at the far end looking out at trees and a neighboring apartment building. To his right in the small kitchen stood a man in boxer shorts and an unbuttoned Hawaiian shirt, frozen in place with his mouth and eyes seemingly stuck open. In his hand was a long glass vial full of liquid.

"Richard, darling, we didn't mean to startle you." Lilah put the groceries on the counter and gently took the vial from Richard. Tony watched as she removed the cap and poured off most of the liquid, leaving only an inch at the bottom and something that looked like a congealing blob of oil. She pulled a bottle of Perrier from the refrigerator, popped the plastic cap from it, and poured the cold mineral water into the vial. The mass in the vial seemed to harden and lose its translucent quality, suddenly becoming a pale white rock almost an inch in diameter, which Lilah removed and placed on a coffee filter. Richard, having come out of his paralysis, picked up a hair dryer that was lined up among an arsenal of accessories between the sink and the stove and commenced to blow hot air at the rock in the filter.

"Hey, close the fuckin' door, okay?" Richard sounded like he was out of practice talking, as if some serious effort were required just to summon and assemble words. A sparse fringe of hair was matted to his head, wet with a perspiration that covered his face and chest with a sheen. He nodded to Tony as Lilah introduced them, his mouth still hanging open.

Tony pulled the Wild Turkey from the bag on the counter and was about to ask Lilah for a glass, but thought better of it and, removing the cap, took a good hard pull from the bottle. Lilah opened the Courvoisier and half-filled two large snifters, which she then placed on the counter. As she put away the other contents from the grocery bag, Richard scooped the white rock from the coffee filter and said, "How about your room?"

Lilah said, "Fine," and put the ice cream in the freezer. "Hey, you can't keep leaving the flame burning on the stove."

Richard didn't appear to have heard; he was already out of the kitchen, moving toward the end of the hallway—toward, Tony presumed, Lilah's bedroom—holding the rock out in front of him as he walked. He held it between his thumb and index finger at about chin level, his head tilted back, seeming to appraise it as he disappeared from view.

Lilah carried the drinks and some of the items she had bought at the market. Tony followed her, carrying the two bottles. The evening had looked so promising; it still had potential, but he had always hated freebasers. Every time he had seen people smoke cocaine, it seemed that they did it obsessively and to the exclusion of all other activity: sex, eating, bathing, conversation.

Richard was sitting on the edge of a king-size bed in Lilah's room, an elaborate glass pipe in his hands. A blue flame hissed out of a butane torch directly onto a white chip that was already melting into a tangle of copper strands—a piece of the scouring pad that Lilah had bought. Suddenly the bulb of the pipe, which was about the size of a tennis ball, filled with a thick white smoke. He watched as the smoke streamed up the glass stem, Richard staring intently at the tip of the flame as he inhaled.

Holding his breath, Richard handed the pipe and the torch to Lilah, who had put the drinks on a bedside stand and pulled Tony to the center of the bed. She took a new chip from a silver dish on the bed, placed it on the wire mesh, and fired it up. When she was through, she offered the pipe to Tony.

"No, thanks. If you're offering, though, I wouldn't mind having some for my nose." On the dresser against the wall opposite the end of the bed, a shining white slab of coke the size of a telephone book sat on a large sheet of blue plastic wrapping.

Lilah passed the glass pipe back to Richard, grinning while she held the smoke in. Then, putting her hand behind Tony's neck, she drew him to her, brought their mouths together, opened soft lips, ran her fingers up through his hair, let her other hand drop to his thigh and slide upward, and filled his lungs with the harsh, sweet smoke.

The next time the pipe came his way, he accepted it.

CHAPTER 56

☇

"Would you please talk to me? What's going on?" Holly was speaking through one of the holes Jeff had gouged in the wall. Startled, he brought the flashlight up and saw her pull away.

"Go pack. We have to get out of here." Suddenly he wanted to be far from this place. Crouching low, he swept the flashlight beam across the entire underside of the building, imagining a deranged Doctor Jack Stanley crawling toward him in the dirt.

When he emerged from the hole in the closet floor, Holly was standing in the hallway, hugging herself as though she were cold.

"What's the matter?" he asked, then realized it was a ridiculous question.

"I was hoping . . ." She faltered.

"What?" He was impatient. It was time to get out of here.

"I think that I really wanted you to prove that I was crazy, delusional. That none of this was really happening." A tear streaked down her cheek; she wiped it away with the back of her hand. "I mean, I don't want to be crazy, but this"—she gestured toward the closet floor—"is a pretty crummy reality."

"One thing . . ." he said.

"What's that?"

"Can you leave the pills behind?"

She hesitated, eyes wide and moist, then nodded.

Ten minutes later they emerged from the apartment, Jeff carrying a suitcase that Holly had packed in a dazed silence. She stepped into the carport and looked apprehensively at the door to the laundry room; to its left, the windows were ominously dark.

He placed the suitcase in the trunk of the BMW and said, "Look, are you okay to drive? Maybe we should go in one car . . ."

Holly faced him in the darkness, put a hand out and touched his arm, left it there. "Thank you for helping me. I'll be all right."

Driving up Fairfax, watching his rear-view mirror to make sure that he didn't lose her, he wondered if, by taking Holly from her apartment, he had blown a good chance at catching Jack Stanley. Maybe they should have turned out the lights and waited for him to return, to burrow under the goddamned building and set up camp on the other side of Holly's living room. He thought of his sister Marilyn and imagined firing the Walther into the wall, firing into the closet door, emptying the clip and then doing it again. He started to play it over again in his mind but something stopped him. It was useless, he realized. Old thinking, part of the world he had left behind. This was the best course, to move away from insanity and toward the sanctuary he had been given, and to bring Holly along.

The canyon air was cool and clean when they left their cars on the gravel drive in front of Ron's home. The porch was lit, but the house inside was entirely dark. The Land Rover was gone.

He carried the suitcase into his room, which he had offered to let Holly use. He would sleep on the sofa in the living room. When he put the suitcase down, he asked Holly how she felt.

"I think I'm ready to fall asleep." She smiled for the first time that night. "In a New York minute."

"Is there anything you need?"

"Yes." She looked at him, pretty now in the soft light from the bedside lamp. She put her hand out and touched his arm like she had done earlier. "Would you stay here and just hold me?"

CHAPTER 57

☟

It was Wednesday afternoon, and Doctor Jack Stanley's rage simmered like sauce in a pot. Every now and then a new bubble of anger rose to the surface. It was infuriating to have to give up a perfectly good name. He had had a good run as Art Bradley, MFCC, and co-founder of SOL. Now that was irretrievably gone. And now the girl was gone.

"Hey, man, you want a hit?" It was the idiot with the glass pipe, exhaling a huge plume of chemical smoke in Lilah's kitchen as he spoke.

"No, Richard, I don't, thank you." Almost time to stop being nice. "When do you suppose Lilah and Tony will come out?" They had been in the back room—Lilah's bedroom—for hours now. Occasionally, noises from Lilah punctuated the interminable rhythmic hammering of the headboard against the wall.

Richard coughed and fell back against the refrigerator, then shuffled out of the kitchen and disappeared through the hallway without replying.

He had tolerated this zoo, as he thought of it, since early Sunday morning, shortly after the debacle at the Malibu pier. He had gone home, glad that Bobbi was in Portland lecturing, and packed a suitcase. When he appeared at the Brentwood apartment, Lilah had opened the door and thrown her arms around him, crying out, "Dahling," and inviting him in. Nobody, himself included, had slept during the next three days, and the moronic behavior of Lilah and her two friends was wearing thin.

He went to the stereo and inserted the Miles Davis CD into the deck, turning it on loud. Time to clean house. The Art Bradley charade was crumbling beyond repair. He had been seen on the pier, the girl was alive, and Joanie, the fool, could put him in line for lethal injection. Worse, Jeff Fenner and Lilah linked him with his past.

He finished his drink and came to a decision. He went out of the apartment and down the hallway. The elevator took him to the underground parking, where the Jag was safely hidden from general view. He took the tire iron from the Jag's trunk and wrapped it in an old red towel he kept over the spare wheel.

When he got back to the apartment, the music had been turned off. He saw Richard sitting on the sofa at the end of the living room, the one area that Jack had staked out as his own. He said, "I'm sure I've asked you to sit somewhere else . . ." for the hundredth time. The mindlessness of it.

"Hey Doc, no reason to get uncivilized." The man sat there in his jockey shorts, lighting a butane torch and adjusting the flame. "I'll get up in a minute." He picked up the glass pipe from the coffee table and, putting it to his lips, aimed the hissing blue flame into the blackened bowl. The cocaine rock ignited with a sizzling sound. "By the way, man—" Richard wheezed—he was holding his breath and puffs of smoke escaped with each word "—your music sucks."

He walked across the living room, flicking the music back on and turning it up as he passed the console. The tire iron had a nice heft to it—he held it at his side by the end that curved back in a U shape. He had never killed a male before. Not directly, anyway, he thought, reflecting that he had always relished the image of his stepfather with a prison shank sticking out of the side of his neck.

Richard sucked mightily at the pipe, his chest heaving as he suppressed the urge to cough, holding it in, eyes intent on the flame vaporizing the bubbling white rock. Jack lifted the metal bar and brought it down on the shiny bald top of the man's head. *There. That was easy.* The torch and the hot pipe fell into Richard's lap, the flame still hissing as it bit into flesh. He let the towel fall to the ground and struck again, methodically, until it was clear that the job was completed.

The torch, its flame extinguished, lay on the sofa next to the glass pipe. He picked both items up, flipped over the sofa cushion so that the bloody side couldn't be seen, then walked to the kitchen and threw the drug paraphernalia in the trash.

There were two bottles of Bushmills left in the refrigerator, plus a beer and a fifth of Jack Daniel's, purchased special for tonight's occasion. He popped the top off the beer and placed the other bottles in a shopping bag, which he left on the counter at the end closest to the front door.

He pulled the body into the spare bedroom, stuffed it into the closet, and closed the sliding door. Next to a scale on the dresser was Richard's massive block of cocaine: he broke off a corner and placed it in a small zip-lock baggy.

Time to get the show on the road.

CHAPTER 58

At three-thirty on a hot summer Wednesday afternoon, lying on her back with her feet in the air and Tony inside her, Lilah O'Hare had a moment of clarity. She realized that Tony didn't care about her, that he couldn't care about her, or anyone else for that matter. In that instant, as she perceived the full extent of his obtuse selfishness, she saw with equal clarity the extent of the madness that was her life: she had flirted with insanity, prison, and death for too long, and now one or more were imminent.

Tony must have sensed something, for he suddenly ceased his mad, sweaty thrusting and looked down at her. "What's with you?" His voice accusing, as though she had taken something belonging to him.

She didn't have an answer ready, so she said, "I need to go to the bathroom."

"Jesus Christ," Tony said. "You can't stop, just like that," and withdrew from her, shaking his head.

She got up and walked toward the bathroom, looking back once to see Tony on the bed, staring sullenly at the wall. Music blared abruptly from the living room—Doctor Jack's weird old jazz.

She closed the door and sat on the toilet, putting her elbows on her knees and resting her forehead against the heels of her hands. If she had one more drug her head would explode; one more drink and she would surely be sick. And yet she felt oddly clearheaded, sober in spite of the toxic condition of her metabolism. She liked the feeling. The music stopped and she breathed deeply in the silence.

"Hey!" It was Tony, yelling from the bed.

"I'll be right out." She kept breathing deeply. Moments went by and it was almost possible to forget the dread she had felt.

"Hey!" Louder this time. "You wouldn't be holding out on me now, would you?" Tony had run out of coke and hit a wall trying to get Richard to extend his tab. He was crashing now, which was when he seemed to get meanest.

Lilah opened the door and stepped back into the bedroom. "No, Tony, for Christ's sake, I'm not holding out on you." He sat against the headboard, head tilted back as he drained his bottle of Wild Turkey.

The music came on again, louder than before. Tony rolled his eyes. "Oh, great. The hip hypnotist is really swingin' now." He put the empty bottle down and glared at her. "Okay, what have you got, you sneaky little bitch? Where's the vial?" He pushed himself up off the bed and stepped toward her.

"There is no vial." She wanted to tell him how she felt, that they were better off without the stuff, that they could just walk away, maybe go to one of those meetings or something. "Really, Tony. If you want to know the truth . . ."

"The truth?" Tony leered. "If I wanna know the truth? You've never told the truth in your life." He reached out and grabbed Lilah by the throat, pushing her against the wall. "You wouldn't know the fucking truth if it was vibrating in your ass."

Tony was hurting her now, his fingers tight on her throat. Suddenly, he pulled her toward him and then slammed her head into the wall. He did it again, and then a third time. There was a look in Tony's eyes that told Lilah he wasn't going to stop.

"Hey!" She said it as a command, focusing her anger into it, and Tony hesitated. "If I tell you where it is, will you stop this?"

He let go of her throat and shook his head slowly in exasperation. "You are so fucking predictable."

She giggled and said, "Come here. I'll whisper it to you."

When Tony bent and turned his head, she reached up and put her face next to his. She opened her mouth and said, "It's in the—" and bit down hard on the soft part of his ear. She bit until the skin gave with a little pop, then put her knee between his legs and hooked her foot around the back of his knee. As Tony jerked back, she pushed.

A piece of dead meat was in her mouth, rubbery and smooth. She spat it down at Tony, who was lying on the floor holding his hand to the side of his head. Something warm and wet trickled over her lip and down to her chin.

There was a knock at the door. She opened it, relieved to see Doctor Jack. He smiled pleasantly, leaned in slightly to get a clearer view of Tony naked on the floor, and said, "My, my. Aren't we getting a little bit carried away?"

Tony glared at him and said, "Get the fuck out of here, you old quack." Still holding his ear, he propped himself up on one elbow, retrieved the earlobe from his chest, and maneuvered into a standing position. Lilah backed away a step. Tony took his hand from his ear and looked at the blood running from his palm down his forearm. "You're dead, you crazy little bitch."

"Now children, violence won't settle anything." Doctor Jack was still smiling. "But this might . . ." She saw him bring forward one of his hands, which had been behind his back, and produce a plastic baggie of with a golf ball-size chunk of cocaine in it. He held it up, dangling from thumb and forefinger, invitingly toward Tony and said, "Lilah, would you kindly excuse us for a moment?"

"Sure, Jack." She was only too glad to get Tony out of the room.

She watched as Doctor Jack made way for Tony to pass through the doorway. She looked at Tony's naked ass and solid, muscular body as he turned into the spare bedroom. Doctor Jack followed, one hand still holding the baggie, the other hidden by his side. Holding something.

She was about to turn back to the bathroom, wash the blood off her face, maybe even shower if Tony would leave her alone long enough, when she heard the sound. It pierced right through the music, a *crack!* of impact, a sound she had never heard anything quite like before. A nightmare sound. And again. And again.

Frozen, she suddenly knew what the sound was, realized what Doctor Jack had been holding. *Unbelievable,* she thought, but saw that at a deeper level she had always known he was crazy enough to do this, that the dread she had felt was legitimate, and that insanity and death were present.

She turned to the bedside table and picked up the phone, stabbing at the buttons to reach 911. The first ring had just begun when she turned to see Doctor Jack in the room, his arm raised.

The first blow crashed down on her arm, causing her to drop the phone, and then grazed her cheekbone. Dazed, as if only able to move in slow motion like in a frustrating dream, she tried to protect herself but felt the second blow strike her forehead. She fell to the floor, oddly aware of being struck several times more but unable to feel it. Unable, for that matter, to feel anything, but still awake. Awake enough to sense Doctor Jack's closeness as he bent over her, rolled her aside, and retrieved the phone from the floor. Awake enough to hear the dial tone and the ringing; to hear him say, "Joanie? Good, you're in. I thought I'd stop by on my way out of town. I've got a little something for you."

CHAPTER 59

B y late Wednesday afternoon the heat had become
intense, making Jeff want to go home, rinse off in a
cool shower and lie down somewhere in the shade, maybe
even nap. The Santa Ana winds had kicked up again and the
darkroom, though cooler by far than outside, lacked air conditioning. His hands were dry and smelly from the chemicals in the
trays, and in the close, still air he had to fight through his lethargy
to clean up the lab so he could be finished for the day.

He had fallen asleep almost immediately the night before,
still dressed, cupped up to Holly, aware of his warm breath on
the back of her neck. Some time later he had awakened to Holly's hand on his skin, caressing his chest, down over his stomach,
hinting with a gentle push at the button of his jeans. They had
made love slowly in the light of a big rising moon and then fallen
asleep as the night air moved in softly through the window and
dried the perspiration from their bodies.

He left Holly sleeping when he got up that morning, and
wrote a note to her and another to Ron. Now, at five fifteen, driving back from the lab in Silverlake, he wondered who would be
there to greet him: he looked forward to seeing Holly, touching
her, but was apprehensive about what Ron's reaction to her presence might be.

Driving up Sunset Boulevard, he saw a dirty brown haze in
the sky, becoming darker somewhere over beyond the hills to
his right. It was the burning season in California, and the Santa

Monica Mountains, already ripe for fire after the long dry summer, were primed by the Santa Ana conditions. Somewhere up by
Mulholland, he thought, people were piling their belongings into
cars. The optimists would wet down their roofs and hang tight.

It was refreshingly cool in the house, which was quiet and
empty. On the kitchen table there were two messages. The first
was from Holly, telling him thanks, that she had gone to swim at
the gym, not to worry, she would be back at seven. And that she
had talked to Ron, and what a nice man he was. The second was
from Ron, saying, "Time for a pow-wow. Seven thirty, at Nick's.
The four of us."

He showered and dried off, then folded a towel on his pillow
and lay down, covering himself with a second towel. Within minutes he dozed off. In a dream he spilled a glass of whiskey, which
spread across a canyon and caught fire. Fingertips touched his
forehead and brushed back through his hair; he opened his eyes
to see Holly sitting on the bed looking down at him.

He tried to pull her to him, but she laughed and shook her
head and pulled him up to a sitting position instead. "We're supposed to meet Ron in twenty minutes."

"Jesus, it's past seven already?" He stood up, wrapping the
towel at his waist, surprised at his new instinct for modesty. "It
seems like I was only asleep for a minute. I was having this crazy
dream . . ." He shook his head and went to the dresser, choosing
fresh jeans and a navy blue golf shirt.

"I'll drive," Holly said. "How far is it to Nick's?"

"We can get there on time if we leave now." He dressed,
grabbed his wallet and keys, and ran a comb through his hair.

He liked sitting in the BMW, with its nice leather seats and
solid feel, the top down and the wind rushing by so they had to
talk loud. The smell of smoke was in the air now, and the pall had
spread throughout the dusky evening sky. For the first time, he
heard the distant wail of sirens, the long, low blare of a fire-truck
horn.

"What's going on, do you know?" He realized he was shouting.

Holly brought up the windows, which made it relatively quiet in the car, with only the air rushing overhead to intrude on conversation. "The radio said it's Nichols Canyon, up by Mulholland. And Thousand Oaks is out of control. I hope it's not as bad as a few years ago."

"Yeah, no kidding."

At the restaurant, they found Ron and Leanne seated at a corner table, speaking with a waiter, who wrote something on a pad and walked away.

"We took the liberty of ordering for you," Ron said.

"Hot sauce on the side," Leanne added, grinning at Jeff.

He introduced Holly to Leanne as they took their seats. He was glad that they could meet; he had a feeling it would be good for Holly to know this woman.

"It smells so good in here. What do they have?" Holly unfolded her napkin and placed it on her lap.

"I'd label it upscale hippy health food," Ron said.

"With Americanized East Indian curry dishes," Leanne added.

"And a killer hot sauce." Jeff sipped at his water. A paper-thin slice of lemon floating above the ice gave it a sweet fragrance.

They made small talk until dinner arrived, touching on the fires, the weather, upcoming elections, laughing as they tried to find music that all of them had in common.

"Elton John," Holly offered. Jeff and Leanne raised their hands, but Ron shook his head. "How about Horace Silver?" he asked.

"Who?" Holly and Jeff replied in unison. They finally all agreed on Ray Charles. "Yeah, the album with 'Georgia On My Mind,'" Jeff said.

"Right," Ron chimed in. "And 'Ruby.'"

When the food came, Holly said, "This looks wonderful." He told her to watch out for the hot sauce and then watched in horror as she poured the evil brown liquid liberally over her rice and ate a spoonful of the drenched mixture. Even Ron and Leanne watched in silent anticipation as Holly chewed.

Holly swallowed, intent on her plate, and began to lift her next bite to her mouth. Suddenly she stopped, her fork in midair. "What?" she asked.

"Jesus, Holly. That stuff could burn the paint off your car." He shook his head in disbelief.

Holly grinned. "One of my secret vices. I eat jalapeños like popcorn. This"—she gestured with her fork—"is a world-class hot sauce." She raised the next bite to her mouth and chewed enthusiastically.

They finished their meal in near silence, punctuating it with comments about the food or how hungry they were. When the waiter returned, Ron asked for a pot of herbal tea and the check. Holly asked if they could get some of the hot sauce to take home and the waiter said he would see. He returned shortly with tea, check, and a Styrofoam cup with a plastic lid on it. Jeff lifted the lid and saw that the cup was half full of the sauce. He lifted it to his nose and said, "Whew! That stuff is evil."

Ron sipped at his tea, then put it down and said to Jeff, "I read your note this morning." He paused. Jeff didn't say anything. "And I want you to know that, as a rent-paying housemate, you have every right to have a guest. So," he turned to Holly, "welcome to our home."

"Thank you." Holly dabbed at her mouth with her napkin. Jeff watched as she looked to Leanne, as if she were seeking a cue or encouragement.

"Okay, we got that settled," Ron said. "But let's not kid ourselves about our situation. We've got a very sick man out there and he's *our* problem."

"You don't know the half of it," Jeff said. He told Ron and Leanne what he had found at Holly's place. Holly filled in details.

"Wait a minute," Leanne interrupted at one point, addressing Holly. "What made you think of tearing up the rug in your closet?"

"I just felt that there was something wrong there. That's where the vulnerable spot was." She shrugged. "You know?"

When Jeff got to the part about the bottles on the dirt floor of the hidden room, Ron asked, "Moosehead and Bushmills—aren't those the brands you told Joe Greiner about? Art's—Jack Stanley's brands?"

He nodded. "He used to stock them by the case. Like a drug addict. He didn't want to run out."

Ron leaned back in his chair and folded his hands at his belly. "Well, that doesn't leave much room for speculation."

"I knew who it was before Jeff found the bottles," Holly said. "I just really wanted . . ." She faltered.

A chiming sound filled the space of Holly's silence. Ron's hand slapped to his side and the chime stopped. He pulled his cell phone from his belt, viewed the caller ID, and then looked back at Holly. "Just wanted what?"

"I wanted to believe I was crazy. That none of this was really happening. I mean, sitting in my own home, feeling like when you're little and there's a monster in the closet, except this one is real—I think I would have preferred for it to have been a delusion. You know, a paranoid psychotic episode or something." She looked at Leanne, this time, Jeff thought, searching for understanding. And, he imagined, finding it.

Ron said, "Excuse me. I need to get this." He indicated the phone in his hand.

As he listened, Ron's face expressed a tension that Jeff could see and feel. It was in the set of his jaw, the silence as he sat and placed his elbows on the table, lightly bouncing his fingertips together. Leanne put her hand on his arm, a concerned look on her face, but said nothing.

"That was Joe Greiner."

"Where was he?" Jeff asked.

"At your friend Lilah's."

"What?" This wasn't making any sense.

"He was at the apartment of your friend Lilah O'Hare, in Brentwood. I called him earlier and asked him to trace a number and go there. She was nearly beaten to death. Two men in the apartment weren't so lucky." Ron turned to Holly. "One of them is your old friend Tony Petracca. Dead now, his head bashed in with a heavy object. Probably a tire iron, Joe says."

Holly's face was white. She closed her eyes and trembled slightly but perceptibly, as though suddenly chilled. From across the table, Leanne reached out and covered Holly's hands with her own.

"Is Lilah okay?" He felt sadness for her, an urgent hope that her manic spunk would see her through this.

"She was alive. Paramedics took her away." Ron paused.

"Who else was there?" He asked.

"Someone named Richard Cahn. They found his body in the closet of a room that had a big brick of cocaine on the dresser. Know him?"

It seemed so insane, the past that he had walked away from intruding like this. Absurdly, he thought of the twelve thousand dollars he owed to a dead man, how the burden of the debt was now relieved. "Jesus. Richard is dead?" was all he could say.

"Who do they think did it?" Holly asked, staring straight down at Leanne's hands on her own.

He watched Ron glance at Leanne, run his fingers through his hair, before he spoke. "The neighbors said that there had been a fourth person staying at the apartment. Someone who drove a green Jaguar."

Holly didn't look up; she just nodded slowly, unsurprised. As she continued to nod it seemed to Jeff she was coming to a conclusion about something, consolidating an inner resolve.

"So," Ron continued, "Joe wants to meet us up at the house. He's on his way now."

They settled the tab and walked out to the street. It was dark now, the air crackling with dry heat from the desert winds. Opening the door of the Land Rover for Leanne, Ron said, "You two go on ahead. I'm running on empty and have to stop for gas. We'll be right behind you."

CHAPTER 60

They drove without speaking, Jeff at the wheel, all the way to Highland, then onto Sunset. Holly had put up the top; now the silence in the car was palpable, filled with a quality that took him some time to decipher. It was anger, he realized, radiating from Holly like heat.

She spoke for the first time as he turned right on Franklin. "I've always hated guns . . ."

He looked over at her, the set of her jaw, her lips pressed together, the cold flash in her eyes as she glanced back at him.

". . . but I'd really like to have one right now."

There wasn't much to say to that. Yes, it would be nice to have the Walther; the police still had it and he wasn't sure if he could get it back. Or if he wanted to.

The wail of a siren made him look in the rearview mirror. Flashing colored lights were overtaking the cars behind him and, as he pulled over to the right, a fire truck bore down on the BMW and passed them, its deep horn blaring. A second, then a third, truck followed.

Six cars were stopped in a line at the entrance to Beachwood Canyon. A fire captain's red sedan was parked at the curb. In the center of the street a black-and-white patrol car had its colored lights strobing. A cop with a flashlight spoke to each driver, waving several of them through. Two had to make U-turns around the patrol car and re-enter Franklin. When Jeff and Holly pulled up, the officer motioned for them to stop. Jeff hit the button to make the window go down. "What's going on?"

"Fire's made it to the top of the hill. Residents only beyond this point."

"That's okay, we live up here." He hoped the cop wouldn't ask for a driver's license.

"What's the address?"

"454 Sycamore." He had found the address easy to remember because there were four hundred and fifty-four grams in a pound. And it rhymed. It struck him that part of his old self would always be with him.

A blast of static and garbled speech came from the red sedan at the curb to their right. He heard the fireman yell something about holding back any more cars. In his rear-view mirror he saw a new line formed behind him.

"Thank you very much, officer." He looked up and nodded as the man waved him through. Driving away slowly, he saw the red sedan in his rearview mirror as it moved diagonally into the place the BMW had just occupied, blocking the line of waiting cars.

It was with a sense of relief that he pulled into the gravel driveway and parked the BMW next to his own car. The darkened house looked peaceful, isolated from the insanity Ron had reported at the restaurant, and he was glad to be home.

He unlocked the front door and followed Holly through the living room as she angled left toward the kitchen.

"How about some coffee?" She seemed relieved to be back also.

"I don't know, it's pretty late," he said.

"I doubt I'll be sleeping any time soon." Holly put the cup of hot sauce and the leftovers from Nick's on the counter, opened a cupboard, and pulled out two coffee mugs. She placed them on the wooden table in the middle of the kitchen.

"There's decaf in the freezer. It's good, vanilla flavored." He sat at the far end of the table, facing the doorway to the living room.

Holly measured the grounds and poured them into a filter, added water to the Melitta, and switched it on. He watched as she took the plastic cap off the cup of hot sauce.

"What should we do with this?" Holly put the cup to her nose and smelled the contents.

"Well, we could save it in case the drain ever gets clogged."

"Very funny." She put the cup down on the counter. "I meant, is there anything I can put it in, like a glass jar?" She surveyed the open cupboard.

"I don't know. I'll look in a little while." He watched her, the way her hair picked up the light, her slender grace as she reached up and pulled down a bag of turbinado sugar. The coffee began to drip.

Over her shoulder, she said, "I like it here. It feels safe."

"I know. I'm glad." A distant siren screamed, and the wind kicked up outside. Something wasn't right. A corollary breeze blew into the kitchen.

"You didn't open any windows before we left, did you?" He was sure he had closed them—in this weather the house maintained a cooler temperature that way.

Holly turned to look at him. "No. In fact I closed the one in the bedroom. Why?"

Even as she spoke, he looked up to see an image he at first rejected as impossible, like a hallucination from a bad drug. He sat paralyzed, vaguely aware—as though from a distance—of a startled yelp from Holly, an intake of breath so abrupt that it created a vocal expression of pure dread.

Doctor Jack Stanley stood in the doorway, the darkness of the living room behind him.

"Knock, knock, knock." He smiled amiably, echoing his words by rapping three times on the doorframe with a long metal bar. In his left hand he held a paper grocery bag. "Isn't this cozy?"

Jeff looked at Holly, who stood frozen with her back to the counter. He tried to picture himself blocking the tire iron, wresting it away, overpowering the man, but his heart was beating too fast, his breath was too short, the will to move was not forthcoming.

"Well, isn't anyone going to invite me in?" Jack stepped forward to the chair opposite Jeff, hooked it with his foot to pull it back, and sat. He put the bag down and let the tire iron rest on the table. The claw end of the shaft of the iron was matted with hair embedded in a sticky-looking rust-colored substance. His rumpled suit was streaked and spattered in the same color. There was a mad, hysterical glint in his eye, but when he spoke he sounded to Jeff like the same old Doctor Jack.

"So. I've got good news and I've got bad news." Jack smiled again, closing his eyes and lolling his head from shoulder to shoulder as though enjoying music that only he could hear. The guy has lost it, Jeff thought. Now. It's time to act.

Jack's eyes snapped open, staring at him. "The bad news," he turned to his right to face Holly, "the very sad news, is that this will be the last of our little times together. I'm sure you know how much I've come to cherish them." He turned back to Jeff. "The good news"—now he reached into the bag—"is that I come bearing gifts." Out of the bag he pulled two squarish bottles, which he placed on the table. One—it was Bushmills, Jeff noticed—was half empty. The other had the familiar black-and-white label of Jack Daniel's.

Doctor Jack let go of the tire iron and removed the top from the Bushmills. He took a long, hard hit from the bottle, staring directly into Jeff's eyes even as he tilted his head back. He put his bottle down, unsealed the Jack Daniel's, and leaned forward to pour from it into Jeff's empty coffee cup. Now, goddammit. Now. At least get the tire iron. But he sat, immobile, unable to grab the part of the shaft that was closest to him, the blood still sticky on the black metal. Idiotically, he wondered whose hair was matted on it.

"Just like old times, isn't it?" Doctor Jack settled back and grinned. "Oh, here, I almost forgot." He reached into the lining pocket of his suit jacket and pulled out a plastic baggie with a large white lump in it, which he then mashed between his thumb and forefinger. Opening the bag, he leaned across the table again and dumped the powder on the table in front of Jeff. "Your favorite, as I recall."

"Art, for God's sake—" Holly began, but the man glanced sharply at her and held up a hand, palm out: Stop.

Jeff found his voice. "I'm not interested in this stuff anymore. Why don't you just go while you can?" He wondered where Ron and Leanne were, if they were stuck at the bottom of the canyon. And Joe, wasn't he supposed to be here?

"I'll be going soon enough. But for right now—" Doctor Jack picked up the tire iron and leaned forward slightly, reaching across the table until the claw end was inches from Jeff's forehead "—drink up."

Jeff didn't move.

"I SAY DRINK UP." Jack stood, yelling now. "DO IT!"

The tire iron slammed down so hard on the table that the bottles rattled and the wood split from end to end. Whiskey spilled from the cup and met the pile of white powder, amalgamating into an amber smear. Doctor Jack raised the iron again, his face looming over the table in a mask of rage.

As if in slow motion, Jeff saw Holly's right hand appear from behind her on the counter, the white Styrofoam cup drawing an arc above the table until it stopped just short of Doctor Jack's face. The cup's contents, the brown liquid from the restaurant, flew into the man's eyes, causing him to bellow in pain. He dropped the tire iron and fell back into the chair, hands covering his eyes.

Holly picked up the weapon and cocked it back behind her. Using her entire body, she swung it around in the same arc as the cup had drawn. The metal connected with a sharp crack just above the Jack's eyebrows. His head snapped back and he fell backward over the chair.

"Jesus Christ!" Jeff got up, walked over to the other end of the table, turned and paced back, too agitated to formulate an action.

Holly stood as she had before, in her position with her back against the edge of the counter. Her face was white and he could see her fist tighten and relax its grip on the iron as she breathed.

"Tie him up so I don't have to hit him again, would you?"

He pulled Jack's body into a sitting position. There was some nylon cord in a utility drawer.

"Christ. I can't stand it." Holly stared at Doctor Jack's inert form, the blood flowing from his forehead. She bent forward and picked up the empty grocery bag from the table, placing it upside down over the man's head. Jeff bound Jack's wrists together behind his back. At a loss for what to do next, he walked around the table to where Holly stood and drew her to him. She resisted stiffly but didn't pull away. After a moment she relaxed slightly into his arms. He could feel his heart pounding against her.

There was a stirring from the table, a rustling from the paper bag. Holly jumped, startled, and said, "This is insane. I can't handle it." He pulled her back, her head nestled on his shoulder, and stroked her hair. For a moment the only sounds were of his breathing, deliberately slow and deep, and hers, still staccato but slowing in rhythm.

CHAPTER 61

⏃

It helped, being held by Jeff, but not enough. She felt consumed with a sense of dread that was nearly paralyzing. When Jeff stepped away and said he was going to call Ron, she fell backwards and had to catch herself against the counter.

Jeff rang off in frustration. "Shit, he must be on the line. Where the hell are they, anyway?" Then he told her, "Wait here. I'm just going out to the driveway to look," and walked out of the kitchen.

She heard the front door open and Jeff's footsteps on the gravel driveway. She leaned against the counter, numb with anxiety, wondering why she didn't feel triumph, vindication, or at least relief. She needed her medication, but it was in the car, and she knew a seizure was coiling like a cobra inside her, ready to strike.

The rustle of the bag startled her. She grabbed a knife from the counter and turned to see the man, grotesque with the bag over his head, fresh blood staining the front of his jacket, strain against the nylon cord and then relax, sitting erect now. A deep, malevolent chuckle issued from the bag and Jack began to gently rock back and forth.

"Bravo, Holly, bravo. Home run." He chuckled again. "All that anger finally found a target outside of yourself."

"You're insane."

Doctor Jack's shoulders raised once, a shrug. "Ah, well. Sanity. Such a delicate thing really, even in the best of men." He was silent for a moment, then said softly, "Holly, trust me. The doctor needs your help."

Holly's lethargy deepened; she struggled to say no but her heart wasn't in it. Nothing mattered and she didn't care. She heard it again, like an echo: "Holly, trust me. The doctor needs your help." She stood over him, paralyzed. A tremor in her hand became a violent shaking; the knife flew out of her grasp and the seizure gripped her like a wolf shaking a rabbit.

CHAPTER 62

▽

Jeff paced to the end of the driveway for the fourth time, checking the street as if it would help speed Ron and Joe's arrival. He tried calling again. The air was hot and dry, and the smell of burning was thick on the breeze. As he turned to go back to the house, movement caught the corner of his vision.

Holly's BMW bore down on him like a strike ball on a leading pin. In an impossible frozen moment he saw Jack hunched forward at the wheel, grinning as he accelerated. He jumped to the side and watched as the car veered by, Holly slack-faced as a sleepwalker in the passenger seat. Gravel kicked up and showered him as he stumbled and then rolled to the side of the driveway.

The car fishtailed out of the driveway and turned right. He knew there was only one house left before the street hit a dead end, and that although it had a long, circuitous driveway, the house was perched just up the hill and next door to Ron's house, sharing a cliffside view of the canyon and the roads below. A narrow trail meandered through dry scrub brush most of the way between the two homes.

He ran to the side of Ron's house and started up the dirt path toward the neighbor's house. He heard the neighbor's dog barking incessantly; to his left, beyond the street, flames consumed the hillside. The wind swept down the canyon, pushing the fire toward him. He sprinted up the last of the trail and found an opening in the hedge that marked the boundary of the neighbor's property.

He crawled through the narrow space. Thorns from the hedge and burrs in the dirt pressed into his hands. He came out into the clear at the juncture of the driveway and the garage: Holly's car sat askew in a flower patch across the driveway, both doors open and the engine still running.

The front door was open. He entered a foyer that led into a huge room. Gold and platinum records lined the walls, and ornate Chinese lacquered furniture rested on expensive oriental rugs. There was no sign of Jack or Holly, but the dog's barking was louder. He turned to his right, walked through the kitchen, and found a door to the side yard. He opened it to find a dog run; the neighbor's huge Akita was on a chain linked to an overhead cable. The dog stopped barking and came to him and sat, as if expecting a treat from his master. He undid the clasp of the chain from the dog's collar, then, as an afterthought, reached up and released the chain from the cable.

The Akita bounded toward the far end of the dog run, then reared up and placed his paws against the house, growling. Jeff followed and saw that the dog was looking through the open half of a Dutch door and into a bedroom. Diagonally, across the room, was a sliding glass door, open, and beyond it, a porch that ran the length of the house, with Jack and Holly struggling at the rail.

The Akita got there first and snapped at Jack's leg. Holly slipped free but tripped over a chaise lounge as she backed away. Jack raised the tire iron high above his head, ready to bring it down on the dog, but Jeff raced through the doorway and swung the chain outward. He watched, fascinated, as it wound itself around Jack's forearm, then yanked hard, ducking as the tire iron swung down and missed his head. He raised his left foot and came down with all his weight on Jack's ankle; there was a satisfying snap of bone that told him at least Holly would get away from this alive. The man roared like a beast and swung his body around, ripping the chain from Jeff's grasp and smashing the glass door behind him as he spun.

Holly was still on the ground where she had fallen. Jack completed his mad, drunken spin and tried to keep his balance on his ruined ankle. Jeff saw that the collapse would land him on top of Holly; he reached out and pushed Jack toward the porch rail, which cracked and splintered and almost entirely gave way, leaving Jack suspended over the sixty-foot drop to the street below.

He picked up the tire iron and raised it as he stepped toward Jack, who was trying to disengage himself from the wreckage of the railing. He heard Holly cry out, "Jeff, no!" and relaxed his grip on the iron. He experienced relief that he wouldn't have to kill the man, followed by a new surge of adrenaline when he saw the chain swing toward his face and Jack begin to lurch upward. As Jeff ducked he heard a low growl and saw the Akita launch itself at Jack, this time completing the job of demolishing the railing.

The growl turned into a high whine and then a pathetic yipping sound as man and dog disappeared from sight. The sickening sound of the almost simultaneous impacts was followed by what seemed like complete silence, until gradually the sound of wind and flames reasserted themselves in the background and the sound of Jeff's own breathing began to dominate. He leaned down to help Holly to a standing position. As they looked over the ruined railing, the screech of brakes accompanied the arrival of the Land Rover, which came to a stop an arm's length from Jack's body, and they watched as Ron and Joe stepped out of the car and looked, first at the bodies, then up at them.

EPILOGUE

⩇

There is a series of jetties, several miles north of the
Santa Monica pier, across the Pacific Coast Highway
from the eroding cliffs of Pacific Palisades. The first, south-
ernmost, of these rocky extensions had once been called the
Lighthouse Jetty, but the lighthouse had been razed for a lifeguard headquarters. Before that, it had been the site of one of the
longest piers on the California coast, and a railroad track once
led to its base. When Jeff had been a boy, before he had become
caught up in it all, long before it had all caught up with him, he
had ridden the waves that formed on the sandbar at the end of the
pile of rocks, by then called simply the Jetty. His sister, Marilyn,
would watch from her favorite boulder at the Jetty's westward tip.

Jeff sat on the tilted flat surface of that same boulder, thinking of Marilyn and how he had lost her—by losing himself—
long before she died. He remembered her when they were kids,
looking up and smiling with joy at her big brother. *If she could see
me now, she would smile like that again.*

It was early November, more than two months since the
insanity of Doctor Jack's murderous binge. Daylight savings was
over, and the days seemed to end abruptly now that summer was
coming to an end. There was a light chop on the water and the
sun sat like an egg yolk split in half on the horizon.

Life, Jeff reflected, even with its losses, was good. He had seen
Lilah in the hospital, her head bandaged so that only a small window opened onto her face. She had smiled wistfully, only the little

girl remaining. She told him he looked good, and that the doctors had told her she would recover. Mostly. When he said goodbye, she said maybe when I'm better you can take me to one of those meetings. He had said yeah, we'll do that, but she must have seen something in his expression because she took his hand and said, "Just as friends."

He had gone to his parents in the spirit of amends, and his mother cried while his father did something Jeff had never known him to do before: wrapped his arms around him, pulled him to his chest, and held him silently for a fine and timeless moment.

"Are you thinking good thoughts?" Holly, who had been squatting on a lower rock by the waterline watching the crabs scuttling in the crevasses, smiled up at him.

"Yeah." He smiled back. "I am."

She climbed up next to him and sat. The tide was high and a wave slid by in a thick hump, spraying water at their feet as it looked for a shallow place to rear up and break. The sea had gone from a deep green to a slate gray as the last sliver of sun melted into the horizon. Looking out at the spot where the sun had been, Jeff felt Holly's arm go around him, her hand settling at his waist. He glanced at her and saw that she was regarding him with an amused look in her eye.

"What?"

"I was just thinking about Leanne . . . You know we talk a lot." Jeff knew this and was glad; it was part of Holly's own healing.

"And I asked her about all this, you know, you and me."

"Really? What did she say?" He wasn't sure he wanted to know.

"She said that you were definitely a fixer-upper,"—Holly grinned—"but she thinks you've got great potential." She drew him closer, kissed him lightly on the cheek and then, perhaps embarrassed by the disclosure, averted her gaze and looked out at the water. Jeff felt a tightening in his throat, the pressure of tears upwelling, the sweet sad pain of gratitude.

He grinned and said, "I hope so. I heard that a lot when I was a kid."

About the Author

Earl Javorsky is the black sheep of his family of artistic high achievers.

Acknowledgments

⏢

To my kids, this time, and to the Howard family.